LADY
SWEETBRIAR

by

Maggie MacKeever

FAWCETT COVENTRY • NEW YORK

LADY SWEETBRIAR

Published by Fawcett Coventry Books, CBS Educational and
Professional Publishing, a division of CBS Inc.

ISBN: 0-449-50270-8

Printed in the United States of America

First Fawcett Coventry printing: February 1982

10   9   8   7   6   5   4   3   2   1

Chapter One

"Egad!" said Lady Sweetbriar. "Whatever are you doing, Avery? I mean, of course I know *what* you are doing, and very glad I am of it, moreover, because you are not the least like any of my flirts in that respect, which has made me wonder if you *truly* wish to marry me! But if you want to kiss me on the grand staircase of the British Museum, in plain view of anyone who comes along, it is quite all right with me!" In demonstration of her liberal attitude, Lady Sweetbriar stood on tiptoe and placed her hands on her companion's lapels, closed her eyes, and prepared to receive his salute.

Looking distinctly sardonic, Sir Avery Clough gazed down upon his captor's lovely heart-shaped face. At almost thirty years of age, Lady Sweetbriar was a bewitching little creature with a tangle of dark curls and skin rendered faintly golden by injudicious exposure to sunlight. "Nikki!" he said aloud. "You are a minx."

In response to this sally, Lady Sweetbriar opened one twinkling eye. "Am I not?" she cheerfully agreed. "You must not raise a lady's hopes only to dash them, Avery! If you do *not* kiss me, after clutching me all this time against your chest—I am not complaining about it, mind! Had you not caught me, I would doubtless have tumbled down the stair, so fascinated was I by the ceiling—Fancy! The Rape of Proserpine! But if you clutch a lady, she must naturally expect that you will next kiss her, and if you disappoint me, I shall be *very* out of sorts!"

With an appearance less of enthusiasm than exasperation, Sir Avery ascertained that the grand staircase was free of visitors, then delivered a chaste salute upon his *fiancée*'s delightful nose. "I hope this is not how you mean to go on *after* we are married, madam," he remarked.

Lady Sweetbriar responded with a roguish smile to this reproof. "Twaddle!" said she, and tripped gaily up the stair, leaving Sir Avery to wonder whether her cryptic utterance was directed at his criticism, or the quality of his embrace. On the landing she paused and turned, looking contrite.

"I should not tease you, Avery! Of course I do not mean to tell you what you must do—I may be a trifle unscrupulous, and my background a trifle exceptionable, but I am *not* a managing female. Or at least not *odiously* so!" As if the three stuffed giraffes displayed upon the landing might eavesdrop upon their conversation, Lady Sweetbriar stepped closer to Avery and continued in a confiding tone: "I do not scruple to confess that I do not understand you! At first I thought you must be smitten, else you would not have allowed me to wheedle you into a betrothal, but since then I have begun to cherish doubts. Perhaps it is a marriage of convenience that you wish. Yet though it will be very convenient for *me* to have money and position, I do not understand how *you* may benefit." Her pretty face was anxious. "You *do* wish to marry me, Avery? I will be the first to admit I am a designing woman—and of precious little use it has been to me in the past! Look at Reuben! Or rather *don't* look at him, not that you would wish to if you *could,* because he is dead! As you know as well as I, else *we* wouldn't be betrothed."

"And that would be the greatest of misfortunes, my dear," Sir Avery responded politely. "Have you noted the man-of-war?"

Lady Sweetbriar glanced obediently at the model of a man-of-war ready to launch, which with diverse other items, including a large marble foot, littered the grand staircase of the British Museum. Then she peeked again at her companion, a trustee of that establishment. Sir Avery Clough was a tall and very aristocratic-looking gentleman of four-and-forty years, whose figure was set off to good advantage by his morning coat of dark blue superfine with plated buttons, striped toilenette waistcoat, canary-colored pantaloons of ribbed kerseymere, and Hessian boots. His hair was sandy, his eyes brown, his manner so detached that it was impossible to guess his thoughts.

In lieu of Sir Avery's thoughts, Lady Sweetbriar contented herself with her own. *"What* a lucky mischance it was by which we met!"* As if in punctuation, she gave her companion's arm a squeeze. "Had I not disguised myself as a boy so that I might attend a prizefight— and what follower of the Fancy would willingly have missed a contest between Tom Cribb, the champion of England, and the Negro, Molyneaux? There must have been quite twenty thousand people present, and not a bed to be had for twenty miles around. Oh, I know I should *not* have gone, and it is very kind of you not to scold me for it—but I make a prodigious good boy, as even you must admit! You would never have penetrated my disguise had I not twisted my ankle and tumbled right into your lap!" In case Sir Avery had a partiality for that which had brought about their acquaintance, Lady Sweetbriar gave her skirts a little twitch.

Sir Avery evidenced neither admiration nor gratification upon thus glimpsing a neatly turned and dainty little ankle; upon his aristocratic features only faint traces of skepticism could be seen. "A providential mishap, to be sure," he murmured.

Sir Avery's ironic tone inspired Lady Sweetbriar to flutter her outrageously long eyelashes at him. "I would not have done such an improper thing, had I not been feeling so dreary and dull!" she confessed. "I had just discovered how Reuben had left things and I was very cross. Oh, I should have expected him to do something odious, because he was prodigious vexed when he discovered he had married an *actress*—and I admit that was stupidly done of me, but he *was* a lordship and dangling at my slipper-strings, and when he threw the handkerchief in my direction, which I did *not* expect— well, I was very young and it went straight to my head! I married before I had time to discover what a devilish
7

ugly customer Reuben was!" Gustily, she sighed. "It is very disheartening to marry a gentleman for his money and then discover it has all been left to your stepson! Not that I begrudge it to Rolf; Reuben made him miserable, too! But I *do* think I might have been allowed to keep my jewels."

Sir Avery's expression was aloof, his attention all for the stuffed giraffes which presented so unfortunate a contrast with the museum's elegant Palladian interior. "My poor Nikki! Shall I promise to behave less shabbily in case I predecease you also?"

"If you predecease me," Lady Sweetbriar said frankly, "it will doubtless be because your inattention has made someone murderously cross! I do not understand you, Avery."

Similar plain-speaking was not forthcoming from Lady Sweetbriar's *fiancé*. "Understanding is not a prerequisite of marriage," said that gentleman, moving closer to a stuffed giraffe. "If it will make you feel better, you may convince yourself that it is midsummer moon with me. Or if that will not serve, then recall that I have been an eligible widower for many years."

"Have all the matchmaking mamas had you in their sights, poor Avery? Well, *that* shall stop immediately we are wed." There was a speculative quality in Lady Sweetbriar's glance. She didn't love her *fiancé*, more was the pity, but all the same— "I know on which side my bread is buttered; if you give me an inch, I shan't try to take an ell! No, and I don't mean to have flirts either, so you needn't concern yourself with *that!*"

By this noble sacrifice—for Nikki to have flirts was as natural as for her to draw breath—Sir Avery did not appear especially moved. Indeed, Lady Sweetbriar thought indignantly, he was paying an inordinate amount of attention to a stuffed giraffe's ear. "I didn't intend to concern myself," said he.

"No?" Lady Sweetbriar arched her delicate brows. "Reuben was not so tolerant, I promise you. But *he* had flirts; why should have I not? At least I didn't set any of them up in little villas, or give them phaetons and such stuff, which I happen to know he *did!* Though I may have wished to, I never overstepped the line." A delicate blush suffused her golden cheeks. "I should not say such things—but I do not stand on ceremony with you! Anyway, *you* are the one who let it be known we met in the Horticultural Gardens, which is as big a clanker as any I've ever told! Not that I have the *habit* of telling clankers, Avery."

"I hope you do not," responded that gentleman, having completed his inspection of the stuffed giraffe. Absentmindedly he patted the beast, giving rise to a great cloud of dust, which inspired Lady Sweetbriar to a sneezing fit. Hastily Sir Avery conducted her into a saloon furnished with a curious selection of miscellaneous objects, among them a vulture's head in spirits, and a stuffed flamingo. "At least I hope you will not tell *me* tarradiddles. Which reminds me: what *do* you intend to do about Sweetbriar's jewels, Nikki?"

In a very defensive manner, Lady Sweetbriar clutched in turn at her necklet of twenty different Wedgewood cameos fastened together by gold chains, matching bracelets, and brooch; and at the same time pressed Sir Avery's fine cambric handkerchief to her stinging eyes and nose. "I shan't give the jewels back! *Any* of them!" She sniffled belligerently. "I *deserve* to keep them! *Never* was I so taken aback as when I heard Reuben's will read—because though he threatened often enough to cut me off without a farthing, I never thought he would *do* it! I should have known better! It was ever his object to make me miserable."

With the least encouragement Lady Sweetbriar was prone to dwell at great length upon her cheese-paring spouse's last iniquitous act, a fact regretfully known by all her acquaintance. Sir Avery concentrated his attention on the excellently preserved vulture's head, and withheld comment.

Whereas Lady Sweetbriar could lay no claim to a well-regulated mind, she was no slow-top. "My conversation is very fatiguing, I know," she handsomely allowed. "But it is not wonderful that I should be on the dangle for a fortune, existing as I do on the merest pittance—*not* that I am a gazetted fortune hunter—or if I *am*, I mean to give good value, I do assure you! And you are handsome, and well-situated, and of the very first distinction, Avery! But I have been doing all the talking! Now you must talk to me."

"Of course, my dear." Sir Avery immediately proffered an accounting of the more pressing concerns of a museum trustee. The floors of the old building were sagging, in many places kept from breaking up altogether only by iron supports, he explained; and furthermore, considerable damage had been caused in the damp basement rooms by dry rot. An unscrupulous dealer had extracted a number of prints from one of the museum's collections, and had sold them to various private parties, which had done nothing to abate the jealous ill will prevalent among the museum's officers. In addition, more and more people clamored to use the Reading Room and to see the private collections, and expressed strident dislike of the strict regulations which were intended to safeguard the great treasures housed therein. About those treasures Sir Avery then waxed enthusiastic, with special emphasis upon the Cottonian library, and the collection of Sir Hans Sloane, and the difficulty of properly cataloguing everything.

"I fear that I am boring you, my dear!" Sir Avery's remark caused Lady Sweetbriar to start and look extremely guilty; during his eloquent dissertation, she had been silently grappling with her own difficulties. Not only must Nikki contrive to satisfy an extravagant nature on a pauper's purse, she must also contend with a deuced inconvenient conscience which was prone to dwell censuriously upon the fact that only as a result of severe bamboozlement would a gentleman affiance himself to a female who'd pitched herself onto his lap during a prize fight. "If you do not wish to hear about the Magna Carta and the Codex Alexandrus, you need only say."

The *what?* wondered Nikki. Nobly she prevaricated: "Oh, no! That is, I was just wondering if I truly *am* a lady—and I do not refer to those old *on-dits* that I only married Reuben so I could call myself one! I have never been certain if I am Lady Sweetbriar or merely Lady Reuben, and one doesn't like to *ask*—not that I care a button for such things!" Curiously she eyed her *fiancé,*

10

who was himself not immune to gossip; various unkind souls had taken leave to wonder how Lady Sweetbriar had contrived to distract Sir Avery from his antiquities long enough to convince him he wished to rewed. Roguishly she whispered: "You must admit I made a handsome lad."

But no compliment was forthcoming regarding her current unboyish walking dress of muslin with bishop's sleeves tied with green ribbon, her white satin Spanish hat with green rim ornamented with a demi-wreath of cornflowers, her green sarcenet mantle or ridicule of shot silk or elegant little half-boots. Beseechingly, Lady Sweetbriar gazed up at Sir Avery. "I need your advice! The thing is, I have been looking at furniture prints all the morning, and I cannot make up my mind! Would you prefer polychrome chintz with floral designs realistically treated in natural colors? Or painted silks imported from China? The latter would go excellently well with an Axminster carpet of Chinese inspiration which caught my eye. You will approve my taste, Avery! Imagine a pattern of pairs of confronting dragons and sacred symbols in shades of gold on a blue ground."

If Sir Avery was annoyed that Lady Sweetbriar had interrupted his preoccupations to discuss a matter so trivial as the stuffs with which she intended to refurbish his ancestral home, he did not say so outright. Instead he led her out of the saloon. "As I have told you before, you must do as you think best, Nikki. Refurnish the house as you like and have the accounting brought to me. There is no need to consult with me about details."

"No need to bother you, you mean!" No lady who had survived marriage with the uncivil Lord Sweetbriar could take offense at so mannerly a rebuff. "Very well, I shall ask Clytie's opinion instead. How odd it will seem to have a stepdaughter so close to my own age— although I already have Rolf, but you know what *he* is!" She paused, so that Sir Avery might comment upon her marvelously youthful appearance.

No such comment was forthcoming. Lady Sweetbriar displayed an enchanting little pout. Sometimes she despaired of inspiring her *fiancé* to enact the ardent swain. Perhaps Sir Avery was shy? Mayhap he feared to cause offense? Somehow Nikki must subtly intimate that a mild display of passion would not come amiss.

"It is the *principle* of the thing," she said aloud, as she stopped dead in her tracks, thereby insuring that Sir Avery also halt. "No lady likes to feel that vulture's heads and stuffed giraffes are more interesting than she! It is my own fault, I know; I should not have interrupted your work—although why you should *want* to work, when you are wealthy beyond imagining, is more than I can credit! But that is quite beside the point. I am leaving now, Avery. Pray forgive me for disturbing you." In hope of disturbing her *fiancé* even more profoundly, Nikki grasped his lapels, rose on tiptoe, and—to the astonishment of several museum visitors even then mounting the grand staircase—awarded him a long and lingering caress. Made aware of the audience, Sir Avery looked even more sardonic than was his wont. Lady Sweetbriar dimpled and giggled and blushed, and tripped blithely down the stair.

Chapter Two

"Quite midsummer moon!" insisted the young gentleman who currently sought the advice of Sir Avery Clough's sole offspring. "I swear it! I've decided it's time I put it to the touch. *Not* that I expect my hopes to be cut up!"

With an ironic expression reminiscent of her father, Miss Clough contemplated the hopeful young man. Very worthy young Lord Sweetbriar was of contemplation, moreover—for Miss Clough's accostor was none other than Lady Sweetbriar's stepson Rolf, who as a result of her papa's entanglement with his stepmama was prone to regard Miss Clough as a companion in adversity. "What is it?" he inquired, attempting to similarly contemplate himself, and very nearly doing himself serious injury with his excessive shirt points. "Have I a smudge? *Not* a loose thread?"

"No, no!" soothed Miss Clough. "You are the very pink of perfection, Rolf!"

In response to this compliment, Lord Sweetbriar lowered his chin into the folds of his snowy cravat, which was tied in that intricate style known as the Gordian Knot, and looked smug. That his companion spoke no more than the truth, Rolf knew. In matters sartorial, he considered himself without peer. And though there may have been those in Oxford Street that day who might quibble with his lordship's high opinion of himself, few could deny the effectiveness of his current ensemble—a Jean de Bry coat with high stand-up collar, and sleeves gathered and padded at the shoulder to give a "kick-up" effect; light pantaloons of knit stockinet with a pattern of broad stripes; calf-high hussar buckskins, and a waterproof silk hat.

But though his opinion of himself was nice, Lord Sweetbriar was not immune to the insecurities which prey upon young lovers: "Tell me, Clytie, is it absolutely *necessary* that I go down upon one knee?" he nervously inquired.

Miss Clough, whose thoughts had wandered to the errands which had brought her to Oxford Street, looked extremely startled at the notion that Lord Sweetbriar might thus comport himself. "Whatever are you talking about, Rolf? Go down on your knee, indeed! I should hope you will *not!*"

"No?" Lord Sweetbriar appeared unconvinced. "I thought that's the way the thing is done. A fellow gets down on his knees and pops the question—but if you say I shouldn't, then I shan't! To own the truth, I'd just as soon not make a cake of myself!"

Generously Miss Clough refrained from pointing out that horizontally striped unmentionables were not prudent garb for a gentleman wishful of avoiding undue notice. Narrowly she regarded Rolf. Though eclipsed by the grandeur of his garb, Lord Sweetbriar's features were passably pleasant; and his figure, though at two-and-twenty already tending toward *embonpoint,* could cause no maiden offense. "So you will offer for Lady Regina Foliot? I wish you joy," she mused. "But if you are in doubt as to how to go about the business, you should apply to Nikki, not to me!"

A very self-centered young man, Lord Sweetbriar did not pause to reflect upon Miss Clough's tacit admission that she was not in the habit of receiving professions of eternal devotion and other romantical high flights. "Apply to Nikki!" he echoed bitterly. "Yes, so she may send me off *again* with a flea in my ear! You will be very sorry if you allow this marriage to take place, as I have told you before!"

"If you do not wish to marry, then you must not, Rolf!" Miss Clough looked very innocent. "But I fail to understand why, if you *don't* wish to marry, you have
14

been asking me whether one should or should not fall down upon one knee! And what have *I* to do with it, anyway?"

"You? Why, nothing!" Lord Sweetbriar's unremarkable features were flushed. "Are you bamming me *again*, Clytie? You should not, you know! Dashed if I know why you refuse to give your papa my advice."

As Miss Clough contemplated the probable reaction of her parent to Lord Sweetbriar's warnings, she wore a slight ironic smile. Not only in outlook did Clytie resemble her father. She also shared the aristocratic family features, brown eyes and sandy hair. "It is very bad of me to tease you, I know! Pray forgive me, Rolf. What has Nikki done to annoy you now?"

"Nikki don't have to *do* anything!" muttered Lord Sweetbriar a trifle sulkily. "As you will find out for yourself. Dreading what scrape Nikki will next tumble into is every bit as fatiguing as rescuing her from the scrape itself!"

Again Clytie thought of her errands, the execution of which would be much more enjoyable than yet another repetition of a conversation held several times before. "Once Nikki is married to my father, your responsibility for her will end," she patiently pointed out. "And you will need no longer be concerned about her scrapes."

"No?" With a wildly rolling eye, Lord Sweetbriar enacted disbelief. "Your father will leave off his studies to keep her in line? He will not, and you know it as well as I! If you are thinking *you* can keep Nikki from cutting rigs, you may think again, Clytie; you ain't a better fellow than I am, and *I* could not! For that matter, neither could my father, or else Nikki wouldn't still have those accursed jewels, and there wasn't any flies on *him!*" It then occurred to Rolf that this was no fit way to speak even of the unlamented dead. Nervously he glanced over his shoulder. "You know what I mean—the deuce!"

Curious as to what had inspired Lord Sweetbriar's outburst, as well as his sudden ashen color and sweat-beaded brow, Miss Clough also turned her head. At first she saw nothing more than the usual confusion of

Oxford Street. Then Miss Clough glimpsed an oddly familiar figure. Possessing less sensibility than Lord Sweetbriar, who was currently gibbering in a wholly demoralized fashion, Clytie merely blinked.

"I knew it!" muttered Rolf, leaning heavily upon Clytie's shoulder. "I knew the minute Nikki first refused to give me back those wretched jewels that Papa wouldn't rest easy in his grave! I told her so, too, but she only laughed. Well, she shan't laugh at this, I'll warrant! Dash it, I'm so overset I don't know what I'm saying! Clytie, tell me that ain't my papa risen from the tomb!"

Though Miss Clough would have liked very much to reassure Rolf on that head, she could not honorably do so; the gentleman who approached them had very much the appearance of the previous Lord Sweetbriar, though fortunately none of the aspect of one who has passed an entire year mouldering above-ground. As opposed to his shroud, the gentleman was dressed carelessly in buckskin breeches and topboots. His brown hair was sun-streaked, his complexion swarthy; his pale blue eyes were almost the exact shade of his jacket of blue *célest* which could only have come from the celebrated Weston of Bond Street.

Because Miss Clough judiciously reserved comment, and because Lord Sweetbriar's concentration was focused wholly on his determination not to swoon, the source of their mutual fascination was the first to speak. That comment, as well as a devastating smile, he directed at Miss Clough. "My nephew is *still* a mooncalf, it seems. Allow me to introduce myself, since Rolf appears incapable. Marmaduke Thorne, at your service, Miss—er?"

Perhaps as result of the bizarre manner of their meeting, Miss Clough took this impudent gentleman in immediate dislike. Turning a cool shoulder on him, she roused Rolf from his openmouthed stupor by means of a sharp pinch. "You may relax, Rolf! It is not your papa risen from the grave to scold."

"Good God!" ejaculated the newcomer. "No wonder the pair of you looked as if you'd seen a ghost. I shouldn't care to meet Reuben's shade myself, not that

16

I imagine they allow much freedom of movement where *he's* gone. Tell you what, young Rolf: if Reuben should take to haunting you, you just tell him Duke's come home." To Miss Clough, who was regarding him with astonishment, Mr. Thorne explained: "Doubtless Reuben would rather haunt me than anyone! Between us there was no love lost."

"I say, Uncle Duke, that's dashed handsome of you!" Enthusiastically Lord Sweetbriar grasped and pumped Mr. Thorne's hand. "But why the deuce, after all these years, have you decided to come home? Not that I ain't glad to see you!" He too addressed Clytie. "Uncle Duke has been living in Russia, doing some sort of diplomatic stuff."

Marmaduke Thorne's most artful missions would be undertaken in the *boudoir*, Miss Clough unappreciatively thought, and then blushed not at her indelicacy but as result of the suspicion that he perfectly understood her thoughts. "How nice," she murmured repressively. "I have errands to execute. If you gentlemen will excuse me—"

"Not yet, Miss—er?" Mr. Thorne insured that his request was obeyed by gently tucking Clytie's hand through his arm. Stunned by such impudence, she only half heard Lord Sweetbriar's belated introductions. "As to why I departed Russia," Mr. Thorne continued blandly, "the rumor is that Napoleon plans to invade Moscow."

"Napoleon?" Lord Sweetbriar echoed blankly, in the same instant as Miss Clough regained her powers of speech. "Unhand me immediately, sir!" she snapped.

"I'm afraid I cannot do that, Miss Clough." Apologetically, Mr. Thorne smiled. "I have not been so long out of England that I have forgotten that it is *most* improper for a young lady to go about without an adequate escort."

At this suggestion that she should be deficient in her grasp of the proprieties, Miss Clough's breast swelled. In Mr. Thorne's blue eye, an appreciative twinkle danced. Had she had both hands free, she might well have boxed the rascal's ears, and to the devil with propriety, Clytie thought.

Oblivious alike to provocation and indignation, Lord Sweetbriar said enthusiastically: "You must stay at the house, Uncle Duke! I'll have a room prepared. Yes, and I must tell Lady Regina also. Dashed if I can think what she'll say to *this!*" Anxious to discover what pearls of wisdom might consequently drop from his beloved's lips, Lord Sweetbriar turned away. Over his shoulder he added: "Come to dinner, Uncle Duke! Maybe *you* can tell me what to do about the jewels!"

"*Definitely* a mooncalf," remarked Mr. Thorne, as with interest he observed his nephew's regal progress down Oxford Street. "And now I shall escort you to your destination, Miss Clough, if you will only tell me where you wish to go."

"We are *at* my destination!" snapped Clytie, who had for some inexplicable reason been evaluating her assets, the grand total of which she suspected was a great deal less feminine pulchritude than her companion was accustomed to, and was consequently very cross. "And I am more than adequately served by my footman. If this is the way you conduct your diplomatic undertakings, sir, there is no question but that Russia will be invaded by the French!"

"And it will be all my fault, I apprehend. Are you trying to deliver me a set-down, Miss Clough?" Ignoring Clytie's reference to her footman, Mr. Thorne conducted her through the portals of the Pantheon Bazaar. "If so, you must do better than that, or I shall fail to take your point. Yes, I know I am abominably provoking, but you look thoroughly adorable when you *glower* at me. Rather like a kitten trying to look severe."

"Odious man!" In spite of herself, Miss Clough began to be amused by her impertinent escort. "Have you never been snubbed?"

Mr. Thorne's swarthy features were ruminative. "I daresay I must have been, but I cannot recall. Now you will accuse me of having an unsuperable vanity, and of being insufferably pushing—or perhaps of holding an excessively high, and highly unmerited, opinion of myself."

"I shall do no such thing! It would be monstrous illbred." Clytie tried very hard to be prim. "Instead I shall
18

content myself with voicing my conclusion that *all* your family is mad!"

"And to accuse a man of lunacy is *not* ill-bred?" Mr. Thorne's blue eyes laughed. "Shame, Miss Clough! But I do not mean to scold you. Indeed, I doubt I shall ever feel constrained to scold you for anything, *ma coccinelle.*"

Not without considerable effort, Miss Clough dropped her gaze to the snippet of ribbon which she had brought to match. "Your *what?*" she gruffly inquired.

"My little ladybug." Mr. Thorne deftly selected the perfect shade of ribbon from a vast display. "It was the freckles made me think of it. You need not look chagrined, Miss Clough! They are very pretty freckles, and very faint, and would only be apparent to the fondest eye."

Abandoning all pretence of nonchalance, Clytie awarded her tormentor her direct, clear gaze. "This cannot be your normal manner of conversation, sir!"

"I've gone too fast for you," Mr. Thorne said comfortably, as he purchased a length of ribbon and presented it with a flourish. "It comes from having spent so much time in Russia. Perhaps you will understand better if I explain to you the legend of the fortieth bear."

"The fortieth bear?" Perhaps Mr. Thorne's erratic style of conversation dazed Miss Clough; for whatever reason she made no protest when he escorted her back out into Oxford Street.

"The Russians are great bear hunters," Mr. Thorne explained. "The cossacks of Siberia actually hunt the beasts with only knife and *ragatina,* a short-handled pitchfork. The details of the business I will spare you; but the hunters fear their fortieth bear the most. Many kill thirty-nine without receiving a scratch—but the fortieth bear will avenge all the others, being Nemesis in disguise."

Dazed or no, Miss Clough was a young woman of great good sense, and not a damsel to be swept off her feet by a gentleman who had just—she thought—likened her to a bear. "Your conversation is very enlightening, sir," she said coolly, "and it would be very remiss

19

in me not to thank you for your escort. Even if I didn't want it! But—"

"There!" interrupted Mr. Thorne, with his beguiling smile. "See how far we have come already: you no longer feel constrained to be *polite!*"

Clytie abandoned all effort to do so. Grimly, she continued: "But only a fool, sir, would trust you one inch!"

"You doubt my word?" Mr. Thorne looked surprised. "Why, Miss Clough? Surely rumor of my, er, other thirty-nine bears has not travelled all the way to London—and even if it has you must not blame me for what transpired before we met! They were but the merest peccadilloes. Unless—" His expression altered. "Surely that cork-brained nephew of mine hasn't been telling you you're platter-faced!"

"Your nephew?" Briefly Miss Clough had forgotten Lord Sweetbriar's existence. "Of course not!"

"Then someone else?" Mr. Thorne delicately inquired. "Tell me who was so shortsighted and I will carve out his heart and lay it at your feet."

"Gracious! Is *that* a Russian custom?" Apprised by Mr. Thorne's amused expression that she had been led up the garden path, Clytie glowered. A second later she recalled his comment on her scowl. "I know I am not platter-faced! I mean, no one said anything of the sort! Oh, I don't know *what* I mean, except that you are conscienceless! What a bizarre conversation we are having! I wish you would go away."

"*Did* I carve out someone's heart, I would doubtless have to go away, so we must both be glad that no one has offered you insult." The quality of the rascally Marmaduke's glance was such that Clytie felt her face grow warm. "You are a very pretty damsel, Miss Clough, as you must know. Perhaps *that* is why you refuse to take me seriously! I am but one among many, alas. You are accustomed to being admired."

Though Clytie did not lack admirers, she had no other of this ilk—if admirer Mr. Thorne truly was, which she took leave to doubt. All the same, and though she had not wavered from her conviction that Mr. Thorne was more than half demented, Clytie wished she'd worn some costume more exotic than her simple straw bonnet trimmed with ribbon, pale blue pelisse, and demure white muslin dress. There was that about Mr. Thorne which made a lady contemplate intimate candelit dinners, and diaphanous silks.

But Mr. Thorne obviously awaited her response. What had they been talking about? Ah yes, her countless admirers. "Nonsense!" Clytie said.

"Oh?" Mr. Thorne looked sympathetic. "Never mind, I shall make it up to you. I trust you will not try to avoid further encounters, Miss Clough."

Clytie wondered if she truly wished to do so. Curious, this pang of disappointment at the realization Mr. Thorne did not mean to actively seek her out. "I do not think I could, sir," she ruefully replied. "Apparently you are not aware that our families are in the way of being connections. Lady Sweetbriar is to marry my father." She paused. "I do not know how long you have been in Russia, sir, but I think you must surely know Nikki."

"You are astute as well as delightful to behold, Miss Clough." An enigmatic expression settled upon Mr. Thorne's swarthy face. "When next you see your stepmama-to-be, you must give her Duke's regards."

Chapter Three

"Midsummer moon, Lady Regina, I promise you!" Lord Sweetbriar gallantly hissed. "I waited this long to pop the question so that you might have time to fix your affections. You look startled. You must have known I was a pretender to your hand! Did you despair of bringing me up to scratch?"

Indeed Lady Regina Foliot did look startled, an expression which sat as excellently upon her classical features as did any other, due to the assiduity with which she had practiced enacting the entire range of human emotions in front of her looking glass. "Sweetbriar!" she hissed in turn. "I beg you will recall yourself! This is no fit time to be making me a declaration; we are at Almack's!"

Though Lord Sweetbriar could lay claim to no superior intellectual endowment, he was not so much the mooncalf that he had failed to take note of his surroundings. In point of fact, he had gone to considerable effort in preparation for his foray into the assembly rooms, had even exchanged his more flamboyant costume for the knee breeches and white silk stockings and black pumps, the long-tailed coat and white marcella waistcoat that were *de rigueur* in King Street. No fondness on his own part for the Wednesday evening subscription balls had prompted Lord Sweetbriar to undergo such self-sacrifice, but the knowledge that Lady Regina would be present. And if a fellow popped the question whilst engaged in dancing, he could hardly be expected to drop down upon one knee.

"*I* know we're at Almack's!" Rolf offered, in his own defense. "What's that have to do with me making you an offer? You mustn't act so surprised. A perfect looby would have known I was fixing my interest!"

For a maiden who had just received a proposal of marriage, no matter how unsuitable the surroundings or bizarre the delivery, Lady Regina looked singularly unmoved. It was not the first proposal she had received, certainly; an acknowledged beauty, Lady Regina could choose among many swains. Yet she did not immediately banish Lord Sweetbriar, no matter how inept his manner of paying his addresses, and his attempts to execute the dance in which they were engaged. "I think, Sweetbriar, that we must talk."

"Talk?" his lordship echoed blankly. "Ain't we doing exactly that? Dash it, have you been playing fast and loose with me?"

Upon receipt of this inelegant accusation, Lady Regina winced, and thought very seriously that perhaps she should not marry a gentleman so obtuse, no matter if his wealth *was* greater than that of all her other suitors combined. "Was there ever anything equal to this?" she wondered aloud. "It exceeds all belief! How *dare* you accuse me of throwing out lures?"

"Deuced if you didn't!" Although Lord Sweetbriar was uncertain how this quarrel had come about, he was determined to hold up his own end. "Because if you *hadn't* hinted that you might like it, I wouldn't have started making sheep's eyes. I ain't in the petticoat line! Yes, and this is an ungrateful way to act toward a gentleman who's wishful of marrying you, my girl!"

"Ungrateful!" Lady Regina closed her eyes, resolved to silently count one hundred before opening them again, lest she unwisely give her wealthiest suitor a strong piece of her mind. Lady Regina had a very high sense of decorum, and prided herself on the correctness of her conduct, and therefore did not like it pointed out when she was in the wrong.

"Have you put yourself in a pucker?" Lord Sweetbriar was somewhat taken aback by the sight of his beloved standing as rigid as a statue in the middle of the dance floor. "I wish you wouldn't! Come, let us withdraw before people start to *stare!*"

"Oh, very well!" That Lady Regina deigned to open her big green eyes prior to achieving her intended count of one hundred was due to no softening of her attitude toward Lord Sweetbriar, but because of his persistent assaults upon her toes. "You may fetch me some lemonade." Relieved, Rolf whisked Lady Regina off the dance floor. Then he disappeared into a side room.

He had been quick to do her bidding, Lady Regina thought. She wondered if his lordship would be so amenable after he was wed. From this useless speculation, she was diverted only by a glimpse of herself in a looking glass.

Blond curls topped by a cap of muslin and lace ornamented with a wreath of roses; soft and languishing green eyes; excellent complexion and enviable figure set off by a fragile white dress of Indian *mousseline de soie*—Regina stared complacently at her own reflection. She was happiest when her attention was focused upon her own exquisite person and the raiment draped thereupon. Unfortunately, the family purse didn't run to expensive wardrobes. As the means by which she intended to repair this omission inserted himself in her line of vision, Lady Regina frowned.

It had occurred to Lord Sweetbriar, whilst executing his errand, that his beloved's manner was something less than enthusiastic. Therefore he said, with resignation. "Have it your way! Since you insist, I *will* go down upon my knee!" Immediately he suited action to words. "Lady Regina, you will make me the happiest—"

"Sweetbriar, do get up!" Lady Regina wished to sink. "A gentleman does not advance his suit with a lady by putting her to the blush! Since you demand an immediate answer, I will tell you frankly that there is only one circumstance which makes me hesitate—but it is a serious matter!" she added hastily as with alacrity Lord Sweetbriar leapt up. "In a word, *Lady* Sweetbriar."

"Lady Sweetbriar? But I ain't—oh! You mean Nikki."

24

Interpreting Lady Regina's comments in the most favorable of lights, Rolf beamed. "There's no need to worry your head about Nikki; she won't be living with us! Nikki has her own little house, though how she contrived to hire it, I don't know—but that's fair and far off! At all events, she's to marry that museum fellow, Clough!"

By this offhand dismissal of her reservations, Lady Regina was not pleased. "I fear your partiality for Lady Sweetbriar has rendered you over tolerant of her faults. Who is it that appears unchaperoned in Bond Street in mid-afternoon? Who gallops regularly in the Park? Who does all manner of imprudent things, including shocking Sally Jersey almost speechless by introducing that scandalous excuse for vulgar behavior—what is it called? The waltz? Mark my words, no person of refinement will ever indulge in so brazen a display!" She shuddered. "And then there are her flirts."

Lord Sweetbriar was put in the uncomfortable position of defending the female whose influence upon his life he was most often prone to bewail. "Nikki ain't so bad!" he protested. "Remember she wasn't born to be a lady, and so she don't *know!*"

"A common actress!" Again Lady Regina shuddered, causing Lord Sweetbriar to wonder if she was prone to ague. "Your father must have been mad!"

As was his habit, Lord Sweetbriar glanced nervously over his shoulder lest injudicious mention of the dead caused dread specters to arise. "My father may have had the devil's own temper, but he wasn't queer in the attic!" Rolf allowed. "But let's not talk about *that!* Nikki ain't so bad as you make her sound—even if she ain't quite the thing, she *is* all the crack!"

"Your stepmother," Lady Regina responded bluntly, "is nothing more than a base adventuress. You will not mind plain-speaking, I know, from one whom you have just asked to be your bride! I will not undertake to express my opinion of Lady Sweetbriar, beyond stating that I do not care to share a name with a female who has made a byword of herself."

The gist of this declaration, Lord Sweetbriar failed to grasp, though in a dim way he comprehended that his beloved was not responding as anticipated to his suit. Perhaps he had not made his intentions sufficiently clear. "Don't you wish to contract a marriage? To form an eligible connection?" he inquired, somewhat plaintively.

Had Lady Regina's family but possessed sufficient wealth to pamper her as she deserved—but they did not. Clearly Regina must be prepared to sacrifice certain lofty ideals if she were to attain her goal. To marry for love as well as money was not to be her fate. "You are impertinent, Sweetbriar," she retorted. "A gentleman does not ask a young lady questions that are so *personal*."

"Personal?" Lord Sweetbriar looked about for a convenient surface on which to deposit his beloved's empty lemonade glass. "There can't be anything more personal than asking you to be my wife! Or ain't I supposed to do that, either?"

"I did not say so." Lady Regina responded, alarmed by the suggestion that her wealthiest suitor was on the verge of flight. "You must give me time to think over your kind offer, Sweetbriar. You realize, I'm sure, that you *should* have applied to my papa."

"Yes, and so I would have done, had I ever found him sober long enough!" His beloved's shilly-shallying did not accord with Rolf's notion of his own consequence. "I'll be hanged if I can see why you're making such a piece of work of it! You must have known I'd pop the question—you hinted often enough that I *should!*"

"*I* hinted—oh!" In that particular moment Lady Regina had much less the appearance of a damsel about to be thrown into ecstatic transports than one about to deliver a sharp set-down. In an attempt to control the latter impulse, she bit her lip.

Sensitivity to the emotions of those around him was not one of Lord Sweetbriar's virtues, as he promptly displayed: "Don't deny it! You hinted that you would like to become Lady Sweetbriar, else I wouldn't have taken the notion—and now that I think of it, you shouldn't be censuring Nikki for *her* flirts!"

"*I* should not—" Lady Regina also superbly enacted

rage. "You dare compare me to that, that—oh! Words fail me, Sweetbriar!"

For that failure, Rolf could only be grateful, having come to a belated recognition of his lack of tact. "Don't take a pet!" he pleaded, looking anxiously around him to see if they had been overheard. "Remember we're at Almack's! Dash it, there's no need to take offense because I compared you to Nikki! I like Nikki! Even if she *does* drive a fellow distracted! Nikki has a way about her, you know. Or maybe you *don't* know, but you may take my word for it!"

More than he realized, Lord Sweetbriar had spoken truth when he thoughtlessly compared his beloved to his stepmama. Lady Regina, too, was on the dangle for the Sweetbriar fortune, even as Nikki once had been— which was precisely why Regina disliked to hear the merest mention of Nikki's name. She, Lady Regina Foliot, was following in the footsteps of a common actress. That Lady Regina's background was unimpeachable made her ignoble motives all the worse.

Lord Sweetbriar realized that his beloved continued to look incensed. "You'll like Nikki, once you learn to know her! Even my father did! Which ain't to say he forgave her for having pulled the wool over his eyes." Rolf recalled his current dissatisfaction with his stepmama. "No, and it ain't to say either that Nikki ain't cursed unobliging sometimes! Look at her jewels!"

"Jewels?" So intrigued was Lady Regina by this reference that she glanced around her before recalling Almack's was among those select establishments to which Lady Sweetbriar would never have the *entrée*. "What jewels are these?"

Unaware that Lady Regina was even more fascinated by jewels than by her own mirrored reflection, Lord Sweetbriar was gratified by her sudden revival of animation. "Why, Nikki's jewels! The ones my father gave her, which she won't give back to me."

"Ah." Lady Regina erased the frown that had for several moments marred the perfection of her marble brow. "Tell me about it, Rolf!"

Vastly flattered by his beloved's use of his given name, Lord Sweetbriar obeyed. The story was not brief

27

in the telling, involving his stepmama's various follies and indiscretions, and his papa's nasty temper, in final demonstration of which he had left Rolf Nikki's jewels. "But every time I try to claim them, Nikki makes me feel so guilty that I allow her to keep the baubles a while longer! Yes, and she could keep them altogether if it was up to me!" He looked uneasy as he realized what he had said. "But it *ain't* up to me! I must honor my father's last wishes! Maybe Uncle Duke will help me sort out the business."

"What kind of 'baubles' are these?" inquired Lady Regina, very casually, as she deftly maneuvered Lord Sweetbriar into a perambulation around the room's perimeters, and away from the gentleman to whom she was promised for the set of country dances just then forming. "And who is this 'Uncle Duke'?"

"Oh, diamonds and emeralds, rubies and sapphires—you know the sort of thing!" Himself immune to the allure of such trinkets, Lord Sweetbriar failed to note the covetous manner in which his beloved suddenly wetted her lips. "As for Uncle Duke, he's my father's younger brother, who's been living in Russia for years and years. He's only come home now because there's a rumor that the French plan an invasion." Thoughtfully, Rolf paused. "I wonder if that is supposed to be a secret. Mum's the word, Lady Regina, just in case! But anyway, a fellow who's lived with the Russians all these years—you know how emotional they are!—should be able to persuade Nikki to give back the jewels."

"How old a man is your uncle?" Lady Regina had not the slightest interest in Russia and its citizens just then. "Is he married? Is he comfortably circumstanced?"

The interest evidenced by his beloved in the family tree upon which she would soon become a twig inspired Lord Sweetbriar's gratitude. "I haven't a notion; he didn't mention a family when we met in Oxford Street. Uncle Duke must be about five-and-thirty years of age. As for his circumstances—" Rolf shrugged. "I doubt he plans to become my dependent. It ain't the sort of thing one ordinarily asks."

So it was not. Unappreciatively Lady Regina thought of the proprieties which circumscribed polite behavior. She would have dealt far more effectively, could she have inquired outright who was and who was not well heeled. Recalling an adage about the relative desirability of birds perched in bush and on hand, she cast Lord Sweetbriar her most alluring glance. "We have strayed from the topic," she hinted gently.

"We have?" For Lord Sweetbriar's confusion, his beloved's languishing green gaze was partially to blame. "What was that? Oh, yes! Lady Regina, say you will marry me."

How best to play her cards? mused Lady Regina, among whose ignoble motives was an intention to claim Lady Sweetbriar's jewels for herself, thereby in a very circuitous manner vanquishing her foe. She issued a small sigh. "Would that I could—because I would like to, I confess. But it is not to be, alas. There are insurmountable difficulties between us, Sweetbriar. In a word—"

But Lord Sweetbriar had caught the gist of Lady Regina's little speech, and it had rendered him extremely indignant. "*Not?*" he echoed, in loud disbelief. "After I have been dancing attendance on you all these months? You can't mean that!"

Of course Lady Regina did not mean it; although in the moment when his loud tones penetrated the hearing of those around them, and various heads turned, she was strongly tempted to bid him to Hades. "I must—and do!—count myself honored," she said quickly. "Under other circumstances, my answer might be different. But I do not wish a stepmama-in-law who will forever be putting me to the blush. I know you cannot agree with me, Sweetbriar, and I do not blame you for it. That detestable female obviously holds you in thrall."

"She does?" With bewilderment Rolf stared.

"Poor boy! You don't even realize." Though Lady Regina had not a sympathetic bone in her graceful body, she still contrived to look sad. "Or perhaps I am

29

mistaken? If so, you must prove me wrong. Did you but convince me you do *not* favor your stepmama over me, Sweetbriar, I would have no reason to refuse to become your bride."

Chapter Four

During those very moments when Lady Regina Foliot sought to convince Lord Sweetbriar that the family skeleton should be denuded of her jewels and locked away in some dark closet forevermore, the object of her malice was enjoying a comfortable prose with Miss Clough. The setting for their conversation was the drawing room of Clough House.

"We have a choice, dear Clytie!" Lady Sweetbriar wandered through the empty chamber, with a knowledgeable eye inspecting the plaster frieze and ceiling, the oak-paneled walls, the columns and pilasters which flanked doors and windows and chimneypiece. "We may have polychrome chintz with a naturalistic floral design, or painted silks imported from China, executed in body color on a white satin ground. *I* incline toward the latter. And with it I would like to see an Axminster carpet of Chinese inspiration, with a pattern of pairs of confronting dragons, and various other symbols, in gold on a blue ground." She moved to the window. "Chinese paper in addition would be too much, I fancy, though I have seen some excellent examples—each roll is printed with a portion of a large design, which requires several panels to complete—trees and flowers, or landscapes and figure subjects, after the manner of tapestry. But it is very expensive, I believe."

At this somewhat tardy concern for expense, Clytie smiled; Clough House had been already turned on its ear in a frenzy of refurbishing and redecorating. Permission to do so had been Sir Avery's gift to his affianced bride, and at the conclusion of the renovations the wedding would take place. If the renovations *were* completed, amended Clytie, who had been living amid chaos for several months. Fortunately, the creator of that disorder had excellent taste. Aloud, Miss Clough said: "You have never counted the cost of anything, Nikki."

"Have I not?" Having reached a decision, Lady Sweetbriar deserted the window, crossed to Clytie, and with that damsel linked arms. "The China paper, I think, and the Axminster rug! You would be surprised at what I have counted. I do not *blame* you for your lack of understanding, mind! You were not married to Reuben. But I was, dear Clytie, and I promise you there was a vast difference between the way things really were with us and the face we presented to the world."

During the past year, Miss Clough had spent considerable time in company with her prospective stepmama, especially in those last few months when Clough House was being turned upside-down and inside-out. Consequently Clytie had learned to decipher Lady Sweetbriar's most cryptic utterances. "Why did you stay with Sweetbriar?" she inquired, as they exited the drawing room. "If he was unkind?"

"He was not *unkind,* precisely," explained Nikki, with a connoisseur's glance at the hallway. "No, and he wasn't kind either, nor did he let loose for an instant of the purse strings! My dear Clytie, I could tell you— but I must not! You would not thank me for making you embarrassing revelations! Reuben didn't divorce me because to do so would be tantamount to making a public admission that he had been duped—not that I deliberately *tried* to make him think I was something I was not! *I* cannot be blamed, surely, if he leaped to the wrong conclusion? At least I *shouldn't* be, but Reuben *did* blame me, and made it his object to make me miserable." Looking glum, she toyed with her jewels, diadem and necklace and earrings of emeralds set in diamonds and hung with the immense pear pearls. "And he succeeded very well! I am *still* miserable, and Reuben is dead!"

"How sad." Miss Clough's tone was heavily ironic. "Papa must make it up to you."

"Oh, it is not your papa who has made me miserable!" Aghast at this misunderstanding, Lady Sweetbriar abruptly halted, thus necessitating that Miss Clough halt also, since their arms were still linked. "In point of fact, I am not *truly* miserable, except when I think that Rolf is to have my jewels, and I try very hard *not* to think of it above ten times a day!" Her fine eyes narrowed, her voice became grim. "To you I will confess I do not mean to give back my jewels, ever! Even my jewels are scant consolation for having been given only the tiniest portion of the Sweetbriar fortune, because if anyone ever deserved a fortune, I do! But I have not abandoned all hope yet!"

"You haven't?" Miss Clough successfully urged Lady Sweetbriar to resume movement and shepherded her toward the morning room, the one chamber which had thus far escaped the renovative chaos which reigned over the rest of the house. "But you will soon have Papa's fortune—already he has placed a considerable sum at your disposal. Isn't that enough?"

"Dear Clytie, had you ever been *impoverished,* you would know that there is no such thing as *enough!*" Lady Sweetbriar's dark eyes flashed. "Beside, it is the *principle* of the thing! One does not like to feel that one has failed to achieve one's object. Oh, I do not want to cheat Rolf out of his inheritance—he deserves it, poor boy! Simply, I do not wish Reuben to have the last word. Not that it will make any difference to him *now.*" In a manner very reminiscent of her stepson, she glanced over her shoulder. "At least I hope it will not!"

The late Lord Sweetbriar must have possessed a truly diabolical disposition to inspire so habitually nervous a remembrance in his survivors, Clytie thought. Yet Nikki managed to dress herself superbly on the mere pittance she had allegedly been left, this evening in a gown of colored crepe with square low neck, short Spanish shoulder sleeves, and a skirt with a demi-train; as well as to maintain a hired house. Miss Clough suspected her stepmama-to-be had a tendency to exaggerate.

With that suspicion, though Clytie could not know it, she did Lady Sweetbriar a grave disservice: Nikki had greatly understated the case regarding her dealings with her late spouse. To maintain her little house, and present an unimpoverished appearance, she had to mightily contrive. This evening's gown, for instance, was in one of its many incarnations—and not for Clytie's benefit had its current resurrection been undertaken. Lady Sweetbriar was bound for a musical party, and had stopped by Clough House only to reassure herself that soon all need for contrivance would end. Or *almost* all need for contrivance. Nikki was not of the philosophy that husband and wife should share everything.

It then occurred to Nikki that the recent exchange with her prospective stepdaughter had been somewhat indelicate. "Dear Clytie!" she cried, and grasped that damsel's hands, which very nearly resulted in an accident, because Miss Clough had been rearranging some flowers in a vase. "I hope you do not *mind* that I am marrying your papa for his money—not that it is any secret! But he is fond of me, I think, and I shall be very good to him, you'll see!"

"I don't doubt that." Nor did Clytie doubt that any gentleman alive must feel some degree of fondness for Nikki. "You needn't explain further. If Papa doesn't mind, I see no reason why *I* should."

"Such a sensible girl! If only I could be similarly practical—but I fear I am a creature of impulse." Miss Clough was gifted with Lady Sweetbriar's roguish smile. "You won't mind having a stepmama who was once an actress? I thought not! What an excellent child you are! I would have felt very badly, had you disapproved the match—not that it would *stop* me from marrying your father, you understand!" Having settled these matters to her satisfaction, Nikki released Miss Clough and turned her attention to the morning room. Though she itched to redecorate it also, this chamber was sacrosanct, having been the refuge of the previous lady of the house. As well as of several other Clough ladies, Nikki suspected. She doubted the room had been

34

so much as redecorated since it was built in the seventeenth century.

Strips of tapestry hung upon the paneled walls, with silver sconces set between them; the wide oak floorboards were covered only by a small central island of carpet. The furnishings included a commode inlaid with ivory and various woods, a table supported on luxuriously carved legs, a few chairs with high arched backs, and a Japan cabinet which sat against one wall. It all appeared very unexciting, in Nikki's sight. If only she might introduce some modern pieces, or at least camouflage the plain casement windows with hangings in the elaborate French style.

Association with Lady Sweetbriar during the past several trying months had rendered Miss Clough cognizant of the implications of the gleam currently existent in her ladyship's dark eye. Therefore Clytie deemed a change of topic advisable. "I encountered Rolf today in Oxford Street. Did you know he plans to wed?"

"*Rolf* does?" Lady Sweetbriar abandoned window curtains for the much more urgent consideration of a new threat to her intended inroads upon the Sweetbriar wealth. "Whatever for?"

To this suggestion that marriage was an undertaking entered into only for practical purposes, Clytie responded with a wry glance. "Because he has a *tendresse* for the young lady, I assume—indeed, so I was told! Which reminds me, Nikki: Rolf is very annoyed because I will not repeat his warnings to Papa. He is very concerned that Papa can't prevent you falling into scrapes."

"And concerned also that I am on the dangle for a fortune?" Lady Sweetbriar inquired shrewdly, as she settled upon a high arched-back chair. "Silly chub! Avery knows I must have wealth, and if *he* doesn't mind, and *you* don't, what does it signify? Doubtless Rolf is afraid I won't give him back the jewels." She looked contemplative. "And so should he be!"

As always fascinated by conversation with her stepmama-to-be, Miss Clough seated herself on a nearby chair. "Why are you so adamant, Nikki? Papa will give you jewels of your own. Wouldn't it be simpler to return those Lord Sweetbriar gave you to Rolf?"

"No, dear Clytie, it would not!" Did a guilty expression flitter across Lady Sweetbriar's heart-shaped face? "Do not ask me to explain! Instead tell me who Rolf is hankering after—I mean, who he wishes to wed!"

Had a person not known Nikki's background was irregular, Miss Clough thought fondly, Nikki would within five minutes of making their acquaintance have betrayed herself. Lady Sweetbriar was not exactly vulgar, even in her occasional lapses of speech; but her outlook was definitely not that of the *crème de la crème*. "Lady Regina Foliot," replied Miss Clough. "You know of her, I think—why, Nikki, you have turned quite pale! Whatever is amiss?"

"Amiss? Everything!" Lady Sweetbriar was not one to mince words. "Rolf might as well allow the gull-gropers to get their talons fast in him as marry that—that stiff-rumped female! I know I should not call her *so*, but a spade by any other name still remains a spade! In the end it will come to the same thing, no matter *what* I call her, and it makes me very melancholy to think that Rolf will never speak to me again!"

"Never speak to you?" Astonished by her stepmama-to-be's violent reaction to mention of Lady Regina Foliot, Miss Clough poured out a glassful of a restorative beverage, by the benefits of which her papa swore. "'Gull-gropers'? I beg you will explain!"

"I had intended to." Nikki took a large swallow of the restorative beverage, which was in large part alcohol, and wheezed. "Gull-gropers, moneylenders, cursed cent-per-cents; *you* know the breed! Not that you know them *personally*, of course, but *I* do." Again Lady Sweetbriar applied to her glass, but this time took a smaller sip. "*Should* you ever have occasion to strike up an acquaintance with such fellows, Howard and Gibbs are the best of the breed—and even they talk on about securities and credentials until one wishes to scream!"

Miss Clough was very impressed by how quickly, as result of her papa's favorite tonic, Lady Sweetbriar's spirits had revived; and she thought that the next time her own mood was despondent she would seek succor by this same means. Presently, other matters were more pressing. "Nikki! Have you been having deep doings?" she asked.

"Deep doings? Piffle!" Despite her quick denial, Lady Sweetbriar wore a distinctly guilty look. "At any rate I am only a *teeny* bit scorched, and will soon come about again. It is nothing to concern yourself about, I promise! Rather, we should both concern ourselves with Rolf. He must marry where he wishes, of course; and if you assure me he is quite *épris* in that direction—but I am very fond of Rolf, even if he *is* determined to take away my jewels!"

Miss Clough sought to discover the source of her companion's distress. "You do not think Lady Regina Foliot is suitable?" she inquired. "Why ever not? Despite the fact of her father's, er, self-indulgence, Lady Regina is unexceptionable."

"Self-indulgence?" hooted Lady Sweetbriar, as with a scornful glance she drained her glass. "Foliot is addicted both to the bottle and the table of green cloth— and Lady Regina has naught in her head but vanity and an ambition to see herself luxuriously bestowed! You will think me dreadfully plain-spoken, dear Clytie, but it is very tedious to be forever trying to be a pretty-behaved female when at heart one is nothing of the sort! No, and nor is Lady Regina Foliot, because if there's anything a fortune hunter learns, it's to recognize another of the same breed!"

"Are you accusing Lady Regina of marrying Rolf merely for his wealth and position?" A certain tension at the base of Miss Clough's neck caused her to think she might have recourse to her papa's tonic sooner than she had anticipated. "You are severe, Nikki! To marry for monetary consideration is not so unusual a thing."

"Silly girl; I know that! Aren't I planning to do it myself for a second time?" Lady Sweetbriar threw back her head, so that she might drain the last drop from her glass, and then scrambled to prevent her emerald and diamond diadem from falling off. Somewhat breathlessly, she added: "But Lady Regina Foliot is an altogether different kettle of fish! She is one of the people who don't *see* me even if I am smack in front of them, and though I do not ordinarily pay attention to such people, one can hardly overlook one's own daughter-in-law! Doubtless the wretch will try and persuade poor Rolf to deal with me similarly." A spark kindled in Nikki's dark eye. "Doubtless she fancies herself wearing my jewels. Well, you have my word on that, Clytie: she *shan't!*"

Miss Clough, who had not hitherto taken seriously Lord Sweetbriar's warnings about his stepmama's tendency to tumble into scrapes, suffered an ominous presentiment. "Oh, Nikki! Why make such a piece of work of it?" she protested. "Surely you must realize that the only reason *any*one would marry Rolf is for his position! As for the jewels, what do they matter? I have told you Papa will give you jewels that are even more fine. For that matter, *I* will give you Mama's, do you but give Sweetbriar's back!"

"What a good child you are!" A little tipsily, Lady Sweetbriar sought Miss Clough's hand. "Tell me, Clytie, have *you* thought of marriage? I wouldn't mind if it was *you* who had the Sweetbriar fortune in lieu of myself, because it would still be in the family! If you made a push, I'll wager you could cut Lady Regina out in a trice."

"And you think also that I would be most understanding about the jewels," Miss Clough responded dryly. "Thank you, Nikki!"

Lady Sweetbriar wore her pretty pout. "You do not take me seriously! Then you may only blame yourself if you are left upon the shelf—not but what, with Avery forever puttering around with his old museum, I shan't welcome your company!"

"On the shelf?" Definitely Miss Clough would have recourse to her papa's tonic, as soon as her future stepmama took her leave. "Nikki, I am only nineteen!"

"Oh?" It was obvious from Lady Sweetbriar's abstracted manner that she was deep in thought. "I *knew* I was not old enough to be your mama—no, or Rolf's either! Poor, poor Rolf! Yes, and poor *me!* I must resign myself to being snubbed by my own daughter-in-law."

Mention of snubs recalled to Miss Clough the swarthy gentleman she had so recently attempted to deliver a set-down, with such little success. With the intention

38

of diverting Lady Sweetbriar from her unhappy thoughts, Clytie said: "It was the drollest thing, Nikki! Rolf thought he espied his papa's ghost walking down Oxford Street this afternoon."

"Reuben's *ghost?*" Though Lady Sweetbriar had unquestionably been diverted, her expression had nothing in it of drollery. "Had you met my husband, Clytie, you would not say such a thing even in jest! I have often thought it would be just like Reuben to haunt us, because he enjoyed setting us on pins and needles, and even he could devise no better way to cut up a person's peace." Perfectly on cue, one of the old windows rattled in its casement. Nikki started and uttered a little shriek.

"Do not excite yourself, Nikki!" This time it was Miss Clough who caught Lady Sweetbriar's diadem before it hit the floor. "It was not his papa Rolf saw. Moreover, Mr. Thorne volunteered himself as target should Lord Sweetbriar display any tendency to *roam!*"

A queer stillness fell over Lady Sweetbriar's lively features. "Mr. Thorne?" she echoed, in a quiet, expressionless voice.

"Yes, Mr. Thorne." If Nikki's odd behavior was result of Sir Avery's tonic, Miss Clough thought she would not indulge after all. "Rolf's 'Uncle Duke.' He was but recently returned from Russia, I believe."

"Duke." Nikki retrieved her diadem from Clytie and placed it at a rakish angle upon her brow. "Duke has come home, egad! Where *is* he?"

"Why, I do not know! He was promised to dine with Rolf this evening." Miss Clough recalled Marmaduke's nonsensical sallies. His little ladybug, was she? The impudence! Self-consciously, she added: "Mr. Thorne asked to be remembered to you, Nikki!" But Lady Sweetbriar had already leaped to her feet, dashed through the doorway, and was halfway down the stair.

Chapter Five

A short time after her abrupt departure from Sir Avery's ancestral home, Lady Sweetbriar restlessly paced through her own little hired house, on the south side of the New Road, in Fitzroy Square. It was an old brick eight-roomed structure, with two rooms and a large closet on the three floors above the basement, in which were a front and back kitchen. Additionally the house boasted a dark-paneled hallway which ended in an archway leading into a tiny garden enclosed by a high brick wall; and a broad staircase with a massive balustrade in the old style.

Down that stairway, Lady Sweetbriar tripped, en route to the first floor drawing room. On the threshold she paused, with a grimace of distaste. Pale green paper on the wall, pale satin hangings at the window, furniture upholstered in the same—to a lady who thirsted for floral designs and stripes, it was very dull stuff. But her surroundings, tedious as she might find them, could not long hold Nikki's thoughts. She moved to one of the great Venetian windows which were the house's saving feature, and looked out into the night. What she glimpsed there caused her to hastily step back, and glance in a somewhat frantic manner around the chamber, and arrange herself in an elegant posture upon a chair with padded arms and overstuffed seat. This dignified demeanor abandoned her immediately upon the withdrawal of the servant who had conducted her caller there. "Duke! You *scoundrel!* Oh, my darling, it has been so *long!*" cried Lady Sweetbriar, and hurled herself into Mr. Thorne's arms.

Though her *fiancé* might have habitually responded with coolness to Lady Sweetbriar's overtures, she did not ordinarily encounter difficulty in arousing gentlemanly ardor. Certainly Mr. Thorne's reaction was quite as enthusiastic as any lady might have wished: he clasped Nikki to him in a very familiar manner, while she rained kisses on his face.

"If only I had pursued my *first* ambition!" cried Lady Sweetbriar, who between caresses continued to talk. "And stayed upon the stage! I might have become another Sarah Siddons, I think—but instead I encountered *you,* you rogue! Which reminds me that I have a crow to pluck with you, Duke!" She drew back sufficiently to award Mr. Thorne a very reproachful glance. "I do think you might have warned me Reuben was a cursed cheese parer! A nipfarthing! A lickpenny! Because your brother left me the merest pittance upon which to exist—*not* that I haven't contrived excellently on what little I *was* left."

Mr. Thorne's blue eyes rested assessingly upon the emeralds and diamonds and pearls which Lady Sweetbriar still wore. "So I see. Since you had just cast me aside in favor of my elder brother, explanations didn't seem entirely appropriate."

"*Not* your elder brother!" Looking very earnest, Lady Sweetbriar stood on tiptoe and placed her hands one on each side of Mr. Thorne's face. "Your elder brother's *fortune!* There is a very great difference! Moreover I was very young, and thought it was a highly flattering alliance." Her glance was shrewd. "And I knew *you* would never marry me!"

"There was always plain dealing between us, Nikki." Though Marmaduke's expression was amused, he made no effort to elude his captor, indeed clasped his own hands around her tiny waist. "You must not blame *me* if you stood on bad terms with my brother. You were quite content to have landed him, as I recall."

"Yes, and had I known what I know now, I wouldn't have tried so hard to keep him from wriggling off my hook!" Lady Sweetbriar released Mr. Thorne's face and

41

rested her hands upon his chest instead. "You need not try and make yourself out so noble; my memory is excellent. You were convulsed with laughter when you learned Reuben had made me an offer; you said you had shown me how to act the lady better than we thought!"

"And so I did." Marmaduke touched a gentle knuckle to his companion's pouting lips. "You *are* a lady now, Nikki. It was what you wanted, all those years ago. Don't you think it a little late to complain that life as a ladyship was not precisely how you had anticipated it would be?"

"Precisely?" Lady Sweetbriar recalled her late spouse's reaction upon discovering he had not alienated the affections of a well-brought-up young woman, but instead had wed the daughter of strolling players, a damsel who had herself trod the boards. "You knew your brother better than I—and consequently must also have known we would ever be at daggers' points! The merest observances of civility were beyond Reuben's prowess, most days; I vow I spent most of my married life trying to coax him out of the sullens! Oh, it was a bad business, and just remembering it puts me out of frame."

Mr. Thorne gazed down upon the dark curls which during this narration had come to rest upon his chest. As if curious, he touched his fingers to Lady Sweetbriar's curls, upon which the diadem still sat. "My memory is also excellent, Nikki!" he retorted. "I only meant it as a prank. Reuben was bound to want you, as soon as he knew you were mine. Marriage was wholly *your* idea."

"So it was." Lady Sweetbriar revealed a roguish eye. "Gracious, but he was enraptured—even if it did not last! Naturally I accepted his offer, Duke; you would have done the same, had you existed all your life in impoverished circumstances, and wished more than anything to be provided for."

Mr. Thorne still contemplated her ladyship's dark curls, with their jeweled crown. "I would have provided for you, Nikki. In fact, as I recall—"

"Hush!" Lady Sweetbriar attempted to look severe.

"We will not talk of *that*, Duke! Not that I wasn't fond of you, because I was—fonder than I have ever been of anyone else! Not that we need worry about being overheard *here*, because the female who lends me her countenance is long abed, and the servants are conveniently *deaf!* That is why I left Sweetbriar's townhouse—I was very tired of being talked about, and in my own little house I need not try to impress anyone, and may be as common as I please! I *said* it was because Rolf and I were near enough in age that if I did not do so people would talk, which in my experience they *do*. Not that I care a fig for such things, you understand!"

"I understand perfectly," Thorne said. "You are still cross with me for taking an abrupt departure, once I saw which way the wind blew. I thought it the only prudent action. I did not imagine Reuben would be pleased to discover he had married my—"

"Friend!" supplied Lady Sweetbriar, with a twinkling wicked glance. "We will not discuss it further. No, and I shall not even scold you for leaving me to abide the consequence. You must tell me all about yourself, Duke, where you have been and what you have been doing all these years. Yes, and you must tell me also what has brought you home *now!* Have you been afraid to face Reuben? Or perhaps you thought he would immediately suspect I was intriguing with you?"

The late Lord Sweetbriar might well have had basis for such a suspicion, judging from the easy manner in which his widow and his brother stood entwined. Mr. Thorne lifted Lady Sweetbriar's hands to his lips. "In Russia, when a man kisses a woman's hand, she returns the greeting with a kiss on his brow."

"Oh, Russia!" Lady Sweetbriar's husky voice suggested a wish for a more personal salute. Then she looked apprehensive. "Duke, do *you* believe in ghosts?"

"You've been listening to my mooncalf of a nephew." Since Nikki had failed to avail herself of his invitation to salute his brow, Marmaduke escorted her to one of the overstuffed chairs. "Was it because you wanted to hear about Russia that you sent that note? Rolf was very curious as to why I was going out after having just said I did not plan to—yes, and wondered who I knew in London after so many years."

"Rolf is a looby." With a gentle shove, Lady Sweetbriar convinced Mr. Thorne to be seated, and then took up her position on his lap. "I was anxious to see you; Miss Clough had just told me you were in town. And now you may tell me about Russia, if you please!"

"It is a barbarous country." If Marmaduke was discomposed by having a female seated on his lap, he made no sign, indeed seemed to have settled into his unusual position very comfortably. Lest Mr. Thorne's sanguinity be overrated, however, his large number of previous conquests must be recalled, as well as the fact that this was not the first time Nikki had perched thusly. "And barbarously governed. The tsar's father and grandfather were both murdered. The prisons are full, the people are starving, and corruption is rife. The country is filled with secret societies. Most of the officers of the Imperial Guard belong to such societies, and the source of their ideas is revolutionary France." His arms tightened around Lady Sweetbriar. "There are rumors of a French invasion. That is why I was recalled."

"Goodness, but you do that well!" said Nikki, some moments later, in response not to Mr. Thorne's remarks, but his ruthless embrace. "If only Avery—" Her bemused expression changed to horror and she leaped to her feet. "Egad! I quite forgot I am betrothed. How *can* you laugh at me, Duke? I wish you would stop! To think I have forgotten Avery for an entire half hour— it is the most mortifying thing!"

"You refine too much upon it. Your memory was overset by the shock of our reunion." Though he had ceased to laugh, Mr. Thorne continued to look amused. "Come sit down here by me, Nikki, and tell me all about this Avery." He patted the plump seat of a nearby chair.

Looking wistful, Lady Sweetbriar declined and took up a defensive position behind a painted tripod table with hinged top and curved feet. "You must not think that I am bamboozling Avery like I did Reuben—or at least not so *very* much! We met at a prizefight, you see, so Avery *knows* how it is with me. Yes, and I understand how it is with him and his museum—it is the most curious place, crammed with all manner of oddities, from marble feet to stuffed flamingoes and giraffes. Not a time do I go there that I do not see something new; the last time it was a preserved vulture's head. Fancy!"

"A preserved *vulture's* head?" Mr. Thorne's tone was most compassionate. "My poor Nikki!"

"Are you *sorry* for me, Duke?" Feeling suddenly shy of the only man for whom she had ever possessed a nonmonetary affection, Lady Sweetbriar could not meet his gaze. "You must not be. Avery and I will rub along together very comfortably. *He* will never make odious inferences, or be forever accusing me of nourishing evil designs! Yes, and I like Avery very well, and can't imagine anyone I'd rather be married to, even if he *is* a trifle preoccupied—but on the other hand, he doesn't mind that I must have a fortune, or that I once trod the boards—though *that* was so very long ago I think I might be forgiven it, since in the meantime I have been very good." She paused. "At least I have *tried* very hard!"

Mr. Thorne thought that Lady Sweetbriar was quick to take up the cudgels in her *fiancé's* defense. Perhaps *too* quick, he mused. "Are you run aground again, Nikki? You never did have the least sense of economy. Shall I help you out?"

In response to this generous offer, Lady Sweetbriar elevated her gaze from the tea cart. Her expression was not happy. "If you are going to tell me you have made your fortune in Russia, I wish you would not, because if I married Reuben when I could just as well have had you—Paugh! The notion is enough to put one devilish out of humor! As for your help, I must refuse it, though I am grateful for the offer."

"*Why* must you refuse it?" Mr. Thorne left the matter of his own finances unresolved. "Do you think your Avery might take offense?"

Lady Sweetbriar looked rueful. "He *should,* certainly; but I don't know that he *would!* I will admit that I don't understand Avery. Not that it signifies, because I *did* understand Reuben, and it made not a jot of difference."

"Then let me help you." Though Mr. Thorne had long been parted from his Nikki, he immediately recognized the signs of a conscience grappling with guilt. "Your *fiancé* need never know."

"*I* would know!" Lady Sweetbriar ventured out from behind the tripod table and moved to the fireplace. Avaricious as she might be, Nikki would accept no investment in her future without giving good value in return. Even the aloof Sir Avery Clough must balk at his intended bride paying out such dividends, she thought. At least she hoped he would. "Oh Duke, you were the best of all my flirts—not that you were a *flirt*, precisely—no, no! Stay your distance! We must put all that behind us now."

For a lady determined to forget her past, reflected Mr. Thorne, Nikki displayed a queer tendency to dwell therein. But he had long ago learned the futility of engaging the fair sex in argument. "As you wish," he therefore responded, and smiled. "You are in looks, Nikki. Are those some of the family baubles you're wearing?"

This chance remark—Mr. Thorne not yet being aware that the Sweetbriar jewels were a point of sore contention between Nikki and Rolf—reminded Lady Sweetbriar of her ill-usage. "Don't try and diddle *me*, Duke: you know perfectly well that these are Sweetbriar heirlooms." She clutched at the gems hung round her neck. "Yes, and you must know also about Reuben's wretched will, and that he left the jewels to Rolf, because Rolf talks about little else! I give you fair warning: Rolf shan't have them back! And it will do you no good to try and cajole me in his behalf. Oh, I recall very well that you once had the knack of getting around me—yes, and look where *that* led us! You to Russia, me to Fitzroy Square, and Reuben to an early grave."

"Cut line, Nikki!" In protest, Mr. Thorne held up his hand. "Rolf said nothing to me about your baubles, or much of anything else except some female he wishes to wed. *Her* praises he sang so profusely I began to wonder why such a paragon would content herself with

46

less than a duke. So you see your fears were for naught, Nikki."

Had they been? wondered Lady Sweetbriar. *Did* she pose imaginary difficulties for herself? After careful assessment of the situation, she decided she did not. Rolf was determined to reclaim the Sweetbriar jewels; she was equally determined he must not. For a year the fate of the gems had hung in the balance—but now Lady Regina Foliot sought to tip the scales. If Rolf had an ally, Nikki thought she must also—and who could better serve than Rolf's own uncle as an agent in the enemy camp?

Thinking to persuade Marmaduke to her viewpoint, Lady Sweetbriar turned to him with her most bewitching smile. Then she uttered a little shriek. While she had been deep in cogitation, he had left his chair.

"Don't act so blasted missish!" Mr. Thorne caught Lady Sweetbriar by the arms before she could back into the fireplace. "I've no intentions of making advances, Nikki."

Looking simultaneously cautious and confused, Lady Sweetbriar frowned up into his swarthy face. "You don't?"

"I don't." Mr. Thorne smiled. "Unless, that is, you *want* me to."

That was a relief, at any rate; naturally a lady affianced to one gentleman could not wish another to pay her court. Wondering how best to wheedle Duke to lend her his assistance, Nikki studied the pristine pleats of his cravat. Lest he accuse her once more of missishness, she refrained from pointing out that he still gripped her arms. She would be modest and maidenly and troubled, Nikki decided. Marmaduke would respond quickly to a lady in distress. Plaintively she raised her eyes— and surprised on his bronzed features an expression of extreme speculativeness. It was gone in an instant, but Lady Sweetbriar knew her Duke, and she would hand over *all* the Sweetbriar jewels without a single demur if he wasn't running some sort of thimble-rig.

Chapter Six

Lady Sweetbriar was not alone in thinking Marmaduke Thorne would serve as an excellent ally; Lady Regina Foliot came to a similar conclusion within moments of making the gentleman's acquaintance, an event which took place at the King's Theatre in the Haymarket. After considerable wracking of his brain in an effort to determine how best to persuade Lady Regina of his devotion, Lord Sweetbriar had hit upon the happy scheme of presenting his uncle. That Mr. Thorne had quite a way with the ladies, his nephew had already observed. He trusted that Marmaduke could wheedle Lady Regina into an acquiescent mood.

Nor had Lord Sweetbriar's trust in his uncle been misplaced. Mr. Thorne was beguiling Lady Regina, her mother, and sisters, with accounts of the opera as performed in St. Petersburg, with special emphasis upon the jealous stratagems of the Nymph of Dnieper, entertainment in which the ancient costumes and music of Russia were admirably displayed. Lord Sweetbriar, who had no interest even in the Mozart opera in which Mme. Catalini was currently between intervals exercising her fine voice, occupied himself with gazing upon his beloved, who was clad for the occasion in a gown of white muslin trimmed with varicolored beadwork. On her yellow curls she wore a coronet made of fine lace decorated with ribbons and flowers, on her arms long white gloves, and white satin slippers on her feet. The overall effect was angelic.

Lady Regina's appearance in that moment was most deceptive. The source of her un-Christian sentiments—who was behaving in a very gay and animated manner that caused heads to turn toward her, and exhibiting not the least concern for the attention that she drew—was seated in an opposite box. "Your stepmama seems to be in excellent spirits," Lady Regina murmured, with a reproachful glance at Rolf. "I must conclude that you haven't attempted to make her understand that she must try much harder to observe the proprieties. Indeed, I *know* you have not, because the *on-dit* is that Lady Sweetbriar has been publicly embracing Sir Avery Clough! Even *you* must admit that such behavior can hardly add to her consequence. Or yours! Much as you may like your stepmama, Sweetbriar, you cannot sanction such indelicate behavior on the grand staircase of the British Museum!"

Had not Lord Sweetbriar been so besotted, he might have received considerable edification from Lady Regina's opinions on romance. "Blast!" he muttered, as he transferred his gaze from the angelic Lady Regina to the opposite box, where his stepmama was one of a very convivial group. "If she's engaging in that sort of thing, maybe she *ain't* on the dangle for the fellow's fortune," he offered hopefully.

Lady Regina did not care for Lord Sweetbriar's apparent determination to think the best of his stepmama. Lest she appear small and petty-minded, however, she could not voice that thought. Instead she allowed a cool expression to settle upon her features, and refrained altogether from comment. It was a very effective maneuver, one which left its victim feeling as if he'd encountered an Arctic blast.

"Talking to Nikki ain't that easy!" Lord Sweetbriar sought to defend himself. "I don't know what you expect me to do about her, anyway! Nikki ain't my dependent, so I can hardly pension her off—no, and wouldn't if I could! Dashed if I see what *you* have against Nikki! You don't even know her. To take a dislike to someone you don't know ain't what I'd call *fair!*"

Sternly Lady Regina reminded herself of the pecuniary embarrassments which beset her family, of the vast contrivances entailed in merely hiring this box, of her feckless father who was even then doubtless overindulging in one of his clubs. All depended upon Regina making an advantageous match. She could not follow instinct and bid her wealthiest suitor to the devil, alas.

"I do not *dis*like Lady Sweetbriar," she responded coolly. "I merely do not care to become her intimate. Dote as you may upon your stepmama, Rolf, you cannot deny that her habits are not altogether elegant, or claim that one may call her painstakingly discreet! You do not care for my opinion, I credit. I shall say no more."

Clearly a presentation of his stepmama's better qualities—kindness, habitually sunny temper, generosity except as regarded the family jewels—would in no way advance Nikki in Lady Regina's opinion. Pondering how best to deal with the ticklish situation in which he found himself, Lord Sweetbriar gazed about the great horseshoe auditorium. From pit to gallery to the five tiers of subscription boxes, the theater was crowded with people in formal evening dress. Rolf himself had risen magnificently to his surroundings in long-tailed coat and white waistcoat and frilled shirt with high points, silk stockings and breeches with knots of ribbon at his knee. Tucked into the folds of his intricately arranged neckcloth was a jewel, and in his hand a quizzing glass. Across the auditorium, Lady Sweetbriar caught her stepson's brooding attention and waggled her fingers at him in what Lady Regina could only consider a positively vulgar way.

"I have wished to talk to you, Mr. Thorne," she murmured, when the other members of the party were distracted by the resumption of the entertainment onstage. "About your nephew. I fear he has fallen into the clutches of a designing female. You will find it difficult to credit that such a thing might happen, but I assure you it is true. And I fear there is a very strong danger of ill consequence."

"You astonish me." Mr. Thorne's expression was enigmatic. "Pray continue."

Lady Regina was nothing loath. As reward for his interest, she allowed Mr. Thorne a view of her perfect profile. "She is a female of equivocal character—the slyest thing in nature, in fact! She is a complete flirt—the most hardened flirt in London, I vow! Prone to paroxysms of imprudence and—and heaven knows what else!" Aware that her voice had risen, Regina took a deep, steadying breath. "I am certain she harbors designs upon the Sweetbriar fortune. I most earnestly conjure you to assist me, sir, in preventing her from squandering it."

No longer was Mr. Thorne's expression enigmatic, but distinctly bored. "I suggest you refine too much upon the matter, Lady Regina," he said bluntly. "Ordinarily I would not say such a thing to a young woman, but since you introduced the subject I will make an exception: my nephew is not the first to have a 'light o' love.' Since you have become aware of the situation—which you should *not* have; I can only assume Rolf is even more of a clunch than I realized—you must try to swallow it with good grace."

"Swallow!" Lady Regina experienced grave difficulty in achieving that feat. "A—a—*Rolf!*"

Thus bid to attend his beloved, in a tone that caused heads in several nearby boxes to turn, Lord Sweetbriar approached. This act roused no demur from Lady Regina's mother or her sisters, even though his lordship's action quite blocked their view of the stage. "How could I have been so deceived in you?" demanded Lady Regina, in a throbbingly dramatic whisper. "All this time you have professed devotion to *me* you have had—oh! I can say no more!"

For that circumstance, Lord Sweetbriar rendered thanks. Bewildered, he glanced at his uncle. As opposed to boredom, Mr. Thorne's expressive features now registered amusement, of an unholy kind. "You are wondering what has caused this contretemps," Marmaduke suggested. "I must tell you that the truth has come out. You must not try and evade the issue, nephew! It is too late for that."

"It is?" With no lessening of confusion, Rolf stared at his ashen-faced beloved, who responded with a visible shudder and a lowered gaze. "Dashed if I know what you're prosing on about."

"Why, your partiality for designing females, nephew!"
Despite his huge enjoyment of the kick-up he had unwittingly brought about, Marmaduke contrived to sound sincere. "My boy, it simply will not *do!* I am not a fellow prone to moralizing, mind, but it has become appallingly clear to me that *someone* must show you how to go on. And I have had some experience in these little matters. In short, it is cruelly unfeeling to ask a young lady of breeding to play second fiddle to your— you will forgive me, Lady Regina—your fancy-piece!"

"My *what?*" Lord Sweetbriar's voice was scarcely softer than a shout. "But I ain't—"

"Tsk, nephew, of course you have! I have it on the best authority, the word of Lady Regina herself." In a very avuncular manner, Mr. Thorne patted that mortified young woman's hand. "You must break with your ladybird, my boy—yes, I *know* it will be difficult! It always *is!* Had you contrived to keep the *affaire* secret—but you did not. In the future, you will perhaps be more discreet." Having delivered himself of this outrageous speech, Marmaduke directed his attention to the stage.

Before either of Mr. Thorne's auditors were capable of speech, some few moments elapsed. Lord Sweetbriar, whose sensibilities were slightest, broke the silence. "Ladybirds!" he marveled. "If that don't beat all!"

Lady Regina slowly unclenched her fists, with which she had been tempted very strongly to push Mr. Thorne over the railing of the box, with the additional wish that in the subsequent tumble he might break his neck. He had been toying with her, she realized; he had taken her measure within moments of their meeting, and had found her suitable material with which to amuse himself. Marmaduke Thorne was ignoble and base, a man visibly used up by dissipation. Regina could only be grateful *she* was immune to his good looks and charm.

"Mr. Thorne mistook my remarks," she responded repressively. "I sought merely to explain the impediment that stands in the way of our union."

"Impediment?" Lord Sweetbriar was rapt in the novel vision of himself as a man of the world. "What impediment is that?"

Had Lady Regina not been so well-informed of the unattractive consequences of such a grimace, she might well have ground her teeth. "What impediment do you *think* it is? There is only one ruinous entanglement that *I* know you are involved in, Sweetbriar!"

Ruinous entanglement? Enlightenment dawned. "Nikki!" ejaculated Rolf. Anxious to share this revelation with his uncle, he twitched at that gentleman's sleeve. "It's Nikki that Regina ain't wishful of playing second fiddle to, Uncle Duke!"

"Nikki?" Mr. Thorne grasped his nephew's quizzing glass and turned it on that unfortunate man. "Good God!"

So embarrassed was Rolf by his uncle's erroneous conclusion that even his ears turned red. *"Not* Nikki!" he protested. "I never even *thought* of such a thing. It ain't decent, somehow—and anyway, she ain't my style. If you don't believe me, you may ask Nikki herself. It's just that Regina don't cotton to the notion of Nikki as a mama-in-law."

"No?" The quizzing glass swung to Lady Regina. "Why not?"

"Nikki *does* sail close to the wind," suggested Lord Sweetbriar, when his beloved vouchsafed no response. *"You* should know that, Uncle Duke! Yes, and she don't care a fig for what people may say about her, or stop to think that they're bound to talk when she acts before she thinks."

"Acts before she thinks." Furious as she was at being made a mockery, Lady Regina could no longer withhold speech. "You are very generous, Sweetbriar. I wonder what Mr. Thorne would say to your stepmama's latest indiscretion—*embracing* in the British Museum!" Triumphantly she awaited a response.

Mr. Thorne directed the quizzing glass at the opposite box, and through it inspected Lady Sweetbriar. Again she wriggled her fingers. "Nikki seems to be wearing a prodigious amount of pearls," he remarked.

Lord Sweetbriar reclaimed his quizzing glass. "So she is," he lamented. "About those pearls, Uncle Duke—"

"Gracious!" Lady Regina tittered angrily. "You are

both to be felicitated on your *tolerance!* Your attitude is even more dismaying than your nephew's, Mr. Thorne. I tell you that Lady Sweetbriar has been kissing Sir Avery Clough publicly, and you comment only on the magnificence of her pearls!"

"But it is Nikki's pearls which are at issue here, is it not?" The action on the stage having temporarily suspended, Marmaduke rose. Once more he glanced at the opposite box; once more Lady Sweetbriar beckoned. "As for the other, Nikki always *did* like kissing," he added, and then took his leave.

"*Now* you've done it!" complained Lord Sweetbriar, as he gloomily watched Mr. Thorne depart the box. "I'll have the devil's own work to persuade Uncle Duke to help me convince Nikki she must give back the jewels, now you've set up his back. Maybe I should just let her *keep* the blasted things!"

Lady Regina had passed a trying interval, during which she knew she had not shown to good advantage, and her spirits were not elevated by her mama's speaking glance. Reluctantly she abandoned speculations upon how she might repay the odious Mr. Thorne for giving her the cut direct. "It is not my place to advise you," she said quietly. "If you wish to disregard your papa's last wishes, so be it."

Lord Sweetbriar looked contemplative. "I always *did* wish to disregard his wishes, but I never dared! Now I think I might! If Papa haunts anyone, it will be Uncle Duke, since he's come home. After all, Uncle Duke and Nikki were once—at least I *think* they were, from something Nikki let fall—but that's fair and far off!" His brief bravado deserted him. "Still, I suppose you're right. One *should* respect the wishes of the dead."

Lady Regina had found a topic of more immediate interest than the Sweetbriar jewels. "Your uncle and your stepmama—er?" she delicately inquired, her gaze fixed demurely on Rolf's cravat.

"'Er'?" Lord Sweetbriar struggled toward comprehension. "Ah! So I've always thought. Don't poker up; she wasn't my stepmama then. Though you may not approve of her, Nikki ain't done nothing so desperately bad as you make out." He shook his head. "Now Uncle

Duke's taken a miff. I don't know why you can't understand that people *like* Nikki. I like Nikki myself!"

Lady Regina had heard quite enough about the female she was rapidly coming to consider her arch enemy. "Then perhaps you should marry Nikki!" she snapped.

"Marry Nikki? Have you gone queer in the attic?" Lord Sweetbriar inquired. He then realized that this was hardly a tactful manner in which to address the maiden whom he wished to make his bride. "I mean, of course I wish to do no such thing! It's *you* I'm devoted to! Wish to make you a present of my hand and heart!"

Lady Regina could only be glad Mr. Thorne was not present to hear his nephew's impassioned declaration; the odious Marmaduke would no doubt have remarked that her affection dwelled less upon Lord Sweetbriar's various appendages than upon the family purse. *"No,* Sweetbriar, I do not require you to get down on your knees!" she hastily remarked. "We have had this conversation before, I think. Nothing has changed in the interim. I cannot reconcile myself to the idea of marriage with a man who favors his stepmama over me."

They had reached that same impasse? Lord Sweetbriar sighed. "But I *don't* favor Nikki!" he protested. "Most of the time I'd like to wring her neck."

"So you *say.*" Lady Regina's voice was sad. "I hold that actions speak fairer truth than words. So far none of your actions, sir, have betokened a preference."

"Then you may blame yourself!" Rolf's own patience was wearing understandably thin. *"You're* the one who keeps preventing me going down on my knees!"

Lady Regina forebore to explain that she wished a more tangible token of esteem than the sight of her admirer engaged in a ridiculous posture. Silently she gazed at the opposite box, wherein Mr. Thorne had joined Nikki. They were laughing and joking together like the greatest of friends, Regina thought. And so they might! Were Rolf's suspicions correct, more than friendship lay hidden in their mutual past. It occurred to Regina that Mr. Thorne's return to London might be used to her advantage. *How,* she was not certain—but given Lady Sweetbriar's flirtatious nature, and Mr.

Thorne's way with the fair sex, and the excellent terms on which they stood—Lady Sweetbriar might even be persuaded to remove from London, were her betrothal broken off.

Lady Regina turned to Lord Sweetbriar, who was deep in a fit of the sulks. "I have been behaving very badly," she confessed. "Pray forgive me, Rolf. The truth is that I am a little envious. Your stepmama always seems so happy, while *I*—" She sighed. "I will not equivocate! You know how it is with Papa."

"Indeed I do!" For all his self-absorption, Lord Sweetbriar had a good heart. "Drunk as a wheelbarrow!" he added, in demonstration of the fact that good hearts are not inevitably accompanied by tact. "You know, it's queer that you should dislike Nikki so much when your own papa is *worse!* At least Nikki ain't a drunkard! Oh, Lord, I didn't mean—that is, I *did* mean it, but—"Anxiously Lord Sweetbriar wracked his brain one final time, lest he be denied all further opportunities to converse with his beloved, let alone prove his devotion, as from her grim expression threatened to be the case. "Tell you what! If I make you a present of Nikki's jewels, *then* will you stop saying I ain't sincere?"

"Oh, Rolf!" Lady Regina was far too clever to display triumph. "I had not expected—you must not imagine—yes, I rather think I would!"

Chapter Seven

Not only Lady Regina Foliot took note of the enjoyment Lady Sweetbriar appeared to derive from the company of Mr. Thorne during Mme. Catalini's rendering up of Mozart at the King's Theatre in the Haymarket. Miss Clough had also been present, and had paid considerably more attention to the drama being enacted in the Foliot box than the entertainment underway onstage. Clytie thought, from what she saw, that Mr. Thorne had delivered Lady Regina a set-down before he joined Lady Sweetbriar's party. Of course he had not noticed Clytie. Foolish to think he might. The impudent Mr. Thorne was distinctly profligate. It was this suspicion which prompted Miss Clough to seek out her father at the British Museum.

Miss Clough passed the armed guards at the cupola'd entry, nodded to the porter, and then went into the museum, which had once been a private dwelling, Montagu House. Built on the lines of a Parisian hotel, the structure was famed for its magnificent staterooms, frescoes, and parquetry floors. Pondering what she was to say to her papa—even to Clytie, Sir Avery was an enigma, she could not anticipate how he might react to a suggestion that Lady Sweetbriar had in some arcane manner interfered with the orderly working of his mind—Miss Clough paused in the entrance hall. Lord Sweetbriar's continued strictures had not fallen on barren soil. *Had* her father become betrothed to Nikki entirely of his own volition? Sir Avery did not seem the sort of gentleman to fall victim to an adventuress. Yet Rolf claimed for his stepmama almost magical powers of persuasion. And undoubtedly Rolf's own mental processes had been grievously interfered with. Upon realizing the extent of her intended presumption, Miss Clough almost wavered; but having come this far, she could not retreat. With a little sigh, Clytie set out in search of her sire.

Through the entrance hall, Miss Clough passed, threading her way between stuffed elephants and polar bears, oriental idols and marble busts; up the broad staircase with its gaily decorated walls and ceiling. The bacchanalian revels enacted thereupon put her inexplicably in mind of the provoking Marmaduke Thorne. Sir Avery was not upon the landing, hobnobbing with the stuffed giraffes, or engaged in contemplation of the saloon's preserved vulture's head. Nor was he discovered in the Department of Manuscripts, the Department of Printed Works, the Department of Natural and Artificial Productions. Clytie did not begrudge her explorations. She enjoyed the Museum, and paused to enjoy such rarities as a stuffed cyclops pig, and a Roman tomb three feet long and eighteen inches deep, which appeared along the way.

At last Miss Clough ran her father to earth, in the Reading Room, a handsome corner chamber with three large windows and several portraits on the wall. Two long tables covered with green cloth extended across the room from north to south, one on each side; and the Superintendent's table faced a marble fireplace in the south wall. Seated at one of the green-cloth-covered tables, bent over a collection of state papers that dated from Tudor times, was Sir Avery. Miss Clough cleared her throat. "Clytie," her father said, with some surprise. "What brings you *here?*"

"I wished to speak with you, Papa." Since Miss Clough had expected no exuberant welcome from her parent, she was not distressed. "It is a matter of some urgency."

"Very well." With a gesture to the hovering attendant, Sir Avery rose and led his daughter into the corridor. "Now, tell me what was so urgent that it could not wait until next we met."

Somewhat wryly, Miss Clough observed her sire, whose abstracted expression suggested that his thoughts still dwelt upon ancient affairs of state, the dust of which liberally adorned his fingers and his chin. "I daresay it *might* have waited," allowed Clytie, as she withdrew a handkerchief from her reticule, "had I a notion of when we *would* next meet. Do not bother to point out that we meet daily across the breakfast cups, Papa! That can hardly constitute an opportunity for conversation, since I am forbidden to speak!"

"Poor puss." Looking rueful, Sir Avery suffered his daughter to remedy the damage done his chin. "I fear I am a dreadful failure as a parent."

"Pooh!" Clytie tucked away her handkerchief. "You are the best of *all* parents! In truth, I do not *wish* to talk to you over the breakfast cups, because I know that upon arising you are always sulky as a bear! But that is about the only time we are *alone,* Papa, so when I wish especially to speak to you, I must seek you out. And I *do* especially wish to speak to you. It concerns—" Her courage failed her. "A matter of the heart."

"A matter of the *heart?*" Sir Avery's preoccupied expression vanished. Shrewdly he assessed his daughter's ankle-length dress of cambric muslin adorned with a band of tambour work at the hem, her spencer of lilac sarcenet and white chip hat tied round the crown with a bow of lilac satin ribbon. "Child, are you *old* enough for that sort of thing? I conclude you *must* be, though I'm damned if I know where the time has passed. So you wish to leave me? Who's the lucky fellow? I trust *he* won't glower at you of a morning—though how could you know?"

Her father's uncritical acceptance of her hypothetical nuptials caused Miss Clough to look even more wry. "Nikki thinks I should set my cap for Sweetbriar. What, Papa, would you say to *that?*"

"Sweetbriar?" Sir Avery obviously searched his memory for a figure to match up with the name. "Ah, the gudgeon. I shouldn't think a gudgeon would do for you, my dear, but you must act as you think best."

"I am *trying* to do just that, Papa." To insure that her father awarded her his full attention, Miss Clough placed herself in front of the Egyptian tomb toward which his eye had strayed. "It has occurred to me that *you* may not be following the inclination of your own heart, Papa!"

"*I?*" Abruptly, Sir Avery's interest waned. "Are you warning me against Nikki? Child, I beg you will not act the pea-goose! If that was all—" Clytie could not ignore so obvious a dismissal. She shrugged and retraced her steps through the Museum until once more she stood outside. She should have known better than to approach her father on so personal a matter, Clytie thought. He was a determinedly private man, and uninclined to share his sentiments with even his own offspring.

About those sentiments, Clytie was concerned. Sir Avery, for all his brilliance of intellect, was an unworldly man. Clytie was fond of her father, and she didn't want to see him hurt. Not that Nikki would deliberately hurt anyone—but Clytie could not rid herself of the remembered camaraderie between Lady Sweetbriar and Mr. Thorne. Too, Clytie recalled Nikki's excitement upon learning of Mr. Thorne's return to England, an excitement Clytie understood all too well, experiencing considerable difficulty in putting that provoking individual from her own mind. Even now, she could conjure up in an instant a vision of his swarthy features and pale blue eyes, could almost hear his mocking tones. "Oh—Hades!" Clytie muttered aloud.

"Hades?" inquired an amused voice, which was not nearly as mocking as Clytie had recalled. Guiltily, she raised her gaze from the pavement to his face. "Shame, Miss Clough! Not that *I* would mind if you said much worse. You do not seem especially pleased to see me, *ma coccinelle.*"

"Why *should* I be glad to see you, sir? You have a very aggravating habit of putting me in the wrong." Because she was no good liar, Clytie lowered her eyes to the important lapels of Mr. Thorne's black coat. "If you will excuse me, I am in a hurry."

60

Unabashed, Mr. Thorne placed a finger under Clytie's chin. Amazed by his temerity, she gasped. "You are telling me whiskers, Miss Clough. Young ladies who are in a great hurry do not spend several moments blankly staring at the pavement. Will you tell me what is troubling you? I am very good at sorting out tangles."

Very belatedly, Miss Clough jerked her head away, and flushed to realized how much she'd enjoyed Mr. Thorne's boldness. Since she could hardly admit Marmaduke himself was no small part of her problems, she said: "It is nothing with which you need to concern yourself."

If Miss Clough had intended that professed disinterest would deflect Mr. Thorne's persistence, she was very rapidly proved wrong. "I must concern myself with everything about you, Clytie," retorted that exasperating gentleman. "Oh yes, I have decided I must call you Clytie. 'Miss Clough' is far too formal, and you do not like to be called my little ladybug. Since I am to call you Clytie, you must call me Duke. Nor must you accuse me of moving too quickly for you; I know I am! But I have followed you all the way here, and waited for you to emerge, and it is very obvious that something exercises your mind."

Fascinated, Miss Clough observed her accostor, who even as he spoke had taken her arm and led her down the street. "Trying it on much too rare and thick!" she retorted. "Do you *often* go off in these odd humors, sir?"

"Odd humors? Miss Clough—Clytie—you have a poor opinion of yourself!" The irrepressible Marmaduke smiled. "In answer to your question, I only take such humors when I see a lady I can't live without, which has never happened before. Yes, I know you think I'm pitching you gammon. Therefore I will not at this particular moment attempt to convince you of how very far I am gone in infatuation, because that would be to go beyond the line of being pleasing, and I would not wish you to take me in disgust."

"I am relieved to hear it," replied Miss Clough drily. "We shall go on much more prosperously if you cease throwing the hatchet at me. You really should not make such flattering overtures to strangers, Mr. Thorne.

Were someone to take you seriously, you would be in a pretty pickle."

Marmaduke arched a brow. "Now *you* are being bacon-brained. No doubt it is due to association with my nephew. Where did I leave my carriage? It's around here somewhere, I'm certain. Unless my man grew so annoyed at the length of time I left my horses standing that he took it upon himself to depart."

"Your carriage?" Mr. Thorne's abrupt conversational leaps, as well as his potent personality, made Miss Clough's head swim. "I thought you wished to speak with *me*. That is—"

"You'll grow accustomed to my ways." Marmaduke demonstrated a quickness of perception which Clytie could not approve. "That, too, may be blamed on the Russians. They grow so deuced *melancholy* with the least encouragement. *You* are not prone to melancholia, are you, Miss Clough?"

At this particular moment, Miss Clough had not the slightest notion of what she was and was not. "Umf!" said she.

His companion's onslaught of muteness did not deter Mr. Thorne. "I thought you were not!" he said comfortably. "Here is my carriage, at last. Allow me to assist you to be seated—there! Now you may tell me what has cast you into the pathetics while I drive you home."

"I am not in the pathetics, exactly." Miss Clough roused from her bemused condition to discover herself being arranged very tenderly in a yellow-upholstered barouche drawn by a perfectly matched pair. She discovered also that Mr. Thorne was regarding her in a very amused way. "Tell me, sir, is it your *habit* to take all by storm?"

"Not necessarily." Expertly, Marmaduke adjusted the bow on her chip hat. "Only in those situations where I think it will suit. If it does *not* suit, you need only tell me so. But *now* you must tell me why, if not precisely in the pathetics, you have been puzzling your head."

Curiously, given leave to do so, Miss Clough did not bid her persecutor desist. Instead, she conceded defeat. "You are the most persistent man! If you *must* know,

I am concerned about my father's betrothal to Lady Sweetbriar."

"Concerned, Miss Clough?" Mr. Thorne's manner cooled. "You do not *approve* of Nikki, is that it?"

Shrewdly, Clytie narrowed her eyes. "Oho! *Did* I disapprove of Nikki, you would find very quickly that you *could* live without me, sir, I think! Set your mind at ease; you have not found in me already something to dislike. I am very fond of Nikki. Anyone must be."

"Not *anyone*." Marmaduke grimaced. "As you would know, had you been privy to the remarks of Lady Regina Foliot. It was those remarks which made me misjudge *you,* my darling—yes, I know I am being forward, but to be a gentleman's darling, Miss Clough, is not so dreadful a thing! As I have every intention of proving to you some of these days—"

"Mr. Thorne," interrupted Miss Clough, embarrassed not so much by Marmaduke's flummery as by the presence of his servant, "I beg you will call me Clytie!"

"I knew you would eventually see it my way." At least, she thought, he refrained from looking smug. "Are you afraid, Clytie, that your father isn't up to Nikki's weight?"

"It is not that, precisely." In an attempt to analyze her feelings, Clytie frowned. "Rolf keeps teasing me to warn Papa about Nikki's scrapes—indeed, to do anything I can to prevent the marriage taking place! He seems to think of poor Nikki as being *infectious* somehow."

"Rolf's problem is that he *doesn't* think," responded Mr. Thorne. "We must not condemn him for the failure, for the lad *does* try. You came to the museum to issue warning to your father, then. What was his response?"

Miss Clough looked rueful. "He told me not to be a pea-goose. You may laugh, sir! I expected no less. First Rolf's warnings, and then *you*—" She fell silent.

"I begin to understand." Undaunted, Mr. Thorne possessed himself of Clytie's hand. "I think you must have been at the opera last night—and that you also know Nikki and I are old friends. To say you may trust me will not serve, I imagine. Shall I carve *Rolf's* heart out?"

"Carve—" Hastily Miss Clough reclaimed her hand, which she had inordinately enjoyed having held. "I think you have not been in Russia, but Bedlam Asylum instead! Why should you wish to do such a thing to poor Rolf?"

"Oh, *I* don't wish it!" Mr. Thorne took no visible offense at being called a Bedlamite. "I merely thought *you* might like it, since he's been plaguing you! My darling Clytie, you attach too much importance to Rolf's complaints. He *is* rather a stick in the mud. Beside, I imagine your father took Nikki's measure within moments of their meeting. The circumstances *were* somewhat unusual."

"They were?" Clytie was among those who believed that meeting had taken place in the Horticultural Gardens, and consequently looked confused.

Mr. Thorne's voice was admiring: "Assuredly! Surely you must know that ladies do not ordinarily attend prizefights, even so exciting a turn-up as that between Molyneaux and Cribb."

"Gracious!" Clytie shifted on the yellow upholstery, the better to observe her companion. "You mean—"

"Nikki *is* prone to fall into scrapes, I fear." Mr. Thorne was contemplative. "Fortunately your father was too much the gentleman to betray her when she tumbled into his lap."

"Tumbled—" In response to the vision conjured up by these words, Clytie closed her eyes.

"She was wearing boy's clothing, so it is not so bad," Mr. Thorne soothed. "If anyone else had penetrated her disguise, the story would be long out. My point is that your father must know what Nikki is! You need not fret that he is being taken in."

"Indeed." Miss Clough's tone, in response, was wry.

Conversation between them briefly faltered, after Mr. Thorne realized he did not know Miss Clough's direction, and she supplied the address. Somberly Clytie regarded her gloves. Marmaduke's efforts at reassurance had had an opposite effect. Lady Sweetbriar's influence over Sir Avery must be remarkably strong, thought Clytie, to persuade him to overlook the unusual circumstances under which they had met.

"You are blue-deviled, Clytie." Miss Clough roused from abstraction to discover herself under close scrutiny by Marmaduke. "I fear I have not calmed your fears. Then I shall divert you instead! What would you like to talk about? Shall I tell you of St. Petersburg, and my apartments overlooking the Neva? The river is always busy with barges and sailing boats and tiny skiffs with striped sails. On the farther shore are the Convent of Smolnoi, and the Tauridas Palace. Or would you prefer that I confine my comments to more immediate matters, such as the delightful contours of your nose, and your pretty eyes?"

That Marmaduke Thorne should truly have a preference for her was impossible, decided Miss Clough. They had known each other so short a time; it was for some reason other than admiration that he sought her out. "Oh, St. Petersburg, please!" she responded, with what she considered praiseworthy aplomb.

Mr. Thorne's appreciation was expressed in his laughing, sidelong glance. "Coward! I do not mind it. You will discover that, when it comes to what I want, I can be a very patient man." He lowered his voice. "And I want you, Clytie."

"There is no doubt of it; you *are* mad as Bedlam!" Miss Clough felt her cheeks flame. "Will nothing persuade you that I do not *like* to hear such stuff?"

Mr. Thorne considered the question. "Frankly, my darling, no! But even in Russia it is ill-bred to argue with a lady. St. Petersburg it shall be. You will be interested to learn than in that city the metal roofs are painted in colors chosen to withstand the rain and snow...."

Chapter Eight

Much later that same evening, when Miss Clough lay sleepless in her bed—it need not be explained, perhaps, that the speculations which rendered Miss Clough wakeful had little to do with which colors of roof paint best withstood the rigors of a St. Petersburg winter—Lady Sweetbriar's repose was set also at naught. Nikki had been dreaming very pleasantly of a rosewood architect's table, inlaid with brass, which she had almost decided to purchase on behalf of her *fiancé*. Perhaps, were his surroundings rendered more congenial, Sir Avery might be persuaded to spend less time pottering among the musty artifacts gathered together at the British Museum, in favor of the more earthly treasures housed under his own roof. In the way of dreams, he was moving very gratifyingly toward that objective, when some slight noise distracted Nikki's slumbering mind, and she awoke with an oath.

As always, when awakening in Fitzroy Square, Nikki was briefly disoriented. Then a slight sound caught her attention. Nikki squinted into the darkness, and frowned. Houses made all manner of strange noises at night, she knew; creaks and groans and other unearthly things—but this was no eerie protest of settling timber. Nor was it the scamper of mice behind the wainscoting, a sound Nikki recalled from childhood. Instead, Nikki thought she heard a sniffle. Intently, she listened. Yes, there it came again. Definitely it was a sniffle. Sniffles hinted strongly at noses, to which bodies were attached. Though Lady Sweetbriar was an arrant flirt, she wasn't accustomed to the presence of strangers in her bedchamber. Slowly, noiselessly, Nikki reached into a compartment of the bedstead and withdrew a loaded dueling pistol, the existence of which cast an illuminating highlight on either her childhood or her married life.

Her eyes had grown accustomed to the darkness, and she could see the intruder's outline. It had none of the appearance of a piece of furniture, much as he might seek to blend in with the background. "You, there, by the tallboy!" Nikki said sternly. "If you move, I shall shoot you. And in case you do not know me, I am a dead shot!"

When Nikki's voice shattered the silence, the intruder started, then froze. "'Twas a mistake!" he responded, in muffled tones. "I came to the wrong house!"

"I think you must have done." Concealed behind the draperies of her bed, Lady Sweetbriar performed a complicated juggling act with pistol, candlestick, and flint. At length she held the pistol in one hand and a lighted candelabra in the other. "There is nothing in this house *worth* stealing. Let's have a look at you." Candelabra outstretched, she inched forward on the bed.

Lady Sweetbriar's bedroom, as revealed in the flickering candlelight, was as blandly decorated as the rest of her hired house. The chamber was hung with pale blue satin, and the furnishings had been chosen with similar restraint, from the veneered wardrobe to the gabled tent bed, its lower posts masked by draped curtains and united by curved rods. One note of incongruity, amidst this studied mediocrity, was struck by the feminine garments flung in wild disarray around the room. Another, even harsher, discord was created by the gentleman surprised in the process of ransacking the tallboy, his hand still in one drawer.

"Egad!" remarked Lady Sweetbriar, as she curiously surveyed her disheveled chamber, from her perch at the foot of her bed. Then she hopped up and set the candelabra on a dressing table veneered with satinwood and decorated with festoons of flowers. As she approached him, the intruder shrank back, very much as if he wished to confine his bulk in one of the tallboy's narrow drawers. "I think you had better tell me what this is all about," Lady Sweetbriar remarked. "In case you are inclined to argue, I think I should also tell you that I was having a very pleasant dream when you interrupted me, as result of which I am feeling fit to blow your brains out!"

This blunt statement caused the intruder to twitch violently beneath his many-caped greatcoat, the hat that was pulled down over his eyes, and the neckcloth drawn up over his mouth. "A mistake!" he repeated, in desperate tones. "I swear it!"

Lady Sweetbriar decided it was no professional criminal with whom she dealt; a seasoned cracksman would never be made so ludicrous. "Your mistake lay in awakening me," she said severely. "Rather, that was your second error. Your first was in deciding to take up a life of crime. Don't you know that a man can be hanged for theft?"

It was obvious, from the intruder's wild convulsions, that this consideration was new to him. "Not *theft!*" he protested, his muffled voice perilously close to a squeal. "I never meant to *steal* anything!"

Lady Sweetbriar glanced pointedly around her disordered chamber, at the garments strewn so carelessly about. "If you did not mean to steal from me, then why—" She realized that those mistreated articles of feminine apparel were of a delicate nature. "Zounds! If *that* is the case, you are the most precipitate of *all* my flirts! You cannot expect me to condone such conduct, surely? If all the gentlemen who took a marked fancy to me behaved in so bizarre a manner, *then* where would I be?"

By the inference that admiration of Lady Sweetbriar had led him to his present undignified position, the intruder was not set at ease. "I *ain't* one of your *beaux!*" he gasped.

"No?" Nikki laid a finger to her cheek, intrigued. "A stranger, are you? An unknown admirer? How vastly flattering! For I am near thirty, and almost beyond such things. I appreciate the honor you do me, sir, and the risk you have taken to secure some token—but a *gentleman* would content himself with a posy from the lady's hand, or a handkerchief or a glove!" The intruder, made belatedly aware that he clutched an extremely intimate item of underclothing, dropped it like a hot coal. "And anyway," concluded Lady Sweetbriar righteously, "I am betrothed!"

"Didn't *want* a token!" muttered the intruder, staring at his feet—or so it seemed, his face being obscured by hat and neckcloth.

"If you didn't want something by which to remember me, and you didn't plan to rob me, then why *did* you come here?" An explanation presented itself to Lady Sweetbriar, as result of which she took firmer grip on her gun. "You didn't think I—you *couldn't* think to—Egad! I *should* blow your brains out!"

There was in Nikki's expression a strong hint that she might do exactly that, which may be what inspired the intruder to shift his weight nervously from one foot to the other and then back again, lending himself the appearance of a large, squat tree swaying in the wind. "Don't put yourself in a pucker! I *didn't* think it!" he begged. "Dash it, I wish you'd put away that gun!"

The necessity of defending her own honor, however, had called forth Nikki's latent dramatic instinct. "Accosted in my own bedchamber!" she lamented, the hand that did not hold the pistol pressed languidly to her brow. "The world is a dangerous place for a female alone and unprotected, alas."

"But you *ain't* unprotected!" The intruder whipped up his flagging courage. "You've got that cursed gun."

"So I do." Lady Sweetbriar abandoned her dramatic pose. "I also have *you*, you rogue! And I think I must turn you over to the authorities unless you tell me what you are doing in my house." She paused. The intruder fidgeted but vouchsafed no response. Nikki's dark eyes narrowed. "Or perhaps I may guess!"

Of all her ladyship's statements, this one struck the intruder as most ominous. He held up his hands, as if to fend off a blow. "Now, Nikki—"

The intruder was not quick enough; his movements were hampered by his many-caped greatcoat, and his vision by his hat. In a twinkling Lady Sweetbriar had knocked the hat aside, and yanked down his neckcloth. "Have you gone off your *hinges,* Rolf?" she acerbically inquired. "I came within an ace of *shooting* you! Yes, and I still may, because it makes me cross as cats to think you would try and filch my jewels!"

"They *ain't* your jewels, precisely," Lord Sweetbriar felt constrained to point out, then regretted the words as soon as they left his mouth. His stepmama still held her pistol, and her expression was murderous. "Don't be looking daggers at me, Nikki; *I* didn't make up that blasted will! If it was up to me, you could have the cursed baubles, but it *ain't!*"

"Fiddlesticks!" Though Lady Sweetbriar's tone was rudely skeptical, she did remove the pistol from her stepson's midriff. "Are you a trifle bosky, Rolf? I think you must be or you would not try and pull the wool over my eyes. You of all people should know I am awake on all suits!"

"I didn't—" Rolf's further protests were cut off by his stepmama's eloquent reading of his character and conduct, which included every unflattering adjective her ladyship could call to mind, from "abominable" to "reprehensible," and concluding with "crack-brained." "Hang it, Nikki, I *didn't* come after the jewels!" inserted Rolf, when she paused to draw breath.

Lady Sweetbriar's dark glance was sharp. "You wouldn't try and teach your own stepmama how to suck eggs, would you, Rolf? If you didn't wish to filch my jewels, and you are not a secret admirer, why *were* you skulking about my bedchamber in the dead of night?"

Mention of secret admirers caused Lord Sweetbriar to become belatedly conversant with the implications of his presence in a lady's private quarters, and to realize that his current position was compromising indeed. If Nikki herself did not believe his excuses, what chance had he of persuading anyone that his conduct did not smack strongly of depravity? Especially with Nikki looking quite seductive in her gown and petticoat of fine calico, and her Duke of York nightcap? "I *ain't* an admirer!" he stated firmly. "Tell you what, Nikki, we'll talk about this some other time! You go back to bed!"

"We'll do no such thing." With her pistol, Lady

Sweetbriar indicated that Rolf should sit upon a delicate rosewood chair. With such alacrity did he obey that the chair responded with an alarming squeak. "We will stay precisely as we are until you have told me why you are acting like a loony, Rolf!"

It had not escaped Lord Sweetbriar's somewhat limited powers of comprehension that his stepmama was sadly out of curl. Nor did he fail to grasp the awkward misapprehensions that would arise were the servants to discover his stepmama holding him at gunpoint. She would not shoot him, he knew, but she was very capable of raising such a ruckus as would bring the whole household down on his aching head. Some explanation must be given on his conduct, obviously. Rolf cudgeled his brain. Nikki had already given him a good indication of how she would react to the truth. Therefore Rolf would not admit that he had indeed come to reclaim the Sweetbriar jewels. Unfortunately, he had failed to allow for such details as the darkness, and his unfamiliarity with the chamber, and the possibility that Nikki might not leave the baubles laying carelessly about. Alternate explanations eluded him. "I wished to talk to you!" he lied.

Lady Sweetbriar was no pigeon for anyone's plucking, having at an early age gleaned an understanding of the harsh ways of the world; certainly she would not be led astray by tarradiddles presented her by the jingle-brained Rolf. She had parted her pretty lips to inform him of this when a possible explanation of his conduct presented itself to her. "I knew it!" She perched sadly on the side of the tent bed. "I told Clytie that stiff-rumped female would wish you to have nothing to do with me!"

"Stiff-rumped—" Lord Sweetbriar scowled. "If you are speaking of Lady Regina in such terms, I cannot allow it. Dash it, Nikki, she ain't done nothing for which you should hold her in such low esteem!"

"Has she not?" Gracefully dramatic, Nikki arose from her bed. "She has sought to estrange us, has she not? She has made it necessary that to speak with me you must enact the cracksman—how *did* you secure entry, by the bye?"

71

Mesmerized, Lord Sweetbriar watched his step-mama approach. "I secured a key from the agent who hired you this house. Told him you lost yours."

"What a clever notion! And one for which I suspect we have Lady Regina to thank. I don't know why it matters if *I* esteem her or not, Rolf; *you* think enough of her for the both of us!" Nikki came to a halt before him, her hands on her slender hips. "You've made a rare mull of it, haven't you, my lad? At least no one may call you a pudding-heart!"

"Regina don't know I'm here!" protested Rolf. He suspected, moreover, that there would be the devil to pay if his beloved found out. "You said yourself she don't want me to have anything to do with you—not that I'm saying she *did* say such a thing, mind! But if she *had* said it, she'd hardly approve me being in your bedchamber—I mean—Nikki, what the devil are you doing on my *lap?*"

"Hush!" Aborting her stepson's attempts to dislodge her by wrapping her arms around his neck, Lady Sweetbriar settled herself comfortably. "You don't want to wake the servants, do you? This way we need not *shout* at each other to be heard. Beside, if you are contemplating matrimony, you should get used to such things."

At the notion of his beloved Lady Regina thusly snuggling, Lord Sweetbriar's imagination boggled. However, he had to concede his stepmama's point. It was not at all unpleasant to have a female cuddled on his lap. Perhaps there might be some solution to his problems whereby his plaguesome stepmama might not be made unhappy. "How would you like to live in the country, Nikki?"

"I would *not.*" Lady Sweetbriar straightened the collar of her stepson's greatcoat. "I grew up in the country, Rolf, and I do not like it. And I do *not* believe you came here at this odious hour with the intention of persuading me to rusticate. You *were* after the jewels, confess! You wish to give them to that starched-up female. I will not have it!" Her voice grew thoughtful. "Now if it were Clytie you wished to have them, I might change my mind."

"*Clytie?*" By this abrupt introduction of Miss Clough

72

into the conversation, Lord Sweetbriar was nonplussed. "What the deuce has Clytie to do with anything?"

Nikki drew back sufficiently to look arch. "Clytie is to be my stepdaughter, silly! And you are my stepson! The two of you have so much in common. Clytie's opinion of you is *very* high, Rolf!"

This convoluted line of reasoning, Lord Sweetbriar did not even try to comprehend. "It's *late,* Nikki!" he lamented. "I don't want to talk about Clytie! I want to talk about Uncle Duke!"

"Duke?" Lady Sweetbriar abruptly sat up, thereby earning from the rosewood chair another protesting squeak. "What about Duke, pray?"

That question, Rolf could not fairly answer himself; he had only Regina's assurance that the ploy would work. "Don't it strike you as queer that after all these years Uncle Duke should decide to come home *now?* After Papa stuck his spoon in the wall?"

Nikki considered this suggestion. "No," she said. "You'd have acted similarly. So should I! In fact, anyone who knew Reuben wouldn't have deliberately set out to encounter him again, unless—" she contemplated her stepson. "Are you referring to the succession? Were something to happen to you, would *Duke* inherit? The devil, Rolf! Surely you can't think—"

At last Lord Sweetbriar could answer honestly. "Don't know *what* to think!"

"I suppose it is just possible." Nikki knitted her brows. "Duke always *was* a scoundrel. But I can't imagine that he would do you harm."

Nor could Rolf imagine such a thing. "Queer goings-on in Russia!" he hinted, all the same. "A man can change."

"So he can." Looking worried, Lady Sweetbriar nibbled at her knuckles. "I cannot like this, Rolf."

Lord Sweetbriar was no fonder of the situation, but his course of action had been clearly spelled out. If he was to win the maiden of his choice, his stepmama must be got out of the way. "Uncle Duke likes you, Nikki!" he suggested. "Maybe if you was to make a push, you could discover what he's about!"

Chapter Nine

As result of her stepson's intrusion upon her slumber, and his revelations, Lady Sweetbriar had no more sleep that night. At length she abandoned her courtship of Morpheus altogether, and occupied herself pouring over a design book—George Smith's *Collection of Designs for Household Furnishings and Interior Decoration*, with 158 plates adapted from the best antique examples of the Egyptian, Greek, and Roman styles—until she could decently arise. After breakfasting, Nikki adorned herself in a carriage dress of white India muslin with a dashing deep flounce, earrings and necklace of garnets, and a butterfly brooch set with pearls and pinheads of enameled gold. On her dark curls she set a straw bonnet trimmed with feathers, and around her shoulders a cloth pelisse made up in Roman flame.

Satisfied with her appearance, Nikki departed her house in Fitzroy Square. Lady Regina Foliot would doubtless have found cause for adverse comment in even this simple act; ladies of good breeding did not pull on their gloves in public. Since Lady Regina was not present to see Lady Sweetbriar commit this indelicacy, however, Nikki's shocking lapse from propriety went unremarked.

Her arrival at the British Museum was not similarly free of incident; this day was not a Monday, Wednesday, or Friday, nor the hour between ten and four. The porter knew perfectly well who Lady Sweetbriar was, of course. Had he not heard the Keeper of the Department of Natural History and the Keeper of Prints in a heated discussion of whether or not trustees of the establishment should be permitted to engage in public dalliance? In point of fact, the porter would not have been amiss to dallying with Lady Sweetbriar himself. Since he dared not suggest such a thing, he instead put forth to her a nostalgic lament concerning the days when entry to the Museum was by application only. Prospective visitors then had to be approved by the Principal Librarian, a process which involved three different visits to the Museum, and several days. Finally, the porter could think of no further excuses to detain her, and Nikki was allowed to pass.

She found her *fiancé* in the South Sea Room, where underlings were repositioning the first kangaroo ever to be seen in Europe, brought back by Captain James Cook. Perhaps it need not be explained that this specimen was stuffed. Other mementoes of Cook's voyages were exhibited in the chamber—numerous animals preserved in spirits, specimens of Polynesian art, a collection of natural and artificial curiosities. If the reaction of the workmen was a fair example, Lady Sweetbriar was the greatest curiosity of them all. Gratified, she winked.

Alerted by the unanimously gawking expressions displayed by his underlings, Sir Avery turned. His aristocratic features expressed neither pleasure nor surprise. "Eek!" squealed Lady Sweetbriar, and promptly turned her ankle. "Minx!" responded Sir Avery, and caught her before she fell. Prudently he dismissed the workmen, then seated Nikki in what she decided must be the South Sea Islanders' version of a throne.

Before he could elude her, Lady Sweetbriar flung her arms around her *fiancé's* shoulders. "Oh, this wretched ankle! But I cannot censure it *too* severely, for if I did not have it, we would never have met!"

"What a melancholy thought!" Sir Avery sought to disengage himself. "Still, I daresay you would have devised some other means to put yourself in my way, had your ankle not served you, my dear."

Lady Sweetbriar took offense neither at her *fiancé's* reading of her character, which, if unflattering was correct, nor at his attempts to free himself. Instead of reading him a scold, she nuzzled his cheek. "'Tis almost *like* when we met!" she whispered. "Except that *I* am seated and *you* are on your feet! Now if you would only—"

"You may save your breath: I shan't!" Sir Avery, who was not nearly so unworldly as his daughter thought him, gently but firmly removed himself from Lady Sweetbriar's clutch. "Not until after the knot is tied. You are a conniving wench, Nikki! No, I do not mind it. So long as you do not try and bamboozle *me*."

Perhaps it was her prickly conscience that caused Lady Sweetbriar to wince, perhaps the bruised ankle upon which she put her weight in an attempt to prevent Sir Avery from moving away. Temporarily defeated, she sank back down on her throne. "I fear I *have* bamboozled you just a teeny bit, Avery! Pray do not interrupt; I must speak. I do not *wish* to, precisely; indeed, I *would* not, did not I think some old cat might recall— Well! You know already that I like prizefights, and that I have trod the boards—but I fear my past is—er, not quite the thing!"

"Now *you* are being a pea-goose. Why should I care for your past, Nikki?" Having achieved a safe distance, Sir Avery folded his arms across his chest and looked saturnine. "What has brought you to me today? China rugs, or bric-a-brac?"

Lady Sweetbriar bade her conscience cease tormenting her; she had *tried* to make a clean breast of her misdemeanors, and had been told to let the subject drop. "If I am keeping you from your work, you need only *say* so, Avery!" Charmingly, she smiled. "Since you ask, I am on my way to Morgan and Sanders of Catherine Street, off the Strand—you know, Trafalgar House! Or so they style themselves, because they supplied furniture to Nelson—and I thought that since I have not seen you for several days, I should seek you out."

"To inquire if I still wish to marry you?" Sir Avery had moved to inspect the results of the workmen's efforts. He gave the kangaroo one last nudge then stepped back. "Should I change my mind, I will inform you,

Nikki. Since I am not prone to vacillation, I think you may set your mind at rest."

Fervently, Lady Sweetbriar wished she could do just that. "I have not the most distant guess *why* you wish to marry me!" she confessed. "But I have decided that you *must*. Otherwise you would not, I think, no matter *how* hard I tried to persuade you." She cocked her head to one side. "Perhaps I may persuade you to cease fussing with that kangaroo if I tell you I surprised a stranger in my bedchamber last night!"

"A stranger?" Sir Avery moved to the fireplace. "I trust, my dear—"

"—that I shall not carry on in such wise after we are wed?" Lady Sweetbriar was indignant. "I should think you wouldn't want me to do so *before!* Not that I *did*, or would even dream of such a thing, unless—" She looked hopeful. Sir Avery shook his head. "It is no wonder I am in the dismals!" Nikki muttered. "I do not scruple to tell you, Avery, that sometimes a mild display of passion would not come amiss!"

"And I am cruel to deny you? My dear, I have already been subjected by my colleagues to some very pointed remarks upon dalliance enacted within these hallowed walls." Sir Avery ceased his inspection of the kava bowls which hung with various implements of war above the fireplace. "Moreover, it sounds to me like you are suffering little lack of ardor. Who was it invaded your bedchamber?"

"La! You sound positively dog-in-the-mangerish!" Vague though may have been Sir Avery's hint of jealousy, by it Lady Sweetbriar's spirits were revived. "You need not fret; it was only Rolf. You look astounded! And so you should! I wondered if he was a trifle bosky myself! It is just like Rolf to have bungled the thing so completely, moreover—but you are no more astounded than Rolf was when I told him if he advanced an atom further I would have his life! He very nearly swooned from the shock."

Lady Sweetbriar had gained Sir Avery's full attention. "I trust you did *not*, ah, have young Sweetbriar's life."

"Silly! Of course I did not!" Nikki giggled. "Though

77

I very well *might* have, had I not realized who he was in time! You will be wondering what he was doing there, as did I. Rolf tried to put me off with a Banbury story about wishing to speak with me, but I suspect he was trying to diddle me instead, and I *do* wish he would not! It is very disheartening when one's own stepson tries to make one out a flat." Speculatively she eyed her *fiancé.* "I just thought of something! When we are married, will Rolf be *your* stepson also?"

"Not if I don't wish it." Sir Avery inspected the mantelpiece, and discovered dust. "And from what you have told me, I do not."

"Oh." Lady Sweetbriar was disappointed by her *fiancé's* uncooperative attitude; especially as concerned the Sweetbriar jewels, she had hoped Avery would take Rolf in hand. "It's Lady Regina Foliot who is behind this outrage, I'll warrant; Rolf has never done such a crack-brained thing before! I cannot think the Foliot chit is a good influence. I am fond of Rolf, and do not want to see him dwell under the hen's foot. No, and I do not want to stand on bad terms with him either, even if he *is* a clunch! Rolf must be persuaded that he and Lady Regina will not suit." Nikki looked coy. "Which brings to mind something I have wished to discuss with you, Avery: your daughter! You have been remiss in not arranging a match."

"And you will happily repair that omission, Nikki? Were Sweetbriar and Clytie to make a match of it, you would no longer need worry about your jewels." Sir Avery's knowledgeable glance flicked over those specimens which currently adorned Lady Sweetbriar's delicious person. "Clytie must marry where she wishes, but Sweetbriar sounds like a commoner Petticoat fo ver, has he? You, Clytie, Lady Regina Foliot—whomever *she* may be!"

Nikki's expression was vague, her thoughts preoccupied with how to prevent Sir Avery demanding outright that she return the Sweetbriar jewels. *That* would be a pretty dilemma, she realized; were such an order issued, she could neither obey it nor refuse. "Petticoat fever? No, that's Marmaduke! Or do I mistake your meaning? I assure you that I have your daughter's best interests at heart!"

"My daughter is capable of looking after her own best interests," Sir Avery responded cryptically. "You need not try and persuade me of your benevolent nature, my dear; I'm not marrying you for *that.*"

By this, the first even vaguely indelicate remark made to her by her *fiancé,* Lady Sweetbriar was considerably taken aback. Not long did she remain at a loss. A roguish smile appeared on her pretty face, and a twinkle in her eye. Wryly, Sir Avery observed her. "It will do you no good to try and turn me up sweet, my dear! I will be perfectly happy to tell you why I decided to marry you, *after* we are wed."

"I think that you must like to put me off my stride, else you would not do it so often!" Despite Lady Sweetbriar's discontent, there was no malice in her tone. "As you will! What were we discussing? Ah! *Has* your daughter spoken to you of Rolf?"

"Not only has she mentioned him—" As Lady Sweetbriar gracefully heaved herself erect, Sir Avery abandoned the mantelpiece and set out on a leisurely tour of the room. "She mentioned him in connection with matters of the heart."

"How did that strike you?" Hastily Lady Sweetbriar set out in pursuit. "Rolf is not *truly* common, you know! *If* he and Clytie should make a match of it, what would you think?"

No true gentleman could ignore a lady limping after him in such determined distress. Looking less than enthusiastic, Sir Avery paused so that his pursuer might catch up. "If Sweetbriar has taken to invading ladies' bedchambers, it's time he was leg-shackled to *some*one!" he remarked, as Nikki clutched his arm. "Is *he* sulky as a bear over the breakfast cups?"

"No, no, that was Reuben!" Since Sir Avery was much taller than his *fiancée,* and his stride correspondingly longer, Nikki had to hurry to catch up. Consequently, she was short of breath. "What, pray, does that signify?"

Whatever thoughts Sir Avery cherished as result of Lady Sweetbriar's determined possession of his arm, his expression gave no clue. "I am poor company of a morning," he explained.

Her *fiancé* was little better company of an afternoon or evening, Lady Sweetbriar thought, but charitably refrained from voicing this ungenerous remark. Roguishly she fluttered her eyelashes. "I'll wager your mood of a morning will be marvelously improved," she murmured, "*after* we are wed! I should not speak *so* to you, I know! I hope you are not cross."

"Not at all," responded Sir Avery politely, and continued his perambulations. Lady Sweetbriar cast him an exasperated glance, and grimly kept pace.

In the South Sea Room, the walls of which were papered with a neat mosaic pattern, were many items of interest. In one corner stood the mourning dress of an Otaheitian lady; opposite it were displayed rich cloaks and feathered helmets from the Sandwich Islands. Also arranged around the perimeter of the chamber were rudely fashioned island idols, and primitive works of art.

As she skipped to keep pace with her long-legged *fiancé*, and listened to his knowledgeable remarks, Nikki's thoughts raced. As if it were not bad enough that Lady Regina Foliot coveted the fortune that by rights should have been Nikki's, now Rolf hinted that Marmaduke nourished similarly devilish designs. If Clytie might be persuaded to steal a march on Lady Regina—but that still left the devious Marmaduke.

"You are very quiet, Nikki!" So abruptly did Sir Avery halt that Nikki missed a step. He caught her before she could tumble into the display of feathered bonnets. "You still have not told me what brought you here today."

"Oh, Avery!" Lady Sweetbriar leaned heavily against her rescuer. "Have you no opinion of yourself? Has it not occurred to you that I might wish to pass some time in your company?"

"I have warned you about trying to bamboozle me." Sir Avery released his *fiancée*, having assured himself she was capable of remaining erect.

Upright Lady Sweetbriar may have been, but she did not long remain so, apparently reading in Sir Avery's words some subtle invitation to cast herself upon his chest. "How well you know me!" she murmured, to his lapel. "There *is* something perplexing my mind: Marmaduke!"

Though Lady Sweetbriar could not see it, her *fiancé's* expression was unsurprised. "Yes," he murmured wryly. "I rather thought he might."

"*Did* you?" Rapt in machinations whereby her *fiancé* might be persuaded to look in the other direction while she sought to disarm Mr. Thorne, Nikki did not remark Sir Avery's tone. "*I* did not! He was always a scoundrel, but not so *much* of a scoundrel as to aspire to Rolf's fortune, as Rolf claims he now does." She frowned. "Rolf could be mistaken, but again he might not! If you should not object, I think I must find out what sort of rig Marmaduke is running, Avery."

Lady Sweetbriar's current rôle as defender of pea-brained youths threatened by wicked uncles earned from Sir Avery a faint smile. "What *am* I to do with you, Nikki?" he inquired.

Lady Sweetbriar was not one to bypass such an opening. "Kiss me, I should think!" she immediately retorted, and turned up her pretty face. Sir Avery obliged with a brief salute, then set her away from him. Nikki pouted just a little, then giggled, and after an exchange of commonplace remarks set out as promised for Morgan and Sanders's establishment in Catherine Street, where she derived temporary distraction from her various difficulties by the purchase of a work-and-game table fashioned of zebrawood.

Chapter Ten

"Dashed if I ain't glad to see you!" announced Lord Sweetbriar to Miss Clough. "Even if I *ain't* quite sure how it came about. I even thought you was avoiding me sometimes—I tell you that, though it will make you laugh!"

Had his lordship paused to ascertain the aptness of his last prediction, he would have discovered his mistake. Miss Clough was not looking the least bit amused. However, Lord Sweetbriar was as usual rapt in contemplation of his own concerns, and thus the need for enlightenment did not arise. So that the reader may not be condemned to share his lordship's woeful ignorance, an explanation is here inserted: the comfortable coze Lord Sweetbriar was currently enjoying with Miss Clough was result of the machinations of his stepmama.

Miss Clough, of a less constricted habit of mind than his lordship, felt ready to spit nails. She should have spoken out more firmly when Nikki first put forth the suggestion that Rolf's affections might be alienated, Clytie thought. She thought also that she would have some very pointed remarks to make to Lady Sweetbriar when next they met.

"You ain't laughing." If belatedly, this circumstance penetrated Rolf's consciousness. "*Is* it a matter of life and death you wished to speak with me about? Nikki said so, but I thought it was all a hum."

The only life-and-death matter currently in Miss

Clough's mind concerned her prospective stepmama; and the only decision Clytie had yet to make was by what means she would murder Lady Sweetbriar. With a certain grim relish, so she announced.

"That ain't very sporting!" Since Lord Sweetbriar had frequently pondered that same topic, his chastisement was strongly reminiscent of pots calling kettles black. "Nikki speaks highly of you. *Very* highly, in point of fact." He turned his head to observe the young lady who shared the seat of his sprung whiskey, a light and elegant conveyance perched upon two great wheels and drawn by one horse. "Hanged if I know *why!*" he added bluntly. "You're a good sort of girl, and well enough in looks, but a diamond of the first water you *ain't!*"

Miss Clough added Lady Sweetbriar's stepson to the list of people she wished alternately to break on the rack and immerse in boiling oil. "Thank you!" she said.

"For what?" Lord Sweetbriar looked extremely vacuous. "You ain't taking a pet because I said you wasn't a nonpareil? Hang it, Clytie, you've got *freckles!*"

"I know I have freckles." Miss Clough had passed considerable time studying those items in a mirror, following a conversation with Marmaduke Thorne. "Pray, try not to be such a dolt."

"A dolt!" So offended was Lord Sweetbriar that he was strongly tempted to set Clytie down. Only horror of what would be said of him by those members of the Upper Ten Thousand currently desporting themselves in Hyde Park prevented him from telling Miss Clough to find her own way home. "What a thing to say! You're miffed because I said you wasn't a nonpareil, I'll wager. Be reasonable, Clytie! I *could* have said you're looking hagged."

Hagged, was she? Miss Clough began to cherish sympathy for Lady Regina Foliot, whose longing for fortune and position were like to condemn her to a lifetime of inane conversations and plain-spoken insults. But Clytie did not care to engage in a turn-up with Rolf, especially in public. "So would you look a little weary, had you passed a next-to-sleepless night."

Lord Sweetbriar's prolonged contemplation of his

companion had resulted in a loss of circulation to his head, so high and stiff were his shirt points. "That's all *you* know!" he muttered, as he turned his attention to the terrain. "I'll go bail you had more sleep last night than I."

Miss Clough—who, in point of fact, looked very pretty in a dress of cambric muslin, pale green shawl and hat of striped sarcenet, her sleeplessness betrayed only by faint shadows under her eyes—shrugged. "I will not argue the point."

"It wouldn't do you any good to argue, because I would win: it ain't likely anyone held *you* at gunpoint!" Lord Sweetbriar was glad to note Miss Clough's astonishment. "If you doubt my word, you may ask Nikki if she wasn't fit to blow my brains out! I tell you, Clytie, I am at my wit's end, what with Lady Regina insisting I favor Nikki, and Nikki refusing to hand over the jewels so I may prove I *don't!*"

To reach his wit's end, Lord Sweetbriar had not far to travel, reflected Miss Clough. "I do not understand. Nikki held you at *gun*point?"

That Miss Clough had voiced no lack of comprehension regarding his stepmama's desire to blow out his brains, Lord Sweetbriar failed to remark. A prudent gentleman would have disclosed to no one his reprehensible actions of the previous evening, he suspected—but Rolf was neither prudent nor prone to contemplate consequence, and he *was* possessed of a strong desire to unburden himself. "She didn't *mean* it!" he explained, lest Miss Clough deduce that Nikki was in the habit of dealing with her stepchildren in this unusual manner. "Didn't know who I was!"

"Nikki did not know who you *were?*" In an attempt at patience, Clytie closed her eyes. "Rolf, *what* are you talking about?"

Lord Sweetbriar looked confounded by this suggestion that his own stepmama was a stranger. "Of course Nikki knows who I am! Whatever you may say about Nikki, it ain't that *she* ain't up to all the rigs! Oh, you are talking about last night! I was trying to explain that to you when you interrupted. It's deuced hard for

84

a fellow to get a story straight when he's being pestered with questions, you know!"

As she silently counted to one hundred, Miss Clough transferred her gaze from Lord Sweetbriar—the height of whose sartorial elegance this day were pale pink stockings and a brown-spotted neckcloth—to the leafy pathways of Hyde Park. Elegant equipages and superbly mounted lords and ladies were everywhere. The park had changed considerably since the days when King James I had ridden out with his favorite hounds to hunt the deer, mused Clytie, as her ironic glance passed over a *vis-à-vis* in which was seated one of the Fashionably Impure.

"But I shan't scold you!" continued Lord Sweetbriar, when his companion failed to respond. "Daresay you meant it for the best! Yes, and so did *I!* But just in case Nikki awakened, I took care to disguise myself."

"Let me understand this, Rolf." Miss Clough's patience was wearing thin. "Did you break into Nikki's *house?*"

"Lower your voice!" Looking agonized, Lord Sweetbriar ascertained whether anyone was within earshot. "I didn't break in, precisely; I had a key." With an economy of words that was quite unlike him, Rolf related the encounter. "Don't you make a kick-up about it, Clytie!" he was prompted by Miss Clough's appalled expression to add. "If Nikki didn't rail at me, I don't know why *you* should!"

"Nikki is hardly in a position to scold anyone for shockingly irregular conduct!" Miss Clough grimly replied. "Gracious, Rolf! Whatever made you think of so outrageous a thing?"

Interpreting his companion's questions literally, Lord Sweetbriar wrinkled his brow. "I can't recall precisely—something Lady Regina said—don't *you* be accusing her of putting me up to it, like Nikki did! She *didn't!*" He looked anxious. "I say, Clytie, you won't tell her about it? Regina don't even like me to *talk* to Nikki. She'd kick up the devil of a fuss if she knew Nikki had been sitting in my lap!"

By the image thus conjured, Miss Clough could not help but be amused. "So I think she might. You need not fear that I shall be indiscreet. Lady Regina and I are not bosom bows."

A pity, that, thought Rolf; he was very much in need of someone to put in a good word on his behalf. "You are still the best of good fellows!" he said generously, despite the fact that Clytie could not assist in his romance. "By the bye, what *is* this life-and-death puzzle that you was wishful of talking to me about?"

"There is no such puzzle, Rolf." Miss Clough's good humor fled. "I fear your stepmama made it up out of whole cloth."

"Whole cloth?" It occurred to Lord Sweetbriar that a conversation might be more easily conducted if his attention was not divided between his companion and his horse. He drew back on the reins. "If that is true, and Nikki has been telling me clankers, it is very bad! I was engaged to take Lady Regina up in my carriage today, and when I had Nikki's note telling me you was in a pickle, and that only I could save you, I was obliged to cry off!"

By Lord Sweetbriar's efforts to play knight errant on her behalf, Clytie could not help but be touched. "That was very good of you, Rolf," she said gently. "But I fear it was for naught. I am in no difficulty." Memory of Marmaduke Thorne's swarthy features sprang unbidden into her mind. "Or no difficulties in which you may assist me."

This effort at reassurance went awry: "I suppose you think I ain't *capable!*" Lord Sweetbriar snapped. "Dashed if I ain't tired of people acting like I have more hair than sense! I don't! Or if I do, it ain't by *much!*" Lord Sweetbriar grimaced as Miss Clough's pointed glance reminded him that his hair had distinctly begun to thin. "Yoo, and I also suppose it was to prevent me driving out with Lady Regina that Nikki thought up this business."

"Not entirely." Clytie thought she might make Rolf her ally. "I fear that Nikki has taken it into her head that you and I might make a match of it."

"You and *I?*" So startled was Lord Sweetbriar by this suggestion that he let his hands drop. Obediently his horse started out at a brisk trot. Some few moments were engaged in his lordship's recovering his seat, self-possession, and control of his steed. Miss Clough, meantime, sought valiantly to choke back a laugh.

"You *ain't* set your cap for me, have you, Clytie?" inquired Rolf. "You *know* I already popped the question to Lady Regina! If you wished me to throw the handkerchief in your direction, you should have said so. A fellow can't be leg-shackled to two females at once."

Due to her strong inclination to fall into the whoops, Miss Clough's voice was strained. "I didn't—" she gasped.

Not without a degree of sympathy did Lord Sweetbriar gaze upon his companion, whose cheeks had turned pink. "I didn't even know you was casting out lures! Another time you want a fellow to know you're *épris,* you'll be more direct! Look at Lady Regina! Even a slow-top would have known *she'd* set her cap at me."

Thought of Lady Regina's reaction to this discussion of her conduct increased Miss Clough's distress. She raised her hands to her gloved cheeks. "Oh, pray stop!" she begged.

Lord Sweetbriar recalled their surroundings, and the tendency of his peers to verbally dissect one another at whim. Were Clytie not persuaded to give over her posturing, his reputation for brutality would be assured. "Don't make such a piece of work of it! It ain't nothing against *you* if I've a partiality for Regina! You mustn't take it to heart."

Miss Clough was not unaware that her odd behavior must occasion comment. With a supreme exercise of self-control she squelched her imminent hysterics. "Pray drive on, Rolf!"

"That's my girl!" His lordship took up the reins. "I mean, you're a great gun! The best of all my friends, even if I *don't* wish to tie the knot! To own the truth, you may look higher than me, Clytie. You ain't at your last prayers, yet."

Could she *not* look higher than Lord Sweetbriar, Miss Clough reflected, she would just as soon not wed. "You do not understand, Rolf. It is not *my* idea that we should suit, but Nikki's."

"Nikki!" With more energy than was necessary, Lord

Sweetbriar flicked his whip. "I should have guessed she was somehow involved in this. She don't want Regina as a daughter-in-law any more than Regina wants *her*. It's a devilish ticklish situation, I can tell you." He heaved a sigh. "There never has been any keeping pace with Nikki."

"No? But I fancy we may do just that—or at least prevent her going to even further lengths." During Lord Sweetbriar's ponderous cogitations, Miss Clough had had ample time to formulate her own conclusions. "Do we but let her think her plans may reach fruition, she may refrain from further mischief. You must speak highly of me to Nikki, Rolf, and I shall speak highly to her of *you*, and hopefully that will be an end to it!"

"Do you think so?" Long acquaintance with his step-mama led Rolf to take a less optimistic view. "Nikki's at home to a peg—but it's worth a try, at any rate! She ain't awake on *all* suits, however; I fancy *I've* put one over on her myself." He looked briefly smug. "Or I *think* I did. Now I'm beginning to wonder if maybe it ain't *true!*"

Lord Sweetbriar was less a potential ally, decided Clytie, than an encumbrance. "Wonder if what ain't—isn't!—true?" she asked.

"If Uncle Duke ain't after my papa's blunt!" Lord Sweetbriar looked irate. "I only told Nikki so because I thought it would take her attention off Regina—once Nikki takes a notion into her head, there's no telling what she may do! I fancied if she was occupied in thwarting Uncle Duke, I might be able to snatch back the jewels. Or so I *think* I fancied. Regina explained it all to me, and I may not have got it right."

Clytie suspected she suffered a similar complaint. "Do I understand you? Lady Regina suggested you tell Nikki that Mr. Thorne covets your father's wealth?"

"Uncle Duke and Papa never *did* get on!" Lord Sweetbriar pointed out in defense of his beloved's strat-agem. "Look at Nikki! I mean, a fellow would never knowingly up and marry his brother's *petite amie*."

"His brother's—" Clytie's voice trailed off. She had known Nikki and Mr. Thorne were acquaintances, but had not guessed *how* close. Her failure to suspect the truth made her feel not only foolish but somehow betrayed. Nikki and Marmaduke— Oddly, receipt of this unwelcome intelligence made Clytie wish to exact vengeance not upon the lovers, but upon her disillusionment's source.

"Why the devil," Lord Sweetbriar inquired plaintively, "are you *scowling* at me? Ain't it bad enough that Uncle Duke and Nikki have joined forces against me? Dashed if I don't think Nikki *called* him back! Your papa's blunt ain't enough for her; she wants mine too! Well, she shan't have it, and that I promise you!"

"Do not excite yourself!" So severe was Lord Sweetbriar's perturbation, and so agitated his hands upon the ribbons, that Clytie feared they might be overturned. "Perhaps I may think of something!"

The ray of hope that with these words pierced the gloom of Lord Sweetbriar's reflections caused him to bite back additional laments. Clytie was a *very* good sort of girl, he thought fondly; offering to help him out of his difficulties scant moments after he had broken her heart. Perhaps he could do something nice for her, once this troublesome business was resolved. Perhaps he might even assist her in discovering someone worthy of her affections. But that was for the future. Presently, Rolf's own problems must take precedence. With bated breath, he awaited Miss Clough's next remarks.

Clytie was not unaware that Lord Sweetbriar breathlessly awaited her pronouncement, but she did not hastily speak. Indeed, she did not trust herself to do so, so severely had the notion of Marmaduke Thorne as villain agitated her mind. Clytie was very much afraid that Rolf's suspicions of his uncle were not without some basis in truth. Even Nikki's surprise upon learning of Mr. Thorne's return could have been feigned. Nikki *had* been an actress, though Clytie had not believed her so good an actress as all that.

Whether originally in complicity with Nikki, however, Marmaduke Thorne was almost certainly her accomplice now; and it made scant difference which of that unscrupulous duo had originated the scheme. The purpose of their alliance, Clytie could not fathom. It sounded very much as if between them Nikki and Marmaduke meant to divest a good portion of fashionable London of its wealth. So they might, and welcome to them, she decided, so long as her own father was spared.

Yet how to protect Sir Avery, who had already proven himself reluctant to heed advice? As if in search of inspiration, Clytie glanced around. Her thoughtful glance lit upon a distant figure. "Aha!" said she.

So long had Lord Sweetbriar held his breath that his plump cheeks were tinged with blue. "Aha *what?*" he queried, hopefully.

Miss Clough did not immediately answer, being deep in contemplation of positively Machiavellian intrigue. For some unexplained reason Mr. Thorne professéd to admire her. Why he should do so, Clytie could not determine. However, she imagined his pretended *tendresse* could be put to good effect.

"Aha," she said finally. "I think I see a means by which we may thrust a spoke in Nikki's wheel."

Chapter Eleven

Miss Clough was not the only maiden to achieve inspiration amid the leafy byways of Hyde Park that afternoon, nor was she the only damsel to gaze with speculation upon Marmaduke Thorne. In point of fact, any number of ladies eyed Mr. Thorne with varying degrees of inquisitiveness. Among them was Lady Regina Foliot.

Forced by Lord Sweetbriar's last-minute disregard of their engagement to take the air in company no more stimulating than her mother and sisters, Lady Regina was in no amiable frame of mind. The remarks of her siblings concerning Sweetbriar's cavalier behavior were largely responsible for her discontent. At least she was mounted on horseback, and could move away from the little cats. Alas, she could not move so far away as to escape their voices wholly. For reasons not entirely monetary did Lady Regina seek to make a good match. It was as one of her sisters commented bitterly upon the parental favoritism that permitted Regina to go on horseback while the rest of them were confined to an outdated carriage, and Regina's mama pointed out the consequences of a public airing of their financial difficulties, that Regina espied respite. Impulsively, she beckoned.

Lady Regina was not the only female to beckon to Marmaduke Thorne in Hyde Park that day; Mr. Thorne received so many invitations, tacit and otherwise, as must have quite turned the head of a gentleman with a less cynical habit of thought. Life among the Russians had left Marmaduke with little appreciation of the dramatic. Moreover, Marmaduke had been the focus of arch glances and knowing looks—not to mention outright propositions—ever since he came of age. Aside from the amusement it afforded him, such stuff no longer held allure.

Now it was Rolf's paragon who sought his attention. Mr. Thorne, whose experience of avaricious young women was not inconsiderable, contemplated ignoring her. A sense of duty prevented him taking that ignoble step—a sense of duty and a lively curiosity about what the young lady might wish to say. Marmaduke had as yet seen no reason to alter his initial impression of the inspiration of his nephew's ardor. Lady Regina was cold, conscienceless, and calculating. Marmaduke wondered what use she thought to make of *him*. In Mr. Thorne's experience, females did not simper in that pea-brained fashion without ulterior motive of some sort.

Lady Regina did not disappoint him, within seconds after general greetings were exchanged edging him aside. "I wish to speak with you, Mr. Thorne!" she said, urgently.

"In that case, Fortune appears to have smiled on you." Already Mr. Thorne regretted his impulse. Lady Regina was an undeniable beauty, and showed to excellent advantage in her riding habit of pale blue cloth, fashioned after a military uniform, and worn with a small fur stable cap, blue kid gloves, and half-boots. But, for Marmaduke, mere beauty had long since palled.

Nor was he especially impressed by her powers of perception. "You *are* speaking to me," he pointed out, when she continued to look blank.

"Oh! You are *teasing* me." Though his familiarity offended, Regina let it pass. "You will be wondering *why* I wished to speak to you, especially since when last we met, you delivered me a set-down. I do not blame you for it! Lady Sweetbriar is your friend. However, you have been long out of the country, and do not know how it is with her and Rolf."

"On the contrary: I know all that I wish to on that head." On onslaught of boredom smote Marmaduke. "And *more!* Nothing could be more tedious."

Though Mr. Thorne might be undeniably attractive, thought Lady Regina, his looks were spoiled by his rude ways. She suspected life among the Russians had exaggerated his innately overbearing nature. To the account already against Marmaduke—the brusque manner in which he had treated her at the opera, as much as accusing her of dangling after Nikki's jewels, and then giving her the cut direct; as well as the damning fact of his close acquaintance with Lady Regina's archenemy—she added his inference that her conversation was dull. Mr. Thorne's repayment, when she figured how to go about it, would be devastating.

But she had not yet determined how best to secure Mr. Thorne's comeuppance, and until she did so, it behooved her to proceed with care. Marmaduke was not without influence. Regina pondered how best to persuade him to wield that influence on her behalf.

As these thoughts passed through her mind, Lady Regina continued to speak. "It is not for me to point out that you have a certain responsibility to Rolf. You must perceive that his situation is most uncomfortable." She arched a delicate brow. "Or perhaps you are not conversant with the manner in which Lady Sweetbriar has wrapped your nephew around her thumb. It is not an association which I can consider *beneficial!* Mr. Thorne, I earnestly conjure you to rescue Rolf from the clutches of that—that adventuress!"

Were his nephew fallen into the clutches of an adventuress, it was not Lady Sweetbriar. Gallantly, Mr. Thorne did not voice this remark. "Nikki is not so bad as all that. You would be much happier if you left off teasing yourself with thoughts of her, you know. What excellent weather we are having! Everyone has come out to enjoy it." Dismissively, he gestured. "This puts me in mind of Moscow, where the favorite amusement is the promenade."

Lady Regina had not the slightest interest in Russia, save as a location whence she wished Mr. Thorne would speedily return. Her wishes had little bearing upon either Mr. Thorne's presence in Hyde Park, alas, or his conversation, which dwelt affectionately upon Moscow. In detail, he described the city—parks and little wooden huts, lakes and market gardens; flocks of crows feeding among the hens, cows wandering through the streets; the spires of the Kremlin swathed in misty moonlight; the *Kitay-Gorod*, or commercial quarter, located near the Spaskiya Gate. Lovingly he dwelt upon the fantastic *Vasiti Blazhennzi*, that cathedral unparalleled because, after its completion, the architect's eyes were put out.

"How interesting!" interrupted Lady Regina, rather faintly, at this point. "Since you miss Russia so much, I wonder that you don't go back."

"Oh, I don't miss it." As had another young lady before her, Regina discovered that Mr. Thorne was impossible to snub. "Russia is a barbarous country. Capital punishment as such doesn't exist; one is merely sentenced to receive corrective treatment. The penalties range from fifty strokes with the knout to running the gauntlet between lines of men wielding birch rods soaked in salt—which is tantamont to being beaten to death."

Regina was beginning to think that Mr. Thorne and Lady Sweetbriar were excellently matched, neither possessing any more sense of delicacy than a stone. "Really, sir! If you should not object, I prefer to speak of happier things!"

Mr. Thorne looked as if he might indeed object. "Tell me," Lady Regina said quickly, *"do* you mean to go back?"

"To Russia, you mean? I think not." An astute gentleman, Marmaduke guessed his interrogator's intent. "And if I *did* eventually return, I doubt Nikki would care to come along. Let us talk without roundaboutation! I fear you are at *point non plus*, Lady Regina. If you mean to have my nephew, you must also have his stepmama."

No advocate of plain-speaking, Regina very nearly took offense. Only thought of Mr. Thorne's influence made her hold her tongue. Could he but be persuaded to speak out on her behalf—yes, but how was the thing to be done? So that Mr. Thorne might not guess at her intentions, Lady Regina turned her face away. In so doing, she had hoped to portray a maiden woefully misjudged.

Briefly, Regina's intention was realized. Then her lips parted and her eyes narrowed and she bit back an oath. Intrigued by his companion's sudden transformation from modesty offended to rage scarce repressed, Mr. Thorne glanced in the direction of her fixed stare. At its terminus was his nephew. "Here's a pretty piece of business!" remarked Marmaduke.

"You've no idea *how* pretty, sir!" So incensed was Lady Regina that she abandoned all pretense. "Sweetbriar was promised to *me,* but he cried off. Now I discover he has taken up another female in his carriage. And he said I *wasn't* playing second fiddle to his—oh, you take my meaning!"

Mr. Thorne, no stranger to the sort of female to whom Lady Regina so delicately alluded, cast his nephew's companion another glance. It was difficult to secure a clear view of the young lady, due to the number of people and carriages in constant movement between himself and the distant whiskey. Furthermore, the damsel in question seemed to be either weeping or giggling into her gloves, which further obscured her face. "She doesn't have the *appearance* of a demi-rep," he said.

"A—oh!" Under other circumstances, Lady Regina would have dealt severely with a gentleman who sullied her ears with such vulgarity. "It distresses me beyond description that Rolf could use me in this monstrous manner. Although I should have expected as much! He *promised* me Lady Sweetbriar's—but never mind that! What sort of gentleman, I ask you, makes a promise he can't keep?"

Mr. Thorne was also distressed, not by his nephew's ill-considered conduct, but that he himself had gotten caught up in the subsequent fuss. Still, he was not an unkind man, and Lady Regina obviously suffered distress. "Poor puss! Do you want my nephew so much as all *that?*"

Lady Regina thought of her wastrel sire and their

increasing debts. "Mr. Thorne," she responded frankly, "you can have no idea!"

Mr. Thorne had no idea either why Lady Regina and his nephew should prefer one another, but since they apparently did, he would do his utmost to promote the romance. The well-traveled Marmaduke had a partiality for romance. "Lady Regina, put yourself in my hands."

"In your hands, sir?" Regina looked confounded, then coy. "Why, Mr. Thorne! I had no idea—can it be that you seek to—a man of substance like yourself! You *are* a man of substance? But I had thought you were seriously angry with me."

"I shall be, if you don't cut line," promptly responded Marmaduke. "I have no desire to pay you distinguishing attentions, my girl. What I *will* do is tell you how to reclaim my nephew's wandering attention—but in turn you must promise to cease plaguing me about Nikki."

Beset by conflicting emotions, Lady Regina lowered her eyes to her horse's mane. She was furious with Sweetbriar for his offhand treatment, and fearful also that while she had sought to persuade Rolf to sever relations with his stepmama, his affection had strayed. Above all, she was mortified by her own conduct as concerned Mr. Thorne. She had practically *hurled* herself at him, and had been sharply rebuffed. "What is it I must do?" she asked, very meekly.

By that meekness, Mr. Thorne was not deceived. "You would like to load me with reproaches, I know," he murmured. "But to do so would accomplish nothing save that I would withdraw my offer of assistance. You would not wish to stand on bad terms with Rolf's uncle."

What Lady Regina wished to do with Rolf's uncle is far too horrifying to here relate. Suffice it to say that boiling oil, and tar and feathers, were in comparison very mild punishments. "You are truly an *abominable* man!" she retorted. "I do not know why I am listening to you."

As expertly as had Lady Regina before him, Mr. Thorne quirked his brow. "Poppycock!" said he. "Had you not sought to lead my nephew such a dance, you would not be in this fix! Do I but manage to fix it up all right and tight for you, you must administer to Rolf's vanity occasionally, instead of expecting that *he* administer to yours! Oh yes, I am being familiar and impertinent, and all manner of odious things—but you did ask my advice. Having explained to you the theory behind our campaign, and what we want to accomplish, I suggest we take the offensive."

Lady Regina had passed beyond such petty emotions as rage and humiliation; Mr. Thorne's frank accusations left her numb. "How do we go about that, sir?"

Mr. Thorne had no desire to wholly demoralize his companion, merely to insure that his nephew dwelt under no hen's foot. "We shall get up a flirtation!" he responded, and revived her spirits with his most disarming smile.

Thus it came about that Lord Sweetbriar was roused from contemplation of his uncle's infamy, as evidenced in lust for the Sweetbriar fortune, by the spectacle of his uncle engaged in animated conversation with Lady Regina Foliot. As first the implications of this spectacle did not burst upon his already overburdened consciousness. "Look!" he said, and nudged his own companion. "There's Uncle Duke!"

Since Mr. Thorne figured largely in Miss Clough's air-dreams, it was with a guilty expression that she elevated her gaze from her hands, clasped tightly in her lap. "Is that not Lady Regina with your uncle?" she inquired.

"Dashed if it ain't!" Ferociously, Lord Sweetbriar scowled. "She was promised to *me* this afternoon. It ain't enough that Uncle Duke is wishful of laying his hands on my blunt!"

"But, Rolf!" As he spoke, Lord Sweetbriar had encouraged his horse to undertake a spanking pace, as result of which Miss Clough was required to clutch in an undignified manner at the carriage seat. "It was *you* who cried off!"

Indignantly, Lord Sweetbriar twitched his shoulders. "Cried off! I did no such thing. Oh, you mean that I am here with you. But that is Nikki's fault!"

Clearly, there was no use in argument. Clytie clung

grimly to her seat and hoped that their headlong progress would result in no injury save to her pride.

At length—having scattered carriages and pedestrians and occasioned a great deal of incensed comment—Lord Sweetbriar drew up his horse. "Hah!" he barked, at his Uncle Duke. "I have caught you out!"

"Have you, nephew?" Mr. Thorne's attention was all for his nephew's companion, whose bonnet during their headlong progress had fallen forward on her nose. What Mr. Thorne could see of her features was tantalizingly familiar, however. "And what have you caught me out *at?*"

Rolf glanced suspiciously from his uncle to his beloved, whose incensed expression he interpreted as indicative of guilt. "As if it were not bad enough that you want Papa's blunt, now you are throwing the hatchet at the lady I wish to make my wife. Don't bother denying you was trying to turn her up sweet. I'll go bail you would have been happy as a grig *had* Nikki murdered me outright!"

"Murdered you, nephew?" Marmaduke looked intrigued.

"When she caught me in her bedchamber. You needn't play the innocent!" Rolf snapped. "You must know very well that I was there. Don't try and pull the wool over *my* eyes, Uncle Duke! Now you're trying to take Lady Regina away from me, too."

"But I don't *want*—" Mr. Thorne, fascinated by the feeble attempts of Rolf's companion to extricate herself from her bonnet, belatedly recalled his offer of assistance. "Ah!"

"'Ah'?" echoed Lord Sweetbriar, in tones of ringing scorn. "'Ah'?! By God, if you weren't my uncle, I'd call you out for that!"

"Take a damper, nephew." Marmaduke's tone was definitely abstracted. "We were merely indulging in a light flirtation. If you wish to, you may flirt with Lady Regina yourself. *I* don't mind!"

"Flirtation?" Lord Sweetbriar's softened tone was due to no abated wrath, but result of his tardy realization that no little attention had accrued to their small party. "I don't *want* to flirt with her. No, and I don't

98

want *her* flirting with you. Dash it, flirting is something of which I can't approve."

"*You* cannot approve? *You!*" Lady Regina could no longer restrain her indignation. "It is *you* who begged off from our engagement this afternoon. A matter of great urgency, you claimed." The look which she flung at Rolf's companion was venomous. "Urgent, indeed! First you admit that you were in your stepmama's bedchamber. Now you cast me aside in favor of a—*a demi-rep!*"

Brief silence greeted this astounding accusation. Most appalled of all was Lady Regina herself. In point of fact, had she not been on horseback, and therefore a great distance above the ground, she might very likely have swooned from the shock of her own lapse from propriety.

The first to recover, Lord Sweetbriar shook his head. "Deuced if I know where you took this notion I'm in the petticoat line! It must be Uncle Duke you're thinking of. He's the only member of the family that I know indulges in such stuff." He frowned. "And I don't *know* that. Papa always said—"

"We will not discuss your papa just now," firmly interjected Mr. Thorne. "I think a great deal of this confusion might be cleared up if you were to persuade your ladyfriend to come out of hiding, Rolf."

"She *ain't* my ladyfriend!" Stiffly, Lord Sweetbriar turned his head to regard the damsel perched beside him on the carriage seat. She was fidgeting with her bonnet in the strangest manner. Tactfully he inquired, "What the blazes?"

Though Lady Regina was mortified by her own outspokenness, her anger was not assuaged. "If she's not your ladyfriend, and not a—er—then who *is* that female, Sweetbriar?"

No longer able to stand idly by while the damsel in question mauled her pretty hat, Mr. Thorne urged his steed forward, rescued and readjusted the bonnet, and pinched its owner's cheek. "Allow me to provide you reassurance, Lady Regina. This young woman is no lightskirt, but merely Miss Clough."

Chapter Twelve

"Dear, *dear* Duke!" exulted Lady Sweetbriar, and availed herself of his arm. "How *good* it is of you to act as my escort. Avery is at some dreary function or other, and anyway, he would not like to come *here!*"

"Here" being a discreet gaming hell equally famed for its ruinous wagers and exclusivity, Mr. Thorne found Sir Avery's attitude not unreasonable. "Your *fiancé* is also apt to dislike me bringing you."

"Dislike?" Lady Sweetbriar's tone was absent, her dark eyes busily inspecting her surroundings, which included facilities for almost every kind of gambling game, set amid brocaded furnishings and gilded mirrors, beneath crystal chandeliers. "Pooh! You do not even know Avery, so you can hardly say what he would dislike. At any rate, I told him I meant to discover— I mean, that you and I are old friends!"

It is perhaps unfortunate that Mr. Thorne was not attending more closely to his old friend's conversation, thereby to be put on the alert. Mr. Thorne's thoughts, however, currently had much more to do with a freckle-faced damsel than with Lady Sweetbriar. Could it be that Miss Clough had taken exception to being described as "merely"? Unless he had misinterpreted the glance she awarded him, it had brimmed with dislike. Marmaduke was not accustomed to being taken in dislike, at least by the gentle sex. If only he had realized it was Miss Clough in his nephew's whiskey, he would never have embarked upon a spurious flirtation with

100

Lady Regina Foliot. So much for unselfish motives! Marmaduke thought wryly. He was denied even the enjoyment attendant upon a flirtation. Exchanging appropriate remarks with Lady Regina was very up-hill work.

"Darling Duke, we were *used* to have a great deal of joking together!" murmured the most accomplished of all flirts, in a very provocative manner, as she squeezed his arm. "Now you have grown positively *stodgy*. We needn't marvel at it; that Foliot female would dampen anyone's *joie de vivre*. But if that is what you want—though *I* would consider her a very poor sort of amusement—still, it leaves Rolf free for Clytie! Come, let us try your luck at macao! Or would you prefer whist?"

"What I would prefer at this particular moment is conversation." Mr. Thorne relieved a passing servant of a glass of champagne. "You mentioned Miss Clough in connection with Rolf. I had thought his affections were firmly fixed on the Foliot chit."

Without appreciable success, Lady Sweetbriar sought to look severe. "You made a dead set at the young woman you believe your nephew to favor? Shame, Duke! Rolf is doubtless a little out of sorts; so would anyone be! But he must someday understand how *good* a turn you served him when you cut out Lady Regina and left him Clytie."

"Let me understand you." Mr. Thorne had the uncomfortable suspicion that he'd made a grave misstep; and Lady Sweetbriar's each renewed assertion concerning her stepson and Miss Clough furthered his unease. "You want Rolf to make a match of it with Miss Clough. *Why*, Nikki?"

"Why not?" countered Lady Sweetbriar, reminded that her escort's motives were not above question. She released him to step back a pace, eyes narrowed suspiciously. "You are monstrous interested in Miss Clough."

So he was, Duke realized. This somewhat startling discovery, he did not feel inclined to air. "She has freckles!" he enigmatically remarked. "What is your pleasure, Nikki? I think I shall play a rubber or two of piquet."

"As you wish." Lady Sweetbriar donned her enchanting pout. "I prefer to watch E.O." With a smile and an apologetic gesture, Marmaduke left her, and took up a position at a table in an adjoining room.

Nikki did not immediately repair to the E.O. stand, but strolled aimlessly through the rooms. Many of the revelers there were known to her, as well as her host, with whom she engaged in a stimulating conversation concerning how he might most advantageously redecorate his house.

Even as she laughed and flirted, Lady Sweetbriar had not forgot her escort. Through lowered lashes, she watched his progress. It struck her as ominous that Duke refused to discuss Miss Clough. If he wished access to the Clough coffers, what better means of entry was there than Clytie herself? Nikki's plans for that young lady's future security were so neatly laid out—or had been until Duke intervened, with what might have been the express intention of cutting the ground from beneath her feet.

Not one to brood silently over injustice, Nikki immediately made her way to the antechamber where Mr. Thorne was engaged in playing piquet, en route passing tables set up for whist and deep basset and macao. Having arrived behind Duke's chair, Nikki leaned down and hissed: "I shan't allow you to queer my game, you—you ingrate! That you should behave so callously after all we have been to one another—and we *were* a lot to one another once, even it it *was* a long time ago! Nothing could be more provoking than your selfishness!"

Since Mr. Thorne's own game was no way improved by the presence of an irate lady murmuring accusations in his ear, he gave up his place. "What the devil *is* all this, Nikki?" he inquired, as he led her away. "If you aren't going to play—or let *me* play!—why did you insist I bring you here?"

"Egad!" The suggestion that a lady with seldom scarce more than sixpence to scratch with should wager her slender resources caused Nikki to look even more put about. "You are a fine one to talk to me of a want of *openness* in one's conduct! I do not hesitate to tell you, Duke, that your own behavior is open to unfavorable interpretations! I am hardly one to talk, you will remind me. And so I am not, and I *would* not, had you not tried to bamboozle *me!*"

Had anyone been bamboozled, Mr. Thorne suspected it had been himself, though he could not decide precisely how, nor to what end. Duke was in the grip of great confusion, and he thought he would not be, were he not victim of a proper take-in. Despite his general bewilderment, one thing remained clear. "Nikki," he said sternly. "You are under the hatches again."

Lady Sweetbriar looked indignant, then contrite. "I do not know why I am perennially short of funds!" she sighed. "I try very hard not to waste the ready, but my best efforts do not serve. Ah well, it is not for much longer now! Once Avery and I are wed, I shall never have to pinch another penny for the remainder of my life. Not even if he predeceases me, poor lamb! He has given me his word." Guiltily, she clapped her hands to her mouth. "I do not *wish* Avery to predecease me, you understand!"

Mr. Thorne understood perfectly: Lady Sweetbriar would not reveal her financial woes. His knowledgeable gaze passed over her half dress of sea-green Italian crepe vandyked around the petticoat, her Norwich silk shawl; lingered on the topaz set which included bracelets and armlets, necklace and tiara, shoe knots set in gold filigree. "Let us talk of other things!" cried Nikki, fidgeting under his scrutiny.

"As you wish." Mr. Thorne promptly, and perversely, obliged with an accounting of a mid-winter journey he had once undertaken between St. Petersburg and Moscow, a trek of four hundred miles across endless steppes and forests. The vehicle utilized for this adventure had been a *kibitka,* a comfortable sledge in which the passenger could stretch out full length on straw and pillows, burrowed under furs. Halfway between the two cities lay the town of Vyshniy-Volochek, notorious as a rendezvous of thieves and receivers of stolen goods. "But you would have no interest in such things."

"In stolen goods?" Lady Sweetbriar clutched at her necklace. "I should think not! Unless you mean to hint that I have as good as stolen Sweetbriar's jewels because I refuse to give them back? That is cruel, Duke! Especially after all—"

"—we have been to each other!" As the servant passed again, Marmaduke secured another glass of champagne. "I take your point."

Lady Sweetbriar immediately appropriated the glass, glanced mischievously over its rim at her escort. "And all," she suggested, "that we might be again."

Accustomed as he was to being the focus of provocation, Lady Sweetbriar's husky pronouncement caused Mr. Thorne to elevate both his brows. "Might we?" he countered. "Would your *fiancé* not mind that, Nikki?"

Briefly Lady Sweetbriar had forgotten the existence of an impediment. "Oh, blast!" said she. "I mean—"

"You mean to lead me up the garden path," interrupted Mr. Thorne. "Yes, and I might be quite willing to follow, did you but tell me *why.*"

Potent as was Mr. Thorne's charm, currently turned on full force, Lady Sweetbriar found it in herself to stand firm, an endeavor in which she was rendered assistance by the contents of the champagne glass. "I will lay *my* cards on the table only if *you* will do so first! And you needn't bother to try and convince me you *aren't* playing with a stacked deck! Otherwise you would never get up a flirtation with Lady Regina Foliot."

"So we come back to that." During their perambulations, Mr. Thorne and Lady Sweetbriar did not fail to pause and exchange compliments with fellow guests. "How did you know I *had* got up a flirtation, Nikki?"

"Lud!" Lady Sweetbriar's glance was wicked. "Have you been away so long that you have forgotten how people *talk?* Considering how they used to talk about *you,* I should think you would not! I doubt there is anyone in all of London who does not know you and Lady Regina passed considerable time conversing in Hyde Park this afternoon—and you may be sure they are all wondering what you found to talk about at such length with a female who is generally accorded a dead bore!"

"Do you really think so?" At the notion of his business upon so many lips, Mr. Thorne suffered distaste.

"Think what?" Longingly, Nikki gazed upon the E.O. stand. If only she might recoup her failing fortunes with a few discreet wagers—but there was nothing left her to wager with. "That Lady Regina is a dead bore? Certainly! How could I do other than dislike her, Duke? She considers my ultimate vanquishment as merely a matter of time." Suddenly Nikki brightened. "Regina can hardly vanquish me if she is being vanquished by *you!*"

"By *me?*" This blithe assumption distracted Mr. Thorne from contemplation of the E.O. table, and the gyrations of the little ball. "You go too fast, Nikki. Lady Regina has no fondness for me."

Lady Sweetbriar knew a clanker when she heard one, and this one was patently absurd. The female did not exist who could regard Marmaduke Thorne without some degree of delight. "Perhaps you have not taken into consideration Lady Regina's natural reserve." Nikki giggled. "Or mayhap you are not aware that *ladies* do not wear their hearts upon their sleeves!"

Mr. Thorne's own lips twitched in response. "A palpable hit!" he acknowledged. "It is you who have not considered, Nikki. It is only to bring Rolf to heel that Lady Regina consented to flirt with me. By the bye, what *was* that mooncalf doing in your bedchamber?"

"*What* mooncalf?" Lady Sweetbriar was indignant. "You of all people should know that I do not—at least, I have not since *you* went away—Egad!" Nikki blushed and dimpled and looked so altogether adorable that several of those present wished very ardently that she *might*. "You mean Rolf! You should have said so! I think, though he would not admit it, that he meant to pinch my jewels."

"It is very likely." Mr. Thorne had been disarmed by Lady Sweetbriar's reference to their shared past. "He promised them to Lady Regina as proof of his regard."

"*Promised! Proof!*" Nikki's adorable confusion gave way to flashing eyes and clenched fists.

105

Lest his companion create a scene, Mr. Thorne applied meaningful pressure to her arm. Absentmindedly, Nikki placed her hand over his own, patted it, and sighed. "What Rolf told me was that *you* are after Reuben's fortune," she confessed. "And I'm not certain but what he may have the right sow by the ear! You're up to something, Duke, and I wish you would tell me what it is."

"So *that's* what the young cawker was raving about." Mr. Thorne looked contemplative. "I wonder who put that particular flea in his ear. Unless—"

Lady Sweetbriar shook her head. "Not I. Although I would have warned Rolf, had I thought it of you. But there is no way you can get your hands on Reuben's fortune without murdering Rolf, and I cannot think you would go so far as that." She recalled the midnight invasion of her bedchamber. "Tempting as the notion may sometimes be! Doubtless it was Lady Regina who planted the idea in Rolf's brain. First she suggests you are after Rolf's money, and then she strikes up a flirtation! What a very odd sort of female she may be— but a diamond of the first water nonetheless!"

Lady Sweetbriar's hasty praise of Lady Regina caused Marmaduke to smile. "She is very near perfection," he agreed. "Perfection, however, has never especially appealed to me."

"Wretch! I am repaid for twitting you about ladies, I think." In the most charming of all imaginable fashions, Nikki wrinkled her nose. "Because I know very well that I did appeal to you once, and therefore must conclude that I am very far from the ideal. Not that I care a button for that. We dealt well together, Duke, did we not?"

"Excellently." Mr. Thorne's expression was wry. "Until Reuben intervened."

"You have not forgiven me for my folly." So mournful was Lady Sweetbriar's countenance that it gave rise to comment. "I have already explained how it was I needed a fortune." She looked annoyed. "For that matter—curse Reuben!—I still do."

"The devil with Reuben!" Marmaduke said impatiently. "You know there is between us no question of forgiveness. All the same, I have not forgotten how you set about cutting a wheedle—and this determination of yours to cast Lady Regina at my head is too smoky by half."

"But, Duke!" Being only as flirtatious as she considered suitable in an affianced female, Lady Sweetbriar trod a very fine line. "It is very simple! Lady Regina must cease dangling after Rolf so he may settle on Clytie."

Mr. Thorne recalled his last glimpse of his nephew and Miss Clough. There had been little in either demeanor to denote budding romance, he thought. Perhaps ardor had been quenched by the intrusion of Lady Regina and himself? No, Rolf had sought them out, and very angry he had been. "Have you any basis for this conviction that Rolf and Miss Clough should suit?" he skeptically inquired.

"Oh, yes!" Nikki immediately responded. "Avery himself told me that Clytie mentioned Rolf in connection with matters of the heart. All that remains is for Rolf to be brought to realize that Clytie is far more suitable." Her dark eyelashes fluttered. "Which is where *you* come in!"

Mr. Thorne's response was immediate: "No!" he said. "I do *not* come in. I want no part of what promises to become a rare bumblebath! Rolf must have whom he chooses, and he had best choose Lady Regina, because any other choice would not accord with my plans. Spare your breath! No matter how you plague me, I will reveal no more."

Nikki could almost be grateful for her escort's sudden reticence; she had already heard enough to confirm her worst fears. Marmaduke sought to breach the Clough fortune through Clytie, and the Sweetbriar wealth by way of Lady Regina Foliot. Had there ever existed so thorough a rogue? Did there exist some means by which she might turn his connivance to her own good use?

Thinking furiously, Lady Sweetbriar sniffled. "Alas! That my first—er, friend!—should be discovered to have no heart. I did not mean to plague you, Duke. And even if I *had,* you would not have said so once. I suppose I am grown an antidote."

"*Once* I would have merely turned you over my knee." Mr. Thorne's voice was both exasperated and affectionate. "Do not look so stricken, Nikki; I did not mean to throw a damper on your spirits. You appeal to me as much as ever you did, I suppose—certainly more than the Foliot chit! Good God, don't cry! Listen, I will engage to persuade Lady Regina that you should keep your jewels. Will that restore me in your good graces?"

It was obvious from the enthusiastic manner in which Lady Sweetbriar hugged her escort that his suggestion met with her support. Vastly relieved, Mr. Thorne dropped a chaste salute on the tip of her ladyship's nose, quirked a quelling brow at those of their fellow gamblers so vulgar as to stare, and then led Nikki off to watch him try his luck at the bones.

Chapter Thirteen

"Merely!" repeated Clytie to her sire. "He said I was *merely* Miss Clough! And he allowed Lady Regina to fawn upon him in the most disgusting manner right in front of poor Rolf—who thinks his uncle nourishes fell designs regarding the Sweetbriar fortune, incidentally."

On the sardonic features of Miss Clough's parent, a faint amusement appeared. "Your Rolf sounds like a jingle-brain."

By this observation, Clytie was put very much in charity with her papa. "Not *my* Rolf!" she protested. "That is all a hum to throw Nikki off the track—she dislikes the idea of Rolf marrying Lady Regina so intensely that she has convinced herself he would suit *me!* That was what gave Rolf the idea of turning the tables on Lady Regina, I imagine. He was furious with her for encouraging Mr. Thorne, and decided to repay her by pretending to prefer me." Clytie looked morose. "I can't see what will be accomplished, but Rolf says this muddle is partially my fault, and I can atone only by cooperating."

Sir Avery awarded his daughter the look he more commonly bestowed upon some unusually bizarre exhibit. "I stand corrected. Sweetbriar isn't a jingle-brain; he's a shocking loose screw."

"You are mistaken, Papa." Reluctantly, Miss Clough took up the cudgels in Lord Sweetbriar's defense. "Rolf is merely a very *middling* sort of person. It is Mr. Thorne who is the loose screw."

So irately rendered was this pronouncement that, for the space of a few moments, Sir Avery withheld comment. Thoughtfully, he regarded his offspring, seated on a marble bench. That bench was located in the peaceful museum garden, which was embellished with a shady grove of lime trees, gay flower beds, and miscellaneous sheds. Miss Clough herself was this day embellished with walking dress of jaconet muslin, lemon cloth pelisse, bonnet trimmed with bands and bows. "I thought it was Sweetbriar you wanted," he remarked.

By the inference that she was partial to Mr. Thorne—for she interpreted her father's comment thusly—Miss Clough was remarkably incensed. "Gracious, Papa! Do you think I have so little sense as to develop a *tendre* for a—a profligate?"

"A profligate?" Sir Avery grew even more intrigued. "Surely not."

"I would not lay odds on it, Papa!" As she gazed at the lime tree grove, Miss Clough pondered Mr. Thorne's association with Lady Regina Foliot and her own prospective stepmama. "Anyway, it does not signify. Whatever Mr. Thorne's true character, he is above *my* touch—not that *that* signifies, either, or him!"

Fleetingly Sir Avery thought of the weighty business from which his daughter had distracted him—the relocation of a collection of Egyptian curios which included twenty-eight pieces in addition to two mummies. "Of course it does not signify!" he soothed. *"Did* you fancy Mr. Thorne, however, I see no reason why you should not *hope,* my dear."

"Oh, Papa!" In response to this display of parental prejudice, Miss Clough sighed. "You are very kind to say so. But even you cannot seriously believe I could compete successfully with Nikki." Belatedly realizing her inference, Clytie flushed. "Forgive me! I should not have said that."

How curious! thought Sir Avery. His own daughter was as great a curiosity as any housed within the museum. "Why should you not have said it?" he inquired. "For that matter, why should you *want* to?"

"Want to?" echoed Clytie, bewildered. "Oh! You mean, why should I want to steal a march on Nikki. I do not! But I would have to, *did* I feel kindly disposed toward Mr. Thorne. I am sorry, Papa; I tried to warn you before! Nikki and Mr. Thorne are very particular friends."

Though Miss Clough eyed her father sharply, she saw in him no discernible response to her blunt pronouncement. If anything, he had grown even more nonchalant. "What maggot have you taken into your brain?" Sir Avery calmly inquired. "It is hardly a matter for conjecture if Nikki is friendly with her own brother-in-law."

Nikki's relationship by marriage to the roguish Marmaduke had not previously occurred to Miss Clough. The revelation did not quiet her fears, but added to them highly improper speculations upon the nuances of incest. "The matter is more serious than you may think it, Papa. Your mind may be of too nice a tone to care for such things, but other people's *aren't!* Mr. Thorne is paying Nikki attentions that are very pointed. Last evening he escorted her to a gaming hell."

"Amazing!" From a pocket, Sir Avery removed a snuffbox that in itself should have been a museum piece. "If only there were some way of harnessing the energy that the pattle-boxes expend in spreading tittle-tattle, the horse would fall into disuse. It is not seemly to glower at your father in that fierce manner, Clytie. If you wish to be taken seriously, you must not talk nonsense."

"Would that it were nonsense!" Grimly, Miss Clough continued. "Will you call it 'nonsense' also when I tell you that the *on-dit* is that Mr. Thorne publicly kissed Nikki on the nose?"

Sir Avery awarded this question his full attention. "Well," he said, "no! I *wouldn't* call it nonsense. Nor can I fault your Mr. Thorne's judgement; Nikki has a very nice nose. You do not like the idea that the gentleman is so free with his favors? Do not judge him too

111

harshly. It's hard to refuse Nikki when she wants to be kissed."

How was Miss Clough to convince her father that Lady Sweetbriar was not what she seemed? Had Clytie not been so fond of Sir Avery, she might have abandoned the task. Not jealousy of Nikki inspired Clytie's efforts, but fear that Sir Avery's feelings might be wounded. It was Marmaduke Clytie held to blame for any mischief in which both he and Nikki were involved. "You don't *mind?*"

"Eh?" Sir Avery's attention had strayed to the sheds in which were stored the Rosetta Stone. "Mind what?"

This was a strange conversation for a young lady to be holding with her father, reflected Miss Clough. But strange conversations were typical of their relationship. "Do you not mind if other gentlemen go about kissing Nikki?"

Sir Avery's ironic gaze shifted from the wooden shack to his distracted-looking daughter. "Plaguesome brat!" he fondly remarked. "It has me quite in a puzzle why you should be bothering me with gossip. Since you *are:* no, I don't especially mind. Nikki likes being kissed. Why should she be deprived just because I'm not handy? I daresay I might mind if she chose to kiss someone else when I *was* handy, but I can't be sure. It hasn't happened yet."

Though no one had had better opportunity to study Sir Avery's eccentricities, his daughter had not previously realized just how much of an original he was. "Heavens!" she said faintly. "I had thought you were *taken* with Nikki. Which reminds me that I have learned the truth of your meeting. *Not* the Horticultural Gardens, but a common prizefight!"

"Not a *common* prizefight!" With her descent into the mundane, Sir Avery's interest in his daughter had begun to wane. "Cribb and Molyneaux. Since you know so much, you will also be interested to learn that Nikki tumbled right into my lap. Was it Nikki you came here to talk about? If so, you should not have."

That Sir Avery did not care to discuss his *fiancée,* he had already made amply clear. "Maybe Rolf is right." Miss Clough persevered as she reflected upon

Lady Sweetbriar's affinity not only for kissing, but gentlemanly laps. "Maybe you *shouldn't* marry Nikki. Oh, this is a dreadful coil!"

Impatient as Sir Avery had grown with his daughter, he did not suggest that the immediate solution to his own exacerbated sensibilities might be her immediate departure. "I shall be very cross with you if you interfere with Nikki!" he warned. "As for the rest—it is no wonder you have fallen into the dismals. Would you like me to straighten out your tangle, my dear?"

At thought of what chaos would result were Sir Avery taken up on this generous invitation, Clytie blanched. In his impatience to be done with what he considered trivial, her father tended to ride roughshod over impediments. "That will not be necessary!" she said hastily. "I will soon see my way clear. Anyway, it is not myself I am worried for, Papa! Rolf has issued so many warnings—but I will plague you no more on that score."

"Mad as Bedlam!" commented Sir Avery. "You may count on it. No, my dear, I do not refer to you. Consider the matter this way, Clytie: would you want someone forever dangling at *your* shoestrings? It would be devilish inconvenient for you both."

Miss Clough had no good argument against this assertion—although to have a certain hardened reprobate dancing attendance on her would have suited very well—and silence descended once more. Since the trustees were very jealous of their little garden, and careful about who might enter, and since the hour was not one during which the museum was open to the public, Clytie and her papa were alone.

"You *don't* want Sweetbriar, then," remarked Sir Avery, with the air of one who has just achieved enlightenment. "I'm just as glad of it, from what you've said. Nikki will be disappointed, you know."

Nikki would be even more disappointed did she realize who Clytie truly fancied, that young lady thought. That discovery was one she would share with no one, not even her papa. Clytie recalled how intent Mr. Thorne had been upon Lady Regina during their disasterous encounter in Hyde Park. How silly she her-

113

self had acted, taking refuge behind her bonnet—and how *dared* he pinch her cheek?

"You have very nice cheeks," pointed out Sir Avery, and Clytie flushed to realize she had spoken out loud. In for a penny, in for a pound, she thought gloomily, and added: "He also called me his little ladybug."

"I take it we are *not* discussing Sweetbriar?" Sir Avery delicately inquired. "I begin to understand what has put you in such a tweak, child. I'm sure that had you made known your preference, Mr. Thorne would have been happy to kiss you, also!"

"Mr.—!" sputtered Clytie, then caught her father's mocking expression. Her own smile was rueful. "You are a very queer sort of parent, sir! I suppose I was foolish to concern myself about you. But one forgets that you are needle-witted, so removed are you from the world."

His daughter's praise of his quick perceptions, Sir Avery acknowledged with a regal inclination of his head. "I was serious," he said. "If you desire a gentleman to kiss you, you must make some indication of your wishes. Otherwise he is very like to do just as your Mr. Thorne has done, and express himself in more conventional means, such as by pinching your cheek." He looked thoughtful. "Perhaps I have been out of the world *too* long. I do not recall that cheek-pinching was the thing."

"You know it is not," retorted Clytie, "else Nikki would have told you so! Pray do not tease me, Papa. This is *serious.*"

Sir Avery rose from the bench. "First you say I am needle-witted, then you infer that I cannot see what is right under my nose. Moreover, I suspect that *were* I to give you advice, you would fail to heed it, as seems to be the way with offspring. Despite having sought me out!"

"Since your advice consists of suggesting I ask gentlemen to *kiss* me, I hardly dare avail myself of it!" Miss Clough responded dryly, as she also rose. "I withdraw my reservations. Providing you can prevent Nikki squandering all your resources, you and she will be excellently matched. I have taken up too much of your time, Papa. I will leave."

"Not yet." As if it were some unusual specimen, Sir Avery took up his daughter's hand. "What a prudish world we live in, when a young lady must be always on guard against having her lesser instincts awakened by the casual touch of flesh on flesh—or so I assume is the reason for these eternal gloves. At least you are not required to eat in them. I wish you would not look so astounded, my dear. No matter whether your preference is for Sweetbriar or Mr. Thorne, we should have this little talk." The derisive quality that was never long absent from Sir Avery made its reappearance in his brown eyes. "Especially, I should think, if it is Thorne."

Miss Clough was touched by her father's concern. She was also quite pink with embarrassment. "Papa, there is no need—"

"Don't interrupt." Sir Avery drew his daughter's hand, offensive glove and all, through his arm. "Truth be told, this isn't any easier for me than it is for you. If only your mother—not that *she* was any authority on the subject! Don't fret, I do not mean to go into detail." Came a pregnant silence. "I trust, Clytie, that you *do* know the details?"

Did she not, Sir Avery was clearly determined to remedy her ignorance. At thought of her aloof papa engaged in an instructive discussion of the mating habits of the higher orders, Miss Clough almost succumbed to giggles. "I believe so, Papa!" she gasped.

"You relieve me." Sir Avery visibly relaxed. "This much advice I *will* give you, Clytie: kissing can be very nice. One needs be somewhat discriminate about with *whom*—"

"—and *where!*" interjected Miss Clough. "It must be a very puzzling business. I would not have thought the museum's grand staircase an appropriate place myself!"

"Am I being pompous?" Sir Avery smiled. "I did not mean to be. It was Nikki who selected the grand staircase, not I. I am not personally keen on public embraces. Your own mother, conversely, would have thought embracing on the staircase of her own home smacked of decadence. You must determine for yourself which point of view most suits."

The viewpoint which best suited her father, thought Clytie, was apparently that displayed by Lady Sweetbriar. She understood that preference better, now that her father had afforded her an illuminating glimpse into his married life. Unfortunately, understanding heightened her dilemma. Should Clytie try to thwart Nikki's romance with Duke? Or should she let the business run its course, thus ultimately bringing her father's romance to naught? About kisses dropped on noses in public gaming rooms, Sir Avery might be blasé; but Clytie did not imagine he would be equally indifferent to a full-fledged *affaire*. "I do not know what to do!" she sighed.

Sir Avery was growing wearied of his offspring, who seemed determined to exhibit all the worst characteristics of her sex; and consequently further violated his own rules regarding parental advice. "Humor the lunatic!" he suggested. "It is always a good rule. If Sweetbriar wishes to make the Foliot chit jealous, you are doubtless the most proper person to assist him in the task. While you are at it, you might try and persuade him that bursting into ladies' bedchambers in the dead of night is not at all the thing." He squeezed his daughter's hand before releasing her. "All of which will leave you no time in which to brood over your profligate. No, I mean to say no more to you about kissing, my dear. Goodbye!"

Having simultaneously done his parental duty and vanquished his daughter, Sir Avery did not immediately return to his indoor tasks. Nor did he repair to the garden sheds. He did not even gaze upon the pleasing prospect of Montagu House, the exterior of which boasted such features as rustic quoins and rich entablatures, lofty roofs in pyramidal and convex, concave and domelike sweeps. Instead he stared absently at the toe of one of his own boots. Unbeknownst to either his daughter or his *fiancée*, Sir Avery numbered among his many acquaintances an individual with a talent for ferreting out obscure facts.

Chapter Fourteen

Mr. Thorne's gaming excesses were not confined to private hells. He also played frequently at White's, through which select portals—set amid Corinthian pilasters in a handsome and well-proportioned façade—he was invited to stroll within days of his return to London, and wherein he conducted himself so unexceptionably that he was soon proposed for membership. For those interested in such details, Dame Fortune smiled on Marmaduke a large portion of the time, which led opponents to assume that the Russian upper classes amused themselves during bad weather—springtime in Moscow, for example, when one dared not venture abroad for fear of being crushed by falling icicles and snow from roof tops—plunging at whist and hazard and macao.

Currently, Mr. Thorne was not engaged at the table of green cloth, but was ingesting a light repast of boiled fowl, oyster sauce, and apple tart. With it he drank only water, in hope of maintaining a cool outlook. Marmaduke suspected he had grave need of such an outlook. Moreover, he suspected also that he stood on very shaky ground, though he was not certain how his unenviable position had come about.

It was as Mr. Thorne pondered the quicksand that threatened to engulf him that his nephew burst in upon his thoughts. "Hah!" cried Rolf, panting slightly from exertion. "*There* you are, Uncle Duke! I've been looking everywhere for you!"

"You have found me, nephew." Another day, decided Mr. Thorne, he would determine whether or not to embrace his threatening fate. "My felicitations! May one inquire why?"

"Why *what?*" Tired of waiting for an invitation, Lord Sweetbriar pulled up a chair. "I wish to talk to you, Uncle Duke! About a delicate subject!"

"Ah." Foreseeing that the conversation would not be of short duration, and anticipating that its course would be tortuous, Mr. Thorne abandoned his resolution to maintain sobriety. "Pray continue!" he suggested, after instructing a waiter to fetch them some wine.

Despite his uncle's generous invitation, Lord Sweetbriar did not immediately speak. No hesitancy about the justice of his intended comments stilled his tongue, nor uncertainty concerning what he wished to say. Several times had Rolf already rehearsed the main thrust of his speech, the last occasion having prompted much comment among the doorman, hall porter, and turbaned Negro page who collected hats and coats, all of whom were unanimously convinced that his lordship was a Bedlamite. No, Rolf's silence was due to neither reticence nor qualm. Simply, his speech was impeded by ingestion of his uncle's apple tart.

Only when the last crumb had been daintily dispatched did Rolf lean back in his chair, rest his plump hands upon the most violently hued, horizontally striped waistcoat ever to be indiscreetly sported by a young gentleman of ample girth, and emit a gentle burp. Having thus expressed his appreciation of the apple tart, he proceeded to the next item on his agenda. "Uncle Duke, I demand to know your intentions!" he proclaimed.

"My intentions?" Mr. Thorne gazed with vast approval upon the waiter who had returned with the wine, and fortified himself with a liberal libation. "Intentions toward whom, nephew?"

"Toward Lady Regina, of course!" Though it had not been offered to him, Rolf grasped the wine bottle. "She ain't one of your straw damsels, Uncle Duke!"

Perhaps it was the wine which prompted Mr. Thorne's

118

next remark, perhaps his nephew's unflattering hints that he was preoccupied with sin. "Not *yet* she isn't!" Marmaduke said, perversely. So that Rolf might not fail to grasp that he shared a table with a villain, Duke adopted a handsome sneer.

Though Lord Sweetbriar did not possess the world's keenest powers of observation, he found his uncle's meaning monstrously clear. Consequently his jaw dropped so far open that his chin rested on his intricately tied cravat. "You don't mean that! You can't! Fiend sieze you, Uncle Duke!"

"What's that?" Mr. Thorne reclaimed the bottle, refilled his glass. "I see what it is! Though your affections lie now with another, you still feel a responsibility for Lady Regina. Your sentiments do you credit, nephew! But you need not concern yourself over the chit."

Nor did Lord Sweetbriar fail to grasp the fact that he was in a pickle. Did he explain to his Uncle Duke that Miss Clough was *not* the focus of his affections, Duke would in turn convey that intelligence to both Nikki and Lady Regina herself. But if he did *not* explain, Rolf had no good reason to take his uncle to task. "The deuce!" he muttered. A horrid possibility struck him. "You ain't thinking of getting leg-shackled, Uncle Duke?"

"To Lady Regina? You may make yourself easy on *that* head!" Mr. Thorne recalled the rôle that he was playing, and reverted to a less appalled tone. "The cream of the jest is that she only took up with me to get a rise out of *you*—she was jealous of your interest in Miss Clough."

Lord Sweetbriar's puzzled features brightened. "She *was?* I say, Uncle Duke!"

"Oh, she isn't anymore!" As result of his deviousness, Mr. Thorne suffered faint pangs of guilt. "I'll warrant I can keep Lady Regina out of your way while you attach the affections of Miss Clough."

"But I don't want—" Constitutionally unsuited to intrigue, Lord Sweetbriar mopped at his damp brow. "That is, you needn't go to all that trouble, Uncle Duke!"

"Poppycock! 'Tis no trouble at all. You *are* my

nephew." What would a true villain do at this point? Marmaduke attempted a lascivious wink. "The chit *is* a tasty piece!"

"A—" So shocked was Rolf by this inelegant description of his beloved that words cannot adequately describe his mental state. Perhaps he had mistook his uncle's meaning? "After I have, er, attached the affections of Miss Clough, *then* what?" he inquired.

Looking very dastardly, Mr. Thorne shrugged. "Lady Regina will not wear the willow long," he predicted indifferently.

By this indication that his uncle meant to play fast and loose with his beloved, Lord Sweetbriar was even more horrified. Indeed, so very angered was he that all vestiges of commonsense fled his overheated brain. Clumsily he leapt to his feet, adopted what he fancied was a pugilistic stance. "I demand satisfaction, Uncle Duke!" he cried.

Upon reception of this invitation to engage in fisticuffs, Mr. Thorne looked less dismayed than amused, though Lord Sweetbriar's sudden display of belligerence did cause several of their fellow diners some digestive distress. "Just like your father!" remarked Marmaduke, eyeing his nephew's posture, which had in it nothing that suggested any familiarity with the noble art of self-defense. "Reuben was prone to take distempered freaks. If you insist on engaging in a brangle with me, so be it, but I doubt Raggett would be best pleased if we got to milling here."

Recalled by these words to a sense of his surroundings, and awareness of the disapproving glances of which he was the focus, Lord Sweetbriar hastily reclaimed his seat. Gloomily he observed his uncle. "I suppose you have a very handy bunch of fives."

"I do." Mr. Thorne made a complacent fist. " 'Gentleman' Jackson complimented me on my science just the other day. Don't fear, nephew, I shan't let *that* stand in our way. Why, just the other day I offered to carve your heart out for someone." He looked thoughtful. "I think it was Miss Clough."

Maybe if no more mention were made of fisticuffs, Lord Sweetbriar's uncle would let his rash suggestion pass. "Why should Clytie want my heart carved out?" wondered Rolf, in plaintive tones inspired by visions of himself receiving a rare pummeling from his uncle's handy fists. "I thought we was friends!"

" 'Friends'?" echoed Mr. Thorne. " 'Friend' is a mighty mild word to describe the object of your affections, Rolf!"

"Was we talking about Lady Regina?" Lord Sweetbriar's confusion was helped to clear by the quizzical look on his uncle's face. "You mean Clytie! Dashed if I don't think at least one of us is foxed, Uncle Duke!" This ignoble suggestion was not without foundation. As they talked, the gentlemen had inbibed apace, and were currently sharing their third bottle of wine.

"One of us is a trifle confused, certainly," allowed Mr. Thorne—who among his other virtues numbered a very strong head. "Which of them *do* you want, nephew? Lady Regina or Miss Clough? I do not mean to stand in your way, but you cannot have them *both*. There is a law against such things. Unless you were thinking of setting up your—"

"Uncle Duke!" By the suggestion that he was desirous of mounting a mistress, Lord Sweetbriar was mortified. "*I* ain't in the petticoat line. Yes, and who is it you're calling bachelor's fare? I'll have you know that Lady Regina is a well-brought-up young woman, sir!"

A certain irate glitter lit Marmaduke's own blue eye. "And Miss Clough is not?" he ominously inquired. "You are very close to going beyond the line of being pleasing, Rolf."

"And you *ain't?*" Lord Sweetbriar unwisely retorted, before recalling his uncle's pugilistic prowess. "That is, Clytie is a very good sort of girl! Fine as fivepence! First-rate! But dash it, sir! You mustn't offer Lady Regina false coin!"

Had Mr. Thorne his preference, he would never again have offered Lady Regina even the time of day. Never had he endured the company of so tiresome a female. Why Rolf wanted her—and that Rolf *did* want her, Duke was now convinced, despite Nikki's declarations that Rolf must have Miss Clough—Duke could not imagine, but he had made his best efforts in the

121

behalf of romance. Privately, he thought he was doing it a little too brown, but Rolf had been slow to rise to the bait. However, he'd finally got the point across. To underscore that point, Duke musingly remarked: "Do you fear Lady Regina will make a nuisance of herself once I have cast her off? There *is* the possibility that she may try to reattach you. Your bride might fairly object to such goings-on—because of course I will not give Lady Regina her *congé* until after you have married Miss Clough." Ruminatively, he tapped his fingers on his wine glass. "Perhaps I *should* invite the chit to toss her bonnet over the windmill. Then she would not dare pester anyone, I think!"

"Windmill? Pester?" Only the need to persuade his uncle against this dastardly plan of action kept Lord Sweetbriar from springing anew to his feet. "Dashed if you ain't a regular out-and-outer, Uncle Duke!"

"Am I to take that to mean you *don't* think it necessary that I offer the Foliot chit a slip on the shoulder?" Mr. Thorne inquired. "You relieve me, nephew!"

Lord Sweetbriar's belligerent expression did not noticeably lighten. "Why the devil you should be relieved, I don't know!" he snapped. "You sound like you don't *want* to seduce Lady Regina! As if she ain't a diamond of the first water! An acknowledged beauty! A—a *nonpareil!*"

"Ah!" Mr. Thorne wore an air of enlightment. "You *do* want me to invite her to toss her bonnet over the windmill, then."

"No, I don't!" Lord Sweetbriar became aware of his uncle's smile. "Uncle Duke! Are you *bamming* me? If you are, it is very bad of you, because I already have quite enough to worry about!"

Though Mr. Thorne could not admit that he had indeed been talking a great deal of nonsense without undoing his own good work, he could refrain from further agitating his nephew's feelings now that his point had been made. Therefore, he changed the subject. "*Why* did you tell Nikki that I'm after your money?" he inquired.

Temporarily diverted from the problems heaped high upon his plate, Rolf stared at his uncle. "*Ain't* you?"

"No, I ain't!" Mr. Thorne grimaced. "I mean, I am not. Shall I give you some advice, Rolf? Let Nikki keep her baubles! In Russia, every woman has rights over her own fortune, totally independent of her husband."

"Good gad!" ejaculated Lord Sweetbriar. "They *are* barbarians!"

To calm his burgeoning impatience, Mr. Thorne embarked upon an artistic rearrangement of dishes and cutlery and empty wine bottles. "Reuben should have left the jewels to Nikki in the first place."

"Yes, but he *didn't!*" It irritated Rolf that everyone, with the exception of his beloved, seemed anxious to take Nikki's part. "And Lady Regina—"

"Curse Lady Regina!" interrupted Mr. Thorne. To speak in such unappreciative tones about the young woman with whom he was engaged in a flirtation, no matter how laborious, was not the thing, he realized. To atone for his outburst, Duke added: "Darling that she is!"

Darling? Certainly Lady Regina was a darling, Lord Sweetbriar's own. Did everyone in the world conspire against them? First Nikki, with her uncooperative attitude toward the Sweetbriar jewels, and now Marmaduke. There must be some way to prevent Regina falling victim of his uncle's evil schemes without revealing that the attendance Rolf danced on Miss Clough was all a sham. Lord Sweetbriar was no saint. Lady Regina had wounded his feelings by the preference she displayed for his uncle. Rolf wanted to wound her feelings a little in return.

All the same, Rolf did not want Lady Regina's feelings to be so badly wounded as they must be by continued exposure to the conscienceless Marmaduke. There was only one solution to this dilemma. Duke must be diverted. Rolf's thoughts flew immediately to the most distracting female he knew. "About Nikki! I don't know if *you* know it, Uncle Duke, but Nikki still nourishes *very* warm feelings for you."

Mr. Thorne's expression was not especially grateful. "Cut line, Rolf!"

"I ain't spinning you a Banbury tale, truly, Uncle Duke!" So anxious was Rolf to persuade his uncle of

123

this untruth that he looked paradoxically earnest. "It is quite midsummer moon with her, I swear it! She wouldn't tell you so herself, lest you didn't share her partiality."

Very hard, Mr. Thorne tried to persuade himself that his nephew had windmills in his head. "You seem to have forgotten Nikki's betrothal."

So he had. How best to explain that most inconvenient detail? "Yes, but you wasn't in the country then!" Rolf reasonably pointed out. "Doubtless Nikki didn't *know* she was still hankering after you because she hadn't seen you in so many years. Everyone knows she and Clough ain't making a love match. But you must not blame yourself, Uncle Duke! Even though I'll be dashed if this ain't the *worst* of Nikki's scrapes."

Chapter Fifteen

Despite his nephew's assurances that he must not blame himself for Lady Sweetbriar's partiality, Mr. Thorne was not absolved. He felt a responsibility for Nikki. Too, he recalled his suspicion that she was under the hatches, a dilemma in which she apparently didn't feel she could apply to her *fiancé* for assistance. That Mr. Thorne should feel culpable as result of his sister-in-law's renewed interest was what Lord Sweetbriar had intended, of course. He had not anticipated, however, that the next day would find his uncle calling not on Lady Sweetbriar, but Miss Clough.

When advised that a gentleman visitor awaited her in the morning room, Miss Clough bit off an annoyed exclamation and dismissed her servant before that worthy could enlighten her as to the caller's identity. Clytie's ill temper was not surprising, in light of Lord Sweetbriar's newly developed habit of treating her home as if it were an extension of his own. Though she was fond of Rolf, Clytie had grown weary of his incessant carping on the topic of Lady Regina Foliot. And so she would tell him! Miss Clough resolved, as she walked down the hallway.

The caller stood at the window, in a glare of bright sunlight. Miss Clough frowned, then blinked. Doubtless she was dazzled by the brightness. For a moment, it seemed Rolf had altered amazingly in outline. "What new disaster has *now* beset us?" she asked. "Or have you come to tell me we may put an end to this absurd charade?"

His mood considerably elevated by this odd welcome, Mr. Thorne stepped out of the blinding sunlight. "If only I might! It will not be much longer, I trust."

Stunned by the magnitude of her error—how could *any*one have mistaken Marmaduke Thorne for his foppish nephew?—Clytie gasped. "I beg your pardon, sir! I thought—"

"I know what you thought!" Marmaduke caught her hands, smiled down into her startled face. "My darling, I already knew you don't care two figs for my nephew. You *couldn't!* In truth, I wonder that anyone might."

In response with these sentiments, which accorded so closely with her own, Miss Clough's lips twitched. Then she recalled the extent of Mr. Thorne's infamy. "Lady Regina *did* care for him!" she sternly pointed out. "Before you alientated—"

"Fudge!" interrupted Marmaduke, as he drew Clytie across the oaken floor and settled her in one of the arched-back chairs. Then he drew up another chair for himself, so closely that their knees almost touched. "I did no such thing. It was *you* who set off this imbroglio."

"I?" Clytie echoed blankly. At such close quarters, Mr. Thorne had a distinctly intoxicating effect. "Fiddlestick! Oh, you mean because Rolf took me up in his carriage when he should have taken Regina instead. That was not my doing, but Nikki's!" Mention of Lady Sweetbriar recalled Clytie's suspicions. Coolly, she added: "If you are looking for Nikki, sir, she is not here!"

"Is Nikki *often* here?" Mr. Thorne inquired, as he casually took possession of Miss Clough's left hand.

"Often?" Perhaps it was her failure to take a nuncheon that left Clytie feeling light-headed. "Daily, I should think! What with decisions concerning China papers and painted silks—to say nothing of bowfronted chests and what-nots—and I am forgetting the most important selection of oval, shield, or heart-shaped chair backs! With fillings of leaves or drapery or vases, honeysuckle or wheat ears! Papa has told Nikki she may refurbish us, sir."

Mr. Thorne had spent the preceding interval in quiet contemplation of his hostess's endearingly faint freckles, lovely sandy hair, and incomparable brown eyes. "*You* do not need refurbishing, Miss Clough."

Miss Clough? Scant moments past she had been his darling. For prudence's sake, this *tête-à-tête* should be brought to a quick conclusion, Clytie decided. Bluntly she inquired what had brought Mr. Thorne to Clough House. "*You* did, Clytie," he replied.

Due to the maddening manner in which her thoughts were prone to wander under the influence of Mr. Thorne, Miss Clough was growing very annoyed with herself. "Why should you seek *me* out?" she snapped. "Aren't Nikki and Lady Regina sufficient— Drat! First you provoke me into saying the most rag-mannered things, and then you laugh! Mr. Thorne, you are a very aggravating man."

"So you have said before, or words of a similar nature." Marmaduke continued to grin. "*What* a merry time we shall have, if ever this bumblebath is resolved! That is why I have come to you, Clytie; so we may put our heads together and see if we can devise some sort of solution to our fix."

Not for the purpose of arriving at solutions did Miss Clough yearn to put her head together with that of Mr. Thorne, an appalling realization that caused her to blush. Marmaduke brushed his fingers across one rosy cheek. Clytie was amazed to feel her skin tingle. A trifle tardily, she jerked away. "*Are* we in a fix?" she feebly inquired.

Not only Miss Clough's skin tingled; Mr. Thorne gazed with some surprise upon his fingertips. "More of a fix than I had suspected!" he replied. "We may blame Nikki for the most of it. She is the one who decided Lady Regina must not have Rolf. Now you are looking wary again, Clytie. Next I suppose you will order me shown the door. Just yesterday Rolf invited me to engage in fisticuffs. Everyone is trying to stir coals!"

"*Did* you engage in fisticuffs with Rolf?" Wary as Miss Clough might look, she had no intention of ordering her guest shown out.

Mr. Thorne sounded rueful. "Have a mill with my

own nephew? *What* a high opinion you hold of me! No, Miss Clough, I did not. Nor will I, no matter how strong the temptation to box the gudgeon's ears. Why, you will ask, did Rolf issue me such an invitation? It was a mere fuss about trifles. My nephew decided I harbor improper intentions toward Lady Regina, and was consequently feeling very cross."

That reaction, Miss Clough understood. "Do you harbor such intentions, sir?"

"Toward Lady Regina? Good God, no!" Mr. Thorne's sincerity could not be held in doubt. His manner abruptly altered. "Were we discussing *you*—"

"But we are *not* discussing me." It took every iota of Clytie's willpower to make her manner so firm. "We were talking about Rolf. Lady Regina is using you to make him jealous, I credit, just as he is using me? As well as to keep Nikki from forcing us upon one another. What a dreadful business this is! I wish we were well out of it—or rather, that *I* was!"

Mr. Thorne gazed in a somewhat morose manner upon one of the tapestry panels set between silver sconces on the wall. "As do I, Miss Clough." So very solemn was his tone that it earned him a startled glance. The situation was even more muddled than Clytie realized, he thought. If only he could explain! But a gentleman's honor forbade him telling one lady that another lady's rekindled ardor threatened to set all at naught.

Her caller looked as if weighty considerations exercised his mind, decided Miss Clough, whose own thoughts were proceeding in a more rational manner now that she had become accustomed to Mr. Thorne's presence in her papa's morning room. Mr. Thorne could only enhance any chamber that he graced, she mused. His muscular figure and swarthy complexion, pale eyes and sun-streaked hair combined to give an exotic effect in comparison with which the ordinary must pale. Certainly all Miss Clough's admirers, in comparison with Marmaduke, seemed sadly commonplace. And she had thought she did not even like him, when first they met. How absurd! No wonder Lady Regina and Nikki—Clytie winced, by her own traitorous reflections caught up short.

"What is it? Have I hurt your hand?" Marmaduke gave it a little pat. "I must have, I think; you are glowering at me. It reminds me of when first we met, but I had hoped to have risen in your opinion since then. No, you do not need to answer. I can see that I have not." He sighed. "Ironic, that I did not appreciate the essential melancholy of the Russians when I dwelt among them—and returned to England only to be made melancholy myself."

In spite of her reservations concerning Marmaduke Thorne's motives, character, and sentiments, Clytie could not help but be amused. "You greatly exaggerate your experiences in Russia, I think."

"Exaggeration, Miss Clough, is not among my sins." Marmaduke's warm glance was invitation to ponder what delightful pursuits his misdeeds might include. "The Russians have every reason to be melancholy; theirs is an anachronistic way of life. *Boyars* of the old aristocracy possess estates and mansions all over Russia, and don't even know how many serfs and villages they own. Then there are the peasants who, if fortunate, live in one-room huts, for warmth laying half naked on the stove. But I should not speak of such things to a young lady. Forgive me."

In point of fact, Mr. Thorne should not have been speaking to Miss Clough at all in the absence of a chaperone, a detail of nice behavior which she chose to overlook. "You have been dancing attendance on Lady Regina too long," Clytie murmured dryly. *"My* sensibilities are not so delicate. Now we are even, sir, because *I* should not have said that! May I speak without roundaboutation? Thank you! I confess that I do not know *what* to think of you, Mr. Thorne."

"That does not surprise me." Marmaduke looked rueful. "I made Lady Regina the object of my gallantry with some notion of persuading her to look more kindly upon my nephew's suit—yes, and to persuade her to leave off plaguing me about Nikki's jewels! For my meddling, I have been more than amply repaid. Had I realized it was *you* in my nephew's carriage, I would

129

never have lent my efforts—but by the time I *did* realize, it was too late!"

A gentleman who *truly* admired a lady would know her even though her features *were* obscured by a bonnet, Miss Clough unfairly felt. "It is not only that," she said coolly. "Rolf thinks you and Nikki have conspired to divest him of his fortune, did you know?'"

"Conspired together?" Mr. Thorne's voice was very like a groan. "That is the version of the tale he told *you*. To Nikki, he announced that I alone lusted—forgive me!—er, pined for my brother's wealth. I suppose he meant to set Nikki and I at odds. Fortunately, Nikki realized that I'm not likely to murder Rolf, which is the only way I could avail myself of Reuben's money—which, for the record, I do *not* want!" His dark features were forbidding. "Although, if Rolf keeps on in this manner, I may well change my mind! Not about my brother's wealth, but my nephew's continued existence."

Among the various ignoble traits which Miss Clough suspected Mr. Thorne of possessing was no ability to take another life. If only she could be equally certain that he was untainted by culpability. "Then there was the gaming hell where you took Nikki!" she remarked.

Never had Marmaduke encountered a female so little susceptible to his charm. Clytie's manner to him was no less distant than upon his arrival—if anything, moreso—even though he had spent the past half hour holding her hand. Reluctantly he released her. "Do you object to gaming hells, Miss Clough?"

"Not especially." Feeling curiously bereft, Clytie gazed at her abandoned hand. "But I must object most strongly if you mean to make a habit of publicly kissing my stepmama-to-be on the nose!"

"Your—" Mr. Thorne looked bewildered, then intrigued. "Are you feeling slighted, my sweet? I would much rather have kissed *your* nose, but you weren't there! And Nikki—well, I have been in the habit of kissing Nikki, you know. It doesn't *mean* anything. However, if you don't like it—"

"I don't!" interrupted Miss Clough. Nor, she suspected, for all his assumed nonchalance, did her papa.

130

About Miss Clough's papa, Mr. Thorne also thought. Rolf had been telling a lot of clankers recently. Perhaps as concerned his stepmama's sentiments toward her brother-in-law, Lord Sweetbriar had also told less than the truth. Devoutly, Marmaduke hoped this was the case. If not, this might well be his own as well as Nikki's worst scrape. "Clytie, I would like to ask you a question. I fear it may sound a little queer."

Miss Clough elevated her gaze from the forlorn hand which Mr. Thorne had once held. What a ninnyhammer she was become! Perhaps she had caught this lachrymose habit of reflection from Lord Sweetbriar. But if Rolf chose to make a cake of himself mourning the perfidy of Lady Regina, that was no reason why Clytie must act similarly bird-witted as regarded Mr. Thorne.

"Sir," she responded, "you have already said several things to me which were *distinctly* queer! I think we need not quibble about one more."

So far was Mr. Thorne from being abashed by Miss Clough's frank rejoinder that he not only reclaimed her hand, but pressed it to his lips. "*Definitely* I will seek you out the next time I am compelled to kiss a lady's nose—or elsewhere! How delightfully you blush, Clytie. If only my nephew were not such a clunch!"

Miss Clough was fully conscious of the compromising picture they must make to anyone entering the morning room, a realization that made her alter her position not one inch. Clytie could have sat that way forever, with Marmaduke's warm attention focused on her, his fingers tenderly gripping her hand. Indeed, she did spend several moments frozen in that posture, before being restored to her senses by a cramp. "I wish you would not throw the hatchet at me, Mr. Thorne!"

"Stuff!" Marmaduke's brusque rejoinder was softened by his smile. "You wish nothing of the sort. Yes, I am the worst of coxcombs to say so, but you have just accused *me* of talking flummery, which I do not. At least not to *you!* Oh, blast all these misapprehensions. I don't suppose, my darling, that you would consider an elopement."

Certainly Clytie would consider an elopement, and a delightful notion it was; but she was not prone to romantical high flights. "Gretna Green?" she murmured ironically. "I am no heroine for such an adventure, Mr. Thorne."

"Of course you are not, and I would not have suggested it, did matters not draw so rapidly to a crisis—and one of which the outcome is not assured." Recalling his own uncertain future, Mr. Thorne released Miss Clough and rose. "I do not mean to sound impertinent, Clytie, but it is very important that I discover how Nikki truly feels about your father."

Was *that* why he had come here? To learn Nikki's sentiments? Surely his advances had not *all* been toward that end! Both curious and indignant, Clytie eyed Marmaduke. He did not *look* like a man with a love of dissipation. Still, had not Shakespeare said a man might smile and smile and yet be a villain? Whoever, if anyone, had said it had made a good point. The devious Mr. Thorne must be held at arm's length.

The better to do so, Clytie moved to the window. She had meant to flirt with Marmaduke, she remembered, to lure him away from Nikki. Now she thought she could do nothing so insincere. "Nikki can tell you her sentiments better than I."

That he had made a severe strategical error, Marmaduke knew, and that there was no way to retrieve his misstep. "My reason for asking is not what it must seem; and there are other reasons why I cannot ask Nikki herself. I wish that you would humor me in this, Miss Clough."

He still wanted Nikki, thought Clytie. Well, what gentleman would not? And what female in full possession of her senses could fail to want Marmaduke? Her papa could not help but be hurt.

Though she could not bring herself to falsely encourage Mr. Thorne, perhaps Clytie might yet champion her father's cause. "I have no reason to think Nikki and my papa will not rub on excellently together," she retorted. "Providing *you* do not interfere with them!"

Marmaduke frowned, as much in response to this thrust as because of the bright sunlight which prevented him a clear view of the barb's source. "It is no more than I deserve, I suppose, that you should hold me in such low esteem. I mean your father no harm. You have my word on that, Miss Clough." She made no answer. Defeated, he walked toward the door. Once there, he turned back, unwilling to leave her on such a final note. "I wish you might trust me."

Clytie wished so also; alas, she could not. Though her expression was obscured by shadows, her tone was unmistakably hostile as she bid her caller a flat goodbye.

Chapter Sixteen

While Miss Clough relieved her pent-up emotions via a good cry into her pillow, and Mr. Thorne repaired to White's, there to imbibe rather more liberally of the grape than was his habit, Lord Sweetbriar underwent a dramatic encounter of his own in Oxford Street. How his lordship came to be strolling along that wide flag-stoned thoroughfare is of no especial importance, nor is the fact that his lordship was so intrigued by the sight of the clown from Astley's Royal Amphitheatre— who periodically drove through the streets in all manner of quaint costumes in an effort to drum up enthusiasm for Astley's equestrian displays—that he walked smack into a lamp post. Once Lord Sweetbriar had unentangled himself from this obstacle, he espied a spectacle even more fascinating than had been Astley's clown. It was no less than his beloved, attended by a gaggle of her sisters, in search of items with which to refurbish their shabby wardrobes.

"I say!" said Lord Sweetbriar, as the Foliot damsels swept by him and trooped *en masse* into the shop of W. H. Botibol, a *plumassier* by trade. Rolf had no desire to traipse after his beloved through fancy feathers and ostrich plumes. "I say!" he uttered again, when the young ladies emerged. Again no response, other than snickers and giggles and noses elevated high into the air, was vouchsafed him. Lord Sweetbriar was not put off by this odd behavior. Clearly, the Foliots had failed to see him. Perhaps the family was shortsighted? It

134

never occured to his lordship that he had received a deliberate snub. He followed Lady Regina into the Pantheon Bazaar.

Though less spectacular than in its original incarnation—the timber-framed cathedrallike hall had burned down many years before—the Bazaar still had in it much to intrigue. Lord Sweetbriar spent several bemused moments contemplating silken stockings before recalling his beloved. Lest he lose sight of her among the different rooms, he set out in hasty pursuit.

Lord Sweetbriar need not have worried; Lady Regina had no intention of evading him, though she did not wish to seem as though she were anxious to engage in speech. Sweetbriar had treated her very shabbily, Regina thought; she was not reconciled by Mr. Thorne's continued assurances that his nephew had no romantic interest in Miss Clough. But here Rolf was, sauntering toward her as nonchalantly as if he passed part of every day browsing among trifles of satin and lace, ribbons and bows. "Ho!" Lord Sweetbriar said amiably, upon achieving her side.

Lady Regina dispelled her giggling sisters with a single quelling glance. "Sweetbriar," she responded coolly. "I am surprised to see you here."

And so she might be surprised, mused Rolf; the Pantheon Bazaar was hardly among his usual haunts. He would not tell Regina that he had followed her, however. Darling that she was, Lady Regina had a slight tendency to puff up with conceit. "Surprised? he said merely. "So am I surprised! Dashed if I expected to encounter you in this place! But I'm glad I have! I don't want to stand on bad terms!"

Nor did Lady Regina deem it politic to continue estranged from the wealthiest of her *beaux*. Even so, she did not mean to forgive him *too* easily. "We would not *be* on bad terms, had *you* not discovered a partiality for Miss Clough."

"A—" Lord Sweetbriar flinched. "I don't have a partiality for Clytie! *You* should know that! Ain't I said I have a preference for *you* any number of times? Clytie's a good sort of girl, but she can't take the shine out of you!" Having, as he thought, reassured his be-
135

loved, Rolf smiled. "There! I'm glad *that's* cleared up! I don't mind admitting I've nigh fretted myself to flinders over this business. Tell me, didn't you miss me just a little bit?"

The object of Lord Sweetbriar's affections narrowed her fine green eyes. Rolf was very sure of her, she thought. Well, Lady Regina was no longer so certain that she must settle for Rolf. "I have been very busy," she replied. "Mr. Thorne—"

"Hah!" interjected Lord Sweetbriar, in such violent tones as made Lady Regina stare. *"Hah!"* he repeated, for good measure. "Certainly Uncle Duke has been busy—leading you up the garden path!"

"The garden—" Lady Regina gasped with outrage. "Not another word, Sweetbriar! I am very displeased with you!"

"You're displeased?" Rolf would not be denied his say. *"You!* You'd be in the very devil of a pucker if you was me! Don't bother to tell me I should not swear in front of a lady; I know it. But you'd swear too if you was me. For that matter, I ain't sure you *are* a lady, because it's sure as check you ain't been *acting* like one! Which reminds me, why did you say Uncle Duke was dangling after my fortune when he *ain't?"*

Only Lord Sweetbriar's last remark saved him from verbal annihilation. "How do you know that he is *not?"* inquired Lady Regina, with clenched jaw.

"Who ain't what?" This reconciliation was not proceeding as Lord Sweetbriar had anticipated it would when he followed Lady Regina through the portals of the Pantheon Bazaar. "Oh! Uncle Duke told me himself that he don't need a fortune, and I don't have any reason to think he was telling me a tarradiddle." His uncle, Rolf reflected, seemed to have a harrowing predilection for the truth.

Lady Regina was also engaged in reflection of which Marmaduke Thorne was the focus. In her view of the world, the only man who didn't need a fortune already possessed ample resources of his own. If Mr. Thorne did not yearn after his nephew's wealth, then he must be already wealthy in his own right. Marmaduke gave the appearance of a gentleman who dwelt in easy circumstances, certainly—but appearances could be very deceptive, as Lady Regina well knew. A perfect example was her own walking dress of white muslin, unadorned by so much as a narrow tuck or colored ribbon, not to mention cambric frills and tambour work. The casual observer might think so uncluttered a creation was the epitome of elegance. Regina knew better. She verged on being a dowd.

Lady Sweetbriar's matched Wedgewood cameos would have made all the difference, Regina realized suddenly. Yes, and such a triumph would also put her siblings' disrespectful noses firmly out of joint. Lady Regina was growing sick to death of her younger sisters, who were prone to go on at great and maudlin length about the selfishness of the family beauty, who had let slip off her hook the plumpest fish in the matrimonial seas.

Regina cast her whispering, snickering sisters a loathing glance, then looked with heightened appreciation upon Lord Sweetbriar. Her own lack of modality was more than compensated by his lordship's violet coat, made up with French riding sleeves and huge plated buttons and skirttails which reached below his knees. "So Mr. Thorne is a man of substance," she mused.

Though Lord Sweetbriar's powers of perception were not especially keen, he had begun to glean a tolerable comprehension of the way in which his beloved's mind worked. "I doubt that Uncle Duke's substance is equal to my own!" he said bluntly. "Duke was a younger son. Moreover, you wouldn't care for his conversation of a morning. Just this day he was talking to me about the St. Petersburg prison over the breakfast cups. People thrown into cells below water level and left there with only a few wisps of straw to sleep on and reptiles for company!" He shuddered. "It's enough to make a fellow wish he'd stayed in bed! How would *you* like to have freezing water poured on your head until your whole body froze into a statue of solid ice?"

For herself, Lady Regina could not like the notion, but she thought it might suit Lord Sweetbriar very well. "It is little wonder that natural deaths are notoriously rare among members of the Russian imperial

137

family," she remarked. "I fail to see what any of this has to do with whether or not Mr. Thorne harbors intentions toward your inheritance."

It was not toward Rolf's inheritance that his uncle harbored intentions, that unhappy young man thought. How best to warn his beloved that she was encouraging the attentions of a gazetted rakehell? Lord Sweetbriar's long suit was not subtlety. "You are encouraging the attentions of a rakehell!" he remarked.

"A—I am not!" Lady Regina wondered if Mr. Thorne's tales of Slavic excess had unhinged his nephew's brain. "Goodness! Can you be referring to your *uncle*? I never heard of such a thing!"

Lord Sweetbriar could not fault his beloved's skepticism; he, too, would have doubted his uncle's aptitude for villainy, had he not had it from Duke's own lips. "My uncle is a very rascally character!" he said, with praiseworthy restraint. "You took up with him to make me jealous. I don't mind owning I *was*, a teeny bit! Even though I knew all along it was a hum! But least said, soonest mended! We'll forget it ever occurred."

By this indication that her transgression had been magnanimously forgiven, Lady Regina was filled with a sense of burning resentment. *Her* attention had not been first to stray. Were anyone to mete out forgiveness, it should not be Sweetbriar. "That settles it! You *are* a jingle-brain!" she unkindly remarked.

Lord Sweetbriar strove for patience. "I may or may not be a jingle-brain, but I'm awake on more suits than *you!* You're wondering if maybe you can attach Uncle Duke for real, now that you know he's plump in the pocket himself." Rolf's quest for patience proved to be in vain. "I was used to think Nikki the most hardened flirt in London! I ain't sure I care to be leg-shackled to a female who's running mad for my own uncle—*not* that he'll be throwing the handkerchief in your direction, my girl!"

"You think not?" Lady Regina did an excellent impersonation of a person who had had the freezing waters of the Neva poured over her head. "I'll thank you, Sweetbriar, to be a little less busy about my affairs!"

"Your—" Upon being gifted with this frank admission, his lordship's feelings so overcame him that even his eyes bulged. "You *admit* to it?" A further disillusioning realization struck him. *"Affaires?* You've, er, gone up the garden path with more than Uncle Duke? Good God!"

Lady Regina, who had endured these perplexing statements in openmouthed bewilderment, now firmly pressed her lips shut. Only after achieving a count of several hundred did she allow them to part again. "Not *affaires,* Sweetbriar! *Affairs!* A-f-f-a-i-r-s! Business! I requested you to be less busy about my business! As to the other, I have *never*—oh! No gentleman who truly cared for a lady could suggest such a thing."

Lord Sweetbriar was stricken with not the slightest pang of remorse. "If he knew what Uncle Duke said to *me,* he could! I ain't wishful of cutting up your hopes, Regina, but someone must. Why, it was all I could do to talk him out of trying to set you up as his fancypiece!"

"His—" Words failed Lady Regina. She pressed her fingers to her brow.

Anxiously, Lord Sweetbriar glanced around them, but no one seemed to have remarked his companion's distress save her sisters, huddled in a giggling cluster a small distance away, and those little cats seemed less anxious than pleased. "Don't poker up!" he begged. "Uncle Duke meant it for the best. He decided I must be hankering after Clytie—don't fly into the boughs! It wasn't *my* idea."

But Mr. Thorne had told her that his nephew *didn't* hanker after Miss Clough. Something very queer was afoot, decided Lady Regina. As regarded Lord Sweetbriar, she may have been a trifle hasty. One did not thoughtlessly toss aside a wealthy suitor in these days of cambric muslins at 1/8 a yard, and damask figured sarcenet at 6, even when it appeared that there might be tastier fish in the sea. "I think you had better tell me all about it, Rolf," she suggested.

By this indication that his beloved meant to be at least sufficiently reasonable as to refrain from enacting high melodrama in the Pantheon Bazaar, Lord Sweetbriar's own worst apprehensions were laid to rest. Briefly he repeated his conversation with his uncle, concluding: "I told him Nikki was still smitten, so that should turn the trick! If he's dangling after Nikki, Uncle Duke can't very well be dangling after you, too!"

Lady Regina could hardly be expected to appreciate this suggestion that any gentleman, given a choice of women after whom to dangle, must automatically choose Lady Sweetbriar. Nor was she gratified to be mentioned in conjunction with the coarse sentiments Lord Sweetbriar had expressed. In point of fact, decided Lady Regina, this entire conversation was a most improper one.

She changed the subject. "You expect me to believe that it is I whom you hold in esteem above all other females, Sweetbriar?"

Rolf interpreted the question in the most favorable of lights. "You know it's midsummer moon with me, Lady Regina; I told you so myself. Don't know what else I *can* tell you! Except that I'll do my best to make you *happy!*"

"And in proof of your professions," Lady Regina hinted, "you have brought me your stepmama's jewels."

"I have?" Looking confused, Lord Sweetbriar patted at himself. "Dash it, I did not! Don't know what put such a notion in your head! Not that I won't, eventually! I ain't had *time* to try and persuade Nikki to hand over the baubles, Regina! I've been too busy trying to prevent her marrying me off to Clytie."

"Nikki!" All the pent-up venom which Mr. Thorne had forbidden Lady Regina to utter in his hearing was released in that one word. "I should have guessed *she* was behind all this. And yet you claim you do not honor her above me. Do not deny it! In all truth you cannot."

It seemed to Lord Sweetbriar that he had had this conversation before. "But—"

"But nothing! First you lavish attentions on another female, then you tell me that for your sake your own uncle means to invite me to toss my bonnet over the windmill! *This* is the way you would treat the woman whom you wish to wed? I think not!" Convinced that she had regained the advantage, Lady Regina gathered up her sisters as a shepherdess might her flock. "Until you can give me proof of your professed affection, I have no alternative but to doubt that affection exists. In short, Sweetbriar, nothing has changed!"

Chapter Seventeen

Unaware that a large number of people were learning to look upon her with varying degrees of resentment, Lady Sweetbriar sallied forth the following morning to Berry's wine shop. There, in the tradition followed by kings and actresses and commoners alike, from the previous century to the current day, Nikki took a glass of wine and was weighed on the great scale. The old machine having no unpleasant surprises for her, Lady Sweetbriar proceeded homeward by an indirect route that meandered through the shopping precincts of Piccadilly and Pall Mall. Upon her eventual return to Fitzroy Square, she was informed that Miss Clough awaited her in the drawing room.

"Clytie!" Having shed her pelisse before learning of her caller, Lady Sweetbriar still wore upon her dark curls an oriental turban ornamented with cock feathers and a single uncurled ostrich plume. "What a *nice* surprise!"

Lady Sweetbriar's turban looked a trifle incongruous in conjunction with her day dress of printed lilac chintz, made with bodice front fastening on the shoulders, and neckline filled in with a white muslin tucker, an effect further heightened by the parasol which her ladyship still carried, made in a pagoda form, with steel stick and telescope. In comparison, Clytie felt positively mundane in her innocuous combination of corded muslin dress, chip straw bonnet, and shawl. However, she had not come to Fitzroy Square to try and outshine its occupant, who was currently regarding her with no little curiosity. "I hope I did not call at an inconvenient time! I had hoped you might be able to help me, Nikki. With, ah, a matter of the heart."

Preoccupied as she might be with more worldly matters—the installation of a cistern in the upper story of Clough House, for example—Lady Sweetbriar was eager to assist her future stepdaughter in pursuit of romance. Few ladies knew more about romance than she, fancied Nikki; had she not courted Cupid for years? Beaming, she settled in the chair nearest Clytie. "Oh, my dear!"

This cooperative attitude made Miss Clough feel a traitor; truth be told, the matters which Clytie sought to discuss dealt not with her own heart. It was her prospective stepmama's sentiments which she wished to discover—but how should she proceed?

Poor child! Lady Sweetbriar thought sympathetically; Cupid's dart had bereft Clytie of speech. It happened that way sometimes. "Has the cat got your tongue, my dear?" Nikki roguishly inquired, after gently nudging the ferrule of her umbrella against the damsel's knee.

Either she speak now or cease to try and interfere. Miss Clough drew a deep breath. "It concerns—" she said, and stopped. Aghast, Clytie realized she didn't want Nikki to confirm her doubts about Marmaduke.

"Silly twit!" Lady Sweetbriar amiably scoffed. "I know who it concerns, and very pleased I am about it, too! You could do far worse for yourself, Clytie."

She could do worse than a confirmed villain? Miss Clough blinked. "I *could?*" she inquired skeptically.

"But of course you could!" Clytie's lack of enthusiasm inspired Lady Sweetbriar to expand upon the subject. "He is a man of substance, with everything prime about him—a regular good 'un! Er, that is, a bachelor of the first stare!"

Things were in worse case than Clytie had imagined if Nikki enthused so freely to her about Marmaduke. Had Nikki forgotten her betrothal to Clytie's father? "I wonder what Papa would think."

"One seldom knows what your papa thinks, dear

143

Clytie." Lady Sweetbriar stroked her parasol. "It is a very unsettling habit until one grows accustomed to it. But in *this* instance I have your papa's own assurance that he wouldn't mind."

Her father had given his blessing to his *fiancée's* blatant flirtation with Mr. Thorne? Here was tolerance indeed! "Are you *certain* that's what Papa said?" Clytie asked faintly.

"Certain?" Lady Sweetbriar nibbled pensively on her lower lip. "Well, no! I do not recall his exact words. You must not fret, my dear! It is a highly flattering alliance. Once your papa understands this is what you truly want, he will come around."

"What *I* want?" Did not Nikki hint at her own association with Marmaduke? How could Clytie conduce such an arrangement, which must cause her papa pain? For that matter, how could her papa condone such a business, as it sounded like he had? Or could it be that Nikki thought *Clytie* had a partiality for Duke? Inexplicably, this absurd misapprehension made Clytie flush. "I *don't* want him!" she snapped.

"You don't?" Lady Sweetbriar's dark eyes opened wide. "How can this be? Obviously he has taken a marked fancy to *you!*"

Upon this startling assertion, Miss Clough's cheeks turned pinker still. "He *has?*" she asked.

"How can you doubt it?" This conversation was very heavy going, Nikki mused. She had never before experienced such difficulty in prosing with Miss Clough. Perhaps if she spoke slowly and distinctly? *"Think,* Clytie! Has he not been dancing attendance on you this age?"

Of one thing Clytie was certain; among the ladies whom Marmaduke Thorne currently danced attendance upon was not herself. Therefore, Nikki must be speaking of someone else. But who—? "Oh, *fiddle!*" Clytie said crossly. "You are talking about Rolf!"

"Naturally I am talking about Rolf!" Sympathetically, Lady Sweetbriar smiled. "You need not *pretend* with me. Rolf has repeatedly told me you are as fine as fivepence, and that is a *very* high accolade! I wish you would not be so missish, Clytie. That is *not* the way to bring a gentleman up to snuff."

Sternly Clytie repressed an impulse to pursue this topic; how to bring gentlemen up to snuff was something Nikki obviously knew. She felt an overwhelming reluctance to go on with pretense. "I am afraid that Rolf and I have been less than honest with you."

"A fig for honesty!" Nikki said gaily. It was clear to Lady Sweetbriar that Miss Clough was undergoing some sort of struggle with her conscience, and the discomfort of such hostilities her ladyship perfectly understood. "I can't imagine that you have done anything so dreadful."

"It is not dreadful, exactly." Warily, Miss Clough eyed her prospective stepmama's parasol. "But you will not like it."

As she puzzled over this dire hint, a tiny frown marred the perfection of Lady Sweetbriar's heart-shaped face. What she would dislike most of all, Nikki decided, was that Lady Regina Foliot should marry Rolf and lay claim to all her jewels. In a very determined manner, Nikki clutched at the specimens which she currently wore—necklace of two rows of fine golden filigree work, the lower hanging below the waist; brooch composed of a spray of flowers and leaves of diamonds set in silver; amethyst motto ring set round with brilliants. Perhaps Clytie might yet be made to see reason. "Rolf is a—"

"Rolf," Miss Clough interrupted grimly, "is a perfect block! It has all been a hum, Nikki. A bubble! A hoax! You were so determined that Rolf and I should make a match of it that we pretended to agree."

Lady Sweetbriar set her parasol point down upon the floor, folded her hands upon the handle, and sat up very straight. "It would have been such a *good* match for you, Clytie. You must not let it weigh with you that Rolf is a bit of a gudgeon. If one but *tries,* one can be happy with even a saphead." It occurred to her ladyship that this was hardly a maternal attitude. "Not a word of this to Rolf, mind!"

"I wouldn't think of it." Her companion's guilt-stricken expression prompted Clytie's smile. "I'm sorry
145

to disappoint you, Nikki, but I do not have a *tendre* for Rolf. Nor shall I develop one. Indeed, I doubt that I would marry Sweetbriar were he the last man on earth!" Came a pause, during which Lady Sweetbriar was heard to mutter ominously about chances frittered away. Added Miss Clough, for good measure: *"No, Nikki!"*

Lady Sweetbriar knew when she was temporarily bested. *"What* a hobble!" she sighed. "I had thought— and now I discover you were only playing a May game! *Why* did you do so, wretched child? While I contrived that you might steal a march on that stiff-rumped Foliot chit, *you* contrived that I be brought to a standstill. *Not* that I mean to pinch at you, or take a pet! Merely, I would like to know why you put forth so much effort to pull the wool over my eyes." She looked rueful. "Was I *such* a nuisance? Reuben was used to say that when I took a bee into my bonnet there was no telling what ill-advised thing I might do. Or if that is not *precisely* what he said—Reuben wasn't one to bandy words—it is what he *meant!"*

"I would not call you a nuisance, Nikki." Miss Clough did not care to agree with the detestable Reuben on any score. "You meant it for the best. As it turns out, Rolf and I simply would not suit. He would not have made such a point of dangling after me, even to mislead you, had not Lady Regina taken it into her head to flirt with Mr. Thorne." A plaintive note had crept into Clytie's voice during that last statement. It earned her a keen glance from her hostess, that authority on romance.

Blew the wind from that quarter? *Here* was a pretty fix! decided Lady Sweetbriar. The enterprising Marmaduke, it would appear, progressed rapidly toward his object. What the scoundrel needed with *two* fortunes, one could not imagine—but not only Lady Regina Foliot was far from indifferent. "Clytie! Has Duke been throwing the hatchet at you?" she asked.

Miss Clough flushed anew. "Not to signify," she murmured.

But flattery from Marmaduke Thorne was seldom lightly received, as Nikki well knew. "He *has* been!
146

And paying you distinguishing attentions to boot, I'll warrant!" She gave the floor an angry little thump with her parasol. "Was there *ever* such a rogue?"

This question, Miss Clough did not feel qualified to answer, her experience with villains being slight. Nor could she determine whether the angry sparkle in Lady Sweetbriar's dark eyes was the result of jealousy or concern on her behalf. The truth of this latter, Clytie thought she must find out. "Distinguishing attentions? Hardly that. Why are you so distressed, Nikki? Is not Mr. Thorne a friend of yours? Most people judge him a fine figure of a man."

"Oh, Duke is well enough in looks." Lady Sweetbriar had not failed to note Miss Clough's wistful tone. Poor child! Perhaps this hopeless passion might be nipped in the bud. "It is his *character* which will not withstand the light of day. You look startled. Are you thinking that because Duke and I are friends I should not speak *so?* But I have known him forever—yes, and many is the time I have had to pull a long face over one of his escapades."

As opposed to long faces, Lady Sweetbriar had—at least within Miss Clough's range of vision—appeared to enjoy Mr. Thorne excessively. Making ladies happy was a philanderer's métier, of course—all the same, something in Nikki's tale did not ring true. Could she in her own turn be trying to put Clytie off the scent, lest Sir Avery came to share his daughter's suspicions? If Nikki thought Sir Avery would pay attention to any suspicions not presented to him in ancient cuniform writing, she did not know her *fiancé* very well.

From Miss Clough's polite silence, Lady Sweetbriar deduced very correctly that the damsel was not convinced. "To use the word with no bark on it, Duke is a devilish ugly customer, my dear! The tales I could tell you—"

"Pray do!" Miss Clough promptly invited. Not only Lady Sweetbriar was perceptive; Clytie had noticed that her companion refused to meet her eyes. "Enlighten me."

Alas, Lady Sweetbriar could not. She knew of nothing against Marmaduke Thorne except this avarice

147

that he suddenly displayed, and it hardly behooved Nikki to castigate someone for dangling after a fortune or two. "I *could* tell you," she said sternly, "were you not a young lady, which you *are!* You must take my word for it that Duke is a very harum-scarum fellow who does things in a very hugger-mugger way. A gay deceiver who will play you false, *just* as he did me, those many years ago."

Definitely Lady Sweetbriar sought to give her a disgust of Marmaduke Thorne, reflected Miss Clough; but why? There seemed only one reasonable reason: Nikki wanted Duke herself. Surely she could not look on Clytie as a rival! "I had the impression that the shoe was on the other foot," remarked Miss Clough.

"The shoe— You mean that I played Duke false!" One could, supposed Lady Sweetbriar, view the matter in that light. Memories overwhelmed her. "It was very stupidly done of me," she murmured.

Stupidly? But Lady Sweetbriar had just finished saying Mr. Thorne was a gay deceiver. Gently, Miss Clough pointed out this fact.

Miss Clough, reflected Lady Sweetbriar, had an aggravating habit of dwelling upon the weak points in an argument. "It was all so long ago!" retorted Nikki with a dismissive wave of one hand. "Perhaps the details have got a little muddled in my mind. All the same, it utterly sinks my spirits to think that *you* might be similarly deceived." The irony of the situation struck her. "My own stepdaughter, forsooth!"

"I am not your stepdaughter yet," Miss Clough pointed out. "And when I *am*, I trust you will not make it your habit to tell me whiskers, Nikki!" Or *if* she became so, Clytie amended silently.

"Whiskers! Next I suppose you will accuse *me* of nourishing some dastardly design." So incensed was Lady Sweetbriar by this eminently reasonable accusation that she hopped up from her chair. Conscience, awakened by Miss Clough's satiric glance, prompted her to add: "At least *I* give good value! Oh, this is such an awkward situation. Clytie, you must perceive that it would be the most ruinous of entanglements were you and Duke—" She closed her eyes in prayer.

Said Miss Clough, in response to this impassioned speech: "Watch out for that chair." Lady Sweetbriar's dark eyes flew open. Directly in her pathway was one of her satin-upholstered, oval-backed chairs. Only by utilizing her parasol as a brake did Nikki avoid pitching head first into its overstuffed seat.

"Thank you!" she said crossly.

"You're welcome!" responded Miss Clough.

For the space of a few moments, the ladies engaged in no further speech. Lady Sweetbriar transversed the perimeters of her drawing room, the feathers of her turban swaying in rhythm with her measured tread. Keenly, Miss Clough observed this progress. Clytie could not determine whether her stepmama-to-be was a conscienceless fortune hunter, or just appallingly indiscreet. Were Marmaduke so wicked as Nikki sought to paint him, she would hardly permit him to publicly kiss her on the nose. Or would she? No, a lady did not criticize a gentleman so severely to another lady without purpose, Miss Clough thought. If only Sir Avery would take a stand! But Clytie knew her papa too well to cling to that forlorn hope. How difficult it was to decide what was for the best.

At least she might pretend to believe Nikki, and thereby gain her future confidence. "I *did* think, when I met Mr. Thorne, that he must be half mad."

"Oh, yes!" Perhaps because they had been conducted whilst in motion, Lady Sweetbriar's thoughts had been much more constructive than those of her guest; and she was very willing to have the silence end. Clytie and Rolf were obviously too young to know their own minds. If only some compromising situation might be contrived—"The entire family is lunatic. Except, that is, for Rolf!"

Miss Clough had heard quite enough about the dandified Lord Sweetbriar for one twenty-four-hour space. Furthermore, she was no closer to her goal than when Lady Sweetbriar had stepped into the drawing room. "Nikki," she asked bluntly, "are you *certain* you wish to marry my papa?"

"Certain?" Wearing a bewildered expression, Lady Sweetbriar once more sat down beside Miss Clough.

"What makes you ask that? Of course I wish to marry your father—oh, you are afraid that *we* may not suit! Silly child, a lady may suit anyone, does she put her mind to it." A very pensive expression settled on her pretty face. "I'll wager even Lady Regina might be brought to accept Rolf's offer, were we to show him how to go about the thing."

Chapter Eighteen

"Are you *sure* this is the way one goes about the thing?" inquired Lord Sweetbriar, whilst attempting to position himself comfortably upon one knee, a process made all the more difficult by the extreme tightness of his breeches, and his excessively high shirt points. "It seems like a very queer business to me!"

Ironically, Miss Clough observed her caller; it was the morning room of Clough House wherein Lord Sweetbriar emulated a contortionist. "Nikki swears that, do you but do as she has written out, you must sweep Lady Regina right off her feet. Admittedly, *I* have never been proposed to quite so poetically minded a manner—but neither have I accepted any of those offers I *did* receive, so maybe Nikki knows what she's talking about."

"'Your eyes are like stars, your face beyond compare—'" Lord Sweetbriar looked up from the piece of paper he clutched in one hand. "I never heard such poppycock. Dash it, you've got *freckles!* It's *my* notion Nikki's got some ulterior motive for making me talk such skimble-skamble stuff."

Miss Clough did not feel up to a discussion of Lady Sweetbriar's motives. It was all she could do to refrain from laughing at the absurd picture Rolf presented. "It's not to *me* you are making your compliments."

"The devil it ain't!" responded Lord Sweetbriar, indignantly rearing back, and consequently very nearly toppling over. "As if I don't know who I'm talking to!

Tell you what, Clytie, you've taken a maggot into your brain! Not that anyone could blame you for it. Nikki has that effect on a person who's around her too long."

Could Nikki be blamed for her stepson's lack of mental prowess, Miss Clough unkindly reflected, then she was a powerful influence indeed. "You are supposed to be sweeping me off my feet in Lady Regina's place, Rolf. We are pretending that I am her, so that you may rehearse your part. Shall we continue? Remember, you are supposed to have taken a fancy to me."

In a less-than-enthusiastic manner, Lord Sweetbriar glanced at his stepmama's instructions, and then grasped Clytie's hand. "'I am mad for you! Absolutely enraptured! I have an income of—'" He faltered. "What the deuce does *that* signify?"

In the case of Lady Regina, Clytie suspected that Rolf's income signified a great deal. How clever Nikki had been to work financial matters into this impassioned declaration—but of course Nikki would know what would most interest Lady Regina. For two ladies who thoroughly detested one another, mused Clytie, Nikki and Lady Regina possessed curiously similar outlooks.

"Never mind!" she soothed. "Pray continue. We must assume Nikki knows what she is about."

"You may be sure *Nikki* knows it!" To his damp brow, Lord Sweetbriar applied a square linen handkerchief with hemstitched border and monogram. "But do *we?* I don't know why we should trust Nikki."

Clytie looked startled. "Why should we not? Practicing your declaration *is* a very good idea, Rolf. What harm can come of it, pray? You are refining too much upon Nikki's wish that *we* should make a match of it, I think."

Lord Sweetbriar thought Miss Clough a veritable innocent as regarded the intricate working of his stepmama's mind. He did not say so, because his own intellect was not sufficient to enable him to verbalize his forebodings. Perhaps he *was* making mountains out of molehills, as Clytie hinted. Once more he studied his instructions, looking resigned.

"'I have a great regard for you,'" he read, in a rapid

monotone. "'There is no other woman with whom I could ever think of settling in matrimony. I trust that you will not think me bold if I most earnestly conjure you to become my wife, nor hold me in lower esteem when I vow that if you do *not* have me I will doubtless succumb to a sickness of the heart. Darling Clytie, say that you will be my bride, so that we may nevermore be forced to endure the anguish of separation again.'"

This was what he was supposed to say to Lady Regina? Lord Sweetbriar's brain reeled. Then a puzzling detail presented itself to him. Frowning, he peered at the paper. "'Clytie'?" he said.

Before Miss Clough could attempt to explain the queer inclusion of her name in an impassioned declaration meant for another lady, a voice behind them intervened. "'Clytie'!" that voice also said. "You told me Sweetbriar *didn't* mean to have her, Mr. Thorne."

The effect of this irate observation was no less staggering than a thunderclap, at least upon Lord Sweetbriar, who in craning his neck to view the newcomers very nearly lost his balance, and in seeking to regain it very nearly dragged Clytie off her own seat. "Lady Regina!" he cried. "You mustn't think—this ain't what it seems—I should never have trusted Nikki! This is all *her* doing! You *must* believe it is all fudge!"

"I will deal with you later, Sweetbriar." The glance he received from Lady Regina made Rolf anxious to wait. She turned back to her companion. "I will not undertake to express my opinion of your perfidy. You meant all along for Sweetbriar to have Miss Clough! Next I will discover you meant also to give me a slip on the shoulder, I suppose!"

"A slip on the shoulder!" This intelligence brought Lord Sweetbriar up off his heels. "I say, Uncle Duke!"

"Must you?" inquired that gentleman, somewhat plaintively. "Spare your breath, nephew, I shan't allow you to call me out. Besides, unless I am mistaken, it was you who put that notion in the lady's head."

Perhaps it was the effect of the handkerchief that he had for several moments been rubbing across his brow that activated Lord Sweetbriar's memory. "Yes, and it was you who put the notion in *mine!* You said you was making sheeps' eyes at her so that I could fix my interest with Clytie, and then that you would cast her off." He frowned. "Or was that when you decided to invite her to toss her bonnet over the windmill?"

"Any gentleman who cares a *button* for a lady would deal very harshly with someone who offered her insult," Lady Regina said bitterly. "Even if that someone *was* his uncle!"

By this announcement, Lord Sweetbriar was posed a very sticky dilemma. Did he not challenge his uncle, Lady Regina would deem him a coward, a courtcard, a milksop. *Did* her persuade his uncle to meet him, however, Duke would doubtless prove the better shot. Lord Sweetbriar could not feel happy about this prospective injury to himself. "Agh!" said he.

If Lady Regina and Mr. Thorne, respectively looking resigned and amused, could find in themselves no sympathy for Rolf's dilemma, Miss Clough was not similarly heartless. "*Most* ladies, if invited by Mr. Thorne to toss their bonnets over the windmill, would be more likely to regard it as a compliment than an insult. Lady Regina is probably miffed because he *didn't* invite her to do. She is also miffed because she caught you paying your addresses seemingly to *me*, Rolf. Set your mind at ease! The lady's honor hasn't been besmirched." Clytie darted a quizzical glance at Mr. Thorne. "*Has* it, sir?"

"No, my darling, it has not!" Marmaduke's smile flashed. "But you must not think I will be similarly forebearing about *yours*, after that glowing testimonial which you so kindly gave me. Tell me, Clytie, *would* you toss your bonnet over the windmill?"

The focus of several eyes, in them varying degress of speculation, Miss Clough wished that she might sink. Alternately, she wished she were less civilized, so that she might express herself via an energetic breakage of bric-a-brac. "I wish you would not be absurd!" she responded crossly. "*I* am not behind this farrago of nonsense."

"No, Nikki is!" Lord Sweetbriar, stiff from prolonged kneeling, tottered across the room. "Dash it, Regina, you must see that I can't marry two females at one time! It was you I asked first—yes, and I was going to ask you again! It was Nikki's notion that I should practice! And that's what we was doing when you came in!" In proof, he waved his instructions. "Look! It's all written out!"

"A likely story!" Sniffing, Lady Regina snatched the paper. Lord Sweetbriar's pretty speech had indeed been written out, complete to the last detail—Clytie's name. Furiously, Regina crumpled up the damning missive. Then, in complete disregard of those ladylike precepts which governed the large majority of her actions, she flung the wadded paper at Miss Clough.

"Oh, I say!" said Rolf, who could not feel that for one young lady to be hurling things at another in the second young lady's morning room was the epitome of good conduct. Nor would it be a comfortable habit in a wife. Just in case Lady Regina *did* become his wife, unlikely as seemed that possibility, Lord Sweetbriar thought it behooved him to nip potential bad habits in the bud. "It ain't *seemly* to be throwing things!"

Lady Regina's fine green eyes fixed on the gilded clock that sat atop the mantle piece, and then moved resolutely away. "You are a fine one to scold me for misbehavior!" she said bitterly.

"Who better?" inquired Lord Sweetbriar, happily unaware of how close he came to being fatally wounded by a chimney clock. "Dash it, I *do* want you to be my wife."

"Me and Miss Clough and who else?" Lady Regina's voice was bitter, her incomparable features chagrined. Sweetbriar had been her ace up the sleeve, or so she thought. How her sisters would roast her for this mortifying development, and her mother scold. Regina turned on her heel, gathered up the tattered fragments of her pride. "I beg that you may remove me from the list."

Lord Sweetbriar wrinkled his brow. "But you have to marry *some*one; everyone knows that! Your papa's pockets are to let! It might as well be me as anyone else, because even if you don't hold me in any special affection, you don't *dis*like me either." It occurred to Rolf that his beloved's expression could well be interpreted as less than fond. What reason Regina might have for taking him in aversion, Rolf could not imagine. Unless—He aimed an accusing forefinger at his uncle. "Aha!"

During the preceding exchange, Mr. Thorne had strolled about the morning room, fetching up at last by the chair where his hostess sat. Judiciously he surveyed his nephew's accusatory stance. "The lad has quite a way with a word!" Marmaduke marveled, to Miss Clough. "No, Rolf. Your suspicions are unfounded. I have not put paid to your romance."

Although he ceased to stab the air with his forefinger, Lord Sweetbriar's doubts were not entirely assuaged. "I ain't saying you *meant* to," he admitted. "Confound it, Uncle Duke, you *are* a dab hand at the game of hearts!"

"So very high an accolade," murmured Mr. Thorne, greatly moved.

"Yes, and from *such* a source!" remarked Miss Clough, in an unsteady voice, an observation which earned her a glance that was very warm.

"Why are you staring at me in that gudgeonish manner?" inquired Mr. Thorne of his nephew, annoyed. Mr. Thorne was growing very wearied by the antics of his family, which might have been expressly designed to alienate him from Miss Clough. "Must I be more plainspoken yet? Very well! I have not the most distant interest in Lady Regina, Rolf. She may be a diamond of the first water, but she's not in *my* style!"

"Oh!" Hectic spots of color flamed in Regina's cheeks. Impotently she glared at Mr. Thorne, who was ignoring her altogether, and then at Lord Sweetbriar, who dared to look relieved. The failure of these gentlemen to enter the slightest distance into her feelings caused Lady Regina to commit her second rude act that day. She stamped her foot. Alas, in so doing, she inflicted excruciating pain upon her opposite ankle bone. "Oh, blast!" cried the much-abused young lady, as she limped toward the doorway. "I vow I shall spend the remainder of my days upon the shelf!"

Here was a threat worse even than that presented by Lord Sweetbriar's uncle; in Regina's voice had been the ring of truth. "Not that!" protested Rolf, as he hobbled after his beloved. Their argument wafted back from the hallway. Lady Regina accused her admirer of being a false deceiver, and lamented her own lack of worldly knowledge, and mourned that she had never thought he would use her in such a heartless way; in response to which Lord Sweetbriar accused his beloved of having windmills in her head. Fortunately, from the viewpoint of their auditors, the voices then passed out of earshot.

No longer under the necessity of having to restrain their amusement, Mr. Thorne and Miss Clough succumbed simultaneously to whoops. For some moments the morning room resounded with giggles and guffaws. Then the merrymakers regained sufficient control of themselves to glance at one another without renewed outbreaks of mirth. Their glances caught, and held. On her part, Miss Clough saw a swarthy gentleman clad in a chocolate-brown cloth frockcoat and beige breeches, whose sun-streaked brown hair was in disarray from hilarity. Marmaduke made a lady feel most deliciously abandoned, she mused, basking in the warmth of his pale blue eyes.

For his part, Mr. Thorne observed a young lady clad in a morning gown of clear lawn trimmed with embroidered frills, seated demurely on the edge of her chair, her hands folded quietly in her lap. Her expression, as she looked at him, was both curious and shy. Lord, but he longed to take her in his arms, kiss every one of her adorable freckles, remove that endearingly absurd cornette of smuggled Parisian lace from atop her curls and tangle his fingers in her brown hair. Yes, and if only he could be certain that his nephew had lied to him about Nikki's affections, he would do exactly that.

But he could *not* be sure that Rolf had told him whiskers, and until Marmaduke could determined that no impediment existed, he could not declare himself. Declare himself? Impediment? Ruefully, Mr. Thorne smiled. He was in a bad way.

That smile, because she could not understand it, recalled to Clytie her own doubts. How *could* she have passed several moments speculating upon the pleasures of abandonment with a gentleman whose every action proclaimed he was wicked indeed? Had he not been flirting outrageously with Lady Regina? Had he not kissed Nikki on the nose? Even if he did not conspire with Lady Sweetbriar to bilk the Upper Ten Thousand of its accumulated wealth—not to mention her own papa!—she had more than ample evidence of his villainy. Why, then, this tingling of the senses when he took her hands and drew her erect? There was only one explanation. She was as depraved as he!

Firmly, if reluctantly, Clytie disengaged herself. "I suppose Nikki bribed the servants beforehand to admit you and Lady Regina unannounced."

"I suppose." Mr. Thorne was a great deal less interested in the behavior of the servants than in what had caused the shuttered expression on Miss Clough's pretty face. That she was not indifferent to him, the vastly experienced Marmaduke could hardly fail to realize. But circumstances forebade he try and ascertain the precise nature of her sentiments. "Do you want to marry my nephew?" he asked.

"I wish to marry Rolf about as much as *you* wish to give Lady Regina a slip on the shoulder, I suspect." Clytie forgot her reservations long enough to grin. "You have been gaining an astonishing reputation, sir. *I* know it is all the fault of the Russians! You lived so long among them that you picked up their little ways."

Strongly against the dictates of his better nature, Mr. Thorne grasped Miss Clough's shoulders and gave her a little shake. Her brown eyes opened wide. *How* he longed to kiss her. "You never answered my questions about windmills," said Marmaduke, in tones that were distinctly strained.

Miss Clough's vocal cords were no less taut. "Umf!" she said. Then she recalled her resolution to save her papa from heartache via embarking herself upon a flirtation with Mr. Thorne. The logistics of that solution, she did not pause to ponder, nor her subsequent realization that she could not act a part so false. Indeed, Clytie paused to ponder very little, except her overwhelming desire to be clasped tight in Duke's arms.

How *did* one go about communicating such a wish? Miss Clough fluttered her eyelashes, placed her palms against Mr. Thorne's chest. "La, sir!" she said, and giggled, and then sighed. "Oh, this is absurd!"

Mr. Thorne had not the least notion what Miss Clough was talking about, or of precious little else but the pretty little hands which felt as though they burned holes through his brown cloth frockcoat, and his waistcoat, and his shirt. He moved his own hand to her waist, and with the other cradled her face.

What *was* the man doing? Had she not made herself clear? "I cannot go through with this!" explained Clytie. Whatever Mr. Thorne was doing, she decided she liked it very well. Definitely, they were a depraved pair. "No matter *what's* at stake!"

Marmaduke cared little in that moment for stakes or scruples, or any other such paltry considerations, including the affections of one-time ladyloves. Nor was he especially interested in this mysterious other matter which Miss Clough felt unable to execute. Whatever it was, he would deal with it for her.

"Never mind!" Duke said kindly, prior to sweeping her into a passionate embrace. "*I* can!" And so in fact he did, so excellently that Miss Clough was left stunned. No wonder Nikki liked kissing, she thought dazedly, when some moments later she was released. With Marmaduke's cooperation, any woman must.

Had Mr. Thorne been in better control of the situation, he might have chosen that moment for an explanation that not all who engaged in the gentle art of kissing reaped such illuminating benefits. However, so very enlightening had been that embrace—and Miss Clough's reaction thereto—that Marmaduke's thoughts were little better ordered. No longer could he doubt the nature of Clytie's feelings, or his own. Regretfully, he gazed upon the damsel who stared so solemnly at him, pink-cheeked, fingertips pressed to her bruised lips. And then he left her, with no explanation other than a groan.

Chapter Nineteen

Whilst Mr. Thorne repaired once more to drink himself under the table at White's, and Miss Clough once more retired abovestairs to ponder what she'd done wrong, Lady Regina Foliot experienced another meaningful encounter, this time with Lady Sweetbriar.

Regina found that lady in the drawing room of her hired house in Fitzroy Square, gazing in a ruminative manner upon a vase and cover with large shaped panels, painted with exotic birds among trees and bushes on a scale-blue ground. Nikki herself was no less worthy of contemplation, in a simple gown of India muslin dressed up by an eighteenth-century necklet of Italian workmanship, which was comprised of twelve links of scroll openwork in tinted gold, with birds and flowers in colored enamels, and earrings to match. On her right hand she additionally wore a marquise ring with clusters of diamonds arranged in an oval form.

The effect of this splendor upon a damsel who had just bid her wealthiest suitor hie to the nether regions in a handcart can easily be imagined. "Lady Sweetbriar!" ejaculated Regina. "You should be ashamed of yourself!"

As result of this stern pronouncement—Lady Regina had far outdistanced the servant who had intended to announce her—Lady Sweetbriar started violently. For one startled moment, she thought her visitor's intimations of culpability applied to the vase which in her surprise she had almost dropped. Then she realized that

Lady Regina had doubtless just witnessed the compromising situation so painstakingly arranged. Narrowly Nikki surveyed her rival for the Sweetbriar fortune. "I don't know," she said bluntly, "why I should be any more ashamed than *you!* At least I *admit* I need a fortune. And I *don't* go about trying to cheat other ladies out of what is rightfully theirs!"

"Oh, no?" Lady Regina dragged her eyes away from Nikki's necklet, at which she had been staring enviously. "*You* only tried to marry Rolf off to a chit he doesn't want, which in my opinion is *worse!*"

Carefully, Lady Sweetbriar set down her vase, lest in her disappointment she utilize it in the commission of some ill-considered act. This haughty miss might well become her stepdaughter-in-law, perish the thought. But perhaps all was not lost. "What," Nikki inquired cautiously, "are you talking about?"

"As if you didn't know! It will serve you nothing to play the innocent with *me,* Lady Sweetbriar. *I* know you for what you are!" Overcome by outrage, Regina committed the day's third rude act and deposited herself without invitation upon one of the satin-upholstered chairs. "Fine feathers make fine birds!"

Lady Sweetbriar wrinkled her nose at her uninvited guest. "I suppose you are hinting that I am feathering my nest," Nikki said. "I wish I knew how I might! That is all the thanks I get for trying to make things come out right. It has not been an easy task to keep Rolf's fortune safe from both you and Duke."

"Flim-flam!" Lady Regina might have sickened for a fever, so hectic was the color in her cheeks. "You wanted it yourself!"

Upon receipt of this sharp accusation, Lady Sweetbriar looked pained. "Why should I not have an interest in Rolf's money? It was almost mine—or part of it, anyway! Imagine yourself in my position. Imagine you had married a man for his money only to discover upon his death that you had been left the merest pittance. I'll lay a monkey that, in such a case, you'd act no differently than I!"

"You would lose your wager, Lady Sweetbriar." Self-awareness was not one of the emotions Regina had communicated with her looking glass. "Moreover, that has little to do with the fact that you *arranged* for Mr. Thorne and I to interrupt Rolf and Miss Clough in very compromising circumstances. Oh! How could you do such a thing?"

Not without difficulty, reflected Nikki, on a sigh. It seemed her efforts had been in vain. "I take it you were not misled?" she hinted.

Lady Regina was not tempted to admit that she had been horror-stricken to discover her favored suitor seemingly paying another young lady court. "Of course I was not. Rolf had already told me you had taken the foolish notion that he should make a match of it with Miss Clough—and that in spite of his preference for *me!* When we walked into the morning room and found Rolf on his knees, vowing he would never again be parted from Miss Clough—" She shuddered with barely suppressed rage. "Of course we knew it was all a hum!"

"He *did* go down on his knees? I thought he would stick at that!" At the vision thus conjured of Lord Sweetbriar playing the gallant courtier, a role for which he was suited neither by temperament or physique, Nikki grinned. "And *then* what happened?"

Lady Regina did not approve her hostess's sense of humor, which would doubtless derive considerable diversion from the confused scene enacted in the Clough morning room as result of her meddling. "Oh, we all agreed that you had grown extraordinarily high-handed!" Regina retorted crushingly. "And *I* decided that it was time someone pointed out to you that you are going on in a *very* bad way."

"For which," Lady Sweetbriar responded drily, "there is none better suited than yourself."

Had she just been insulted? Regina could not be sure. Just in case she *had* been, she would return tit for tat. "No one with a proper way of thinking would do what you have done—not that you can be blamed for *that!* Your upbringing did not acquaint you with the ways of *our* world. You cannot be expected to have the nicety of judgement that is part of the upbringing of a *respectable* female."

Looking pensive, Lady Sweetbriar arranged herself

in a distant chair. Her visitor's comments confirmed what Nikki had long suspected: respectable females with nicety of judgement weren't necessarily also pretty behaved. Rolf *wished* to marry this viper-tongued miss? He was sunk deeper in infatuation than Nikki had supposed. "Oh, yes!" she said, amiably. "My behavior has always merited the severest reproof. But you did not come here to merely tell me that, I think."

"No." Lady Regina knew she was behaving very badly, a circumstance which she unhesitantly lay at Nikki's door. "I will not stand on ceremony with you, Lady Sweetbriar."

"I am glad to hear it!" interrupted Nikki, whose good temper was growing strained. "Allow me to return the compliment! If you continue to grimace in that extraordinary manner, you will soon grow platter-faced. I would not wish Rolf to waken some morning to find himself leg-shackled to a female who is platter-faced. Odd as it may seem in me, I am fond of my stepson."

Lady Regina bridled: "And you think I am *not?*" She paused, somewhat startled to discover that in fact she was. "More to the point, *he* is fond me!"

"So you have said." Wondering how she might bring this unpleasant interview to a speedy termination, Lady Sweetbriar toyed with her diamond ring. "But if you *truly* care for Rolf, you shouldn't flirt with Duke! Yes, I know it is difficult *not* to flirt with Duke, does he will it—but casting out lures to one gentleman will *not* bring another up to snuff, no matter what tales you may hear to the contrary."

The only tales Lady Regina had heard recently, she reflected, concerned her hostess's predilection for kissing gentlemen in gaming hells and on the staircase of the British Museum. Upon further reflection, Lady Regina realized that during their pseudo-flirtation, Mr. Thorne had not offered her a single occasion for insult. Doubtless the story that Rolf had told her of his uncle's intentions was so much poppycock. Was this disappointment that she felt? "Your Mr. Thorne told Rolf he wished to set me up as his fancy-piece!" she complained.

"Not *my* Mr. Thorne!" reproved Lady Sweetbriar, as she raked her guest with a knowledgeable eye. One could only conclude Duke's tastes had radically changed. Then she recalled Duke's claim to have plans for Miss Clough. What might those plans consist of? Duke's dastardly intentions must be thwarted, naturally; but one could not fail to appreciate the ambition of the rogue. "I'd have Rolf, if I were you, Lady Regina—rather, *I* wouldn't, but *you* should! A wife must always take precedence over a light o' love."

Only with superhuman effort did Lady Regina prevent herself from committing another rude act and commenting that Lady Sweetbriar was admirably well qualified to explain the differences between wife and ladylove. Since to accomplish this miracle of self-restraint she had to bite her tongue, her next words were somewhat indistinct. "I *intend* to have Rolf!" Regina said grimly. "No matter what you may do to prevent it. I came here today to tell you that your attempts to estrange us have induced me to look more kindly upon his suit."

Nikki frowned. It was the opposite of what Nikki had intended, of course. She had failed to take into consideration the fact that Lady Regina was perverse. And she should have guessed at that quirk in the young lady's nature, thought Nikki, as she gazed gloomily at her guest. Fond as she was of her stepson, Nikki realized there had to be something queer in the makeup of any female who wished to marry Rolf.

"Do you take my meaning?" Fortunately Lady Regina was not privy to her hostess's conclusion that she had a screw loose. "I *do* mean to have Rolf. And I mean to have him on *my* terms, which means that he will not spend more time thinking about you than he does *me*, and worrying about your scrapes!"

"Does he worry?" Nikki looked sympathetic. "Silly chub! I must tell him he need not. Though I *do* tumble into scrapes, I always manage to climb out again."

Having numbed one foot by continuous tapping, Lady Regina applied the other to the floor. "You are to be felicitated!" she snapped. "It is quite wonderful that on a subject so enormously dreadful as your own misconduct, you should be able to be so *cool!* Oh, I know I should not say so, but *some*one must! It is very bad of you to be trying to manipulate everyone for your own gain. Do not deny that you have done so, Lady Sweetbriar! No one has been safe from your machinations—Rolf, myself, Mr. Thorne, Sir Avery, and Miss Clough!"

Was she such a slyboots? Nikki pondered her own recent actions, and winced. For most of her meddling, there was selfless reason—she had wished to save Rolf from Lady Regina, and Clytie from Marmaduke, and to preserve both the Clough and Sweetbriar fortunes. As for Sir Avery—Nikki's conscience twinged. "I *didn't* bamboozle him!" she cried.

Lady Regina narrowed her eyes at the woman who stood between her and the Sweetbriar fortune, which had gotten confused in Regina's mind with Lord Sweetbriar himself. The greatest of Nikki's sins, Regina had failed to mention—that of thwarting her ambition to drape herself about with jewels. Enviously her green glance lingered on the openwork necklet. "*Who* didn't you bamboozle?" she inquired skeptically. "Sir Avery? Well, you may tell yourself so, if you wish. It is not for *me* to point out that such a gentleman would hardly have betrothed himself to you *except* as result of severe bamboozlement. That is between you and your conscience, Lady Sweetbriar. I *will* point out, however, that it is not your place to criticize my conduct, when yours has been much *worse!*"

Feeling very melancholy, Nikki pleated the fabric of her gown. How many other woes, she wondered, would come to roost upon her weary head? Lady Regina was not to be swayed from her determination to marry Rolf. So be it. If Regina was destined to be her stepdaugher-in-law, Nikki must try to be civil to the chit.

"Very well," said Nikki. "I still think Rolf would be *happier* did he settle on Clytie—and happiness, no matter how insignificant it may seem in comparison to a fortune, is nothing to sniff at! But since he does not wish to marry Clytie, I will say no more on that score. Come, let us cry quits."

"Cry *quits?*" As if it were a poisonous snake, Regina flinched from her hostess's outstretched hand. "Never! You have totally failed to take my meaning, Lady Sweetbriar."

"Have I?" Since Lady Regina seemed to find it so distasteful, Nikki glanced also at her hand. She saw nothing there to account for her visitor's ungracious remark. Perplexed, Nikki returned her hand to her lap. "I think I must have misunderstood you, as you say. Perhaps if you were to speak plainly, I might be able to make some sense of all this!"

In response to this, Lady Regina drew herself erect. "I shall be delighted to speak plainly!" she snapped. "Indeed, I thought I *was* doing so. Since you have asked for it, you must not censure me for what I am going to say."

Lady Sweetbriar contemplated asking her uninvited guest to leave. Curiosity won out, however, over her growing desire to withdraw altogether from the world. Lady Regina looked excited and uncomfortable and queerly triumphant, very much like a hen about to lay an especially large egg. "Open your budget!" invited Nikki, good humor restored.

Had Lady Sweetbriar *giggled*? How *could* the creature be amused? wondered Lady Regina, whose mirror had failed to reveal her resemblance to a pretty broody hen. At any rate, Lady Sweetbriar would not long continue so merry. "The Foliots may no longer be wealthy, but our lineage is among the best in the land. You will understand my reluctance to ally myself with a family upon whose escutcheon there is a blot."

This was her caller's notion of enlightenment? The only revelations thus afforded Nikki had concerned Lady Regina's manners, which could have stood refurbishing—or perhaps shabby conduct was a privilege of venerable lineage. But until her point was made, Rogina obviously had no intention of taking her leave. So as to hasten that event, Nikki thought very hard. "Is it Rolf's, er, escutcheon you're talking about? I'll go bail there's no blot on it so bad as all that. Reuben was a devilish ugly customer, but no worse than your own papa, from what I hear."

Though Nikki made a pretty picture, her heart-shaped little face tilted inquiringly to one side, a fingertip to her lips, Lady Regina was not disarmed. "I am not referring to Sweetbriar's papa," she responded coolly.

"No?" Nikki chewed thoughtfully on her fingertip. "Then it must be Duke. But Duke has done nothing for which he may be so thoroughly censured." She recalled her various suspicions. "Yet!"

"Nor am I referring to Mr. Thorne," retorted Lady Regina, more coolly still. "I believe that leaves only one other possibility."

No wonder Rolf was determined to marry Lady Regina, and vice versa; she was as crackbrained as he. "If you think Rolf is a blot on his own escutcheon, then why—" The puzzlement cleared from Nikki's face. "Egad! You mean *me!*"

Finally the point had been taken. Lady Regina inclined her head. "I have nothing against you personally," she said. "If you were someone in whom was found nothing for which to blush, I would not fuss. But you must yourself admit that you are hardly a model of good breeding. I do not want a stepmama-in-law who will be forever making me wish to sink, and to that I shall hold fast!"

Though no lady could relish so uncharitable a reading of her character, Nikki was afraid that there was in it much with which to agree. The reflection did little to endear her denouncer to her. "So *I* am the impediment that stands in the way of your happiness," she murmured.

"Mine—and Rolf's." Pleased by Lady Sweetbriar's sensible attitude, Lady Regina rose, permitted herself a last covetous glance at Nikki's jewels. Soon that Italian openwork set would adorn her own ears and throat, she exulted. Her gaze moved to the diamond ring.

Around that item, Lady Sweetbriar's hand protectively closed. "How do you propose I remove myself from your pathway?" she inquired ironically. "Perhaps by putting a period to my life?"

Lady Regina pursed her lips. "I do not think it necessary to go to such lengths," she responded, at last. "It would be sufficient if you just removed from town. Sir Avery will be relieved when you break off your betrothal; you'll see! And you'll have the satisfaction of knowing that for once you did what was *right!* But I do not expect you to arrive at a decision straightaway. Sleep on it and you will see that I am right in saying we shall all go on much better without you." One last time, Regina glanced at Lady Sweetbriar, who had turned very pale. Nikki made no comment, merely stared unseeing at her blue vase. Regally Regina swept out of the drawing room, content to have had the last word.

Chapter Twenty

With the last words bestowed upon him by his beloved—a forcibly rendered desire that he might be banished to perdition—Lord Sweetbriar was far from content. Since Lady Regina had failed to inform Rolf of her determination to become his bride, that young man thought his romance was in dire straits. Rolf did not despair, however. He fancied he knew the way to reinstate himself in Lady Regina's affections. All that he need do was present her Nikki's jewels.

It was for that purpose that his lordship skulked about Fitzroy Square. For the first time he rejoiced that his stepmama's hired lodgings were so close to Jermyn Street, where he dwelt in state behind forged iron rails and a tall red brick façade. Lord Sweetbriar had entered with enthusiasm into this bold venture. Already he thought in terms of a successful get-away. But before one could triumphantly exit, one must first enter. "Eyes like stars!" he muttered. "A face beyond compare! Absolutely enraptured! Fudge! Her temper ain't so incomparable! There was no need for her to wish me to the devil just because I said she had windmills in her head! What do *you* think, Mr. Brown?"

Mr. Brown, that most starched-up of manservants, thought very frankly that it was his young master whose mental processes were impaired. Only in an attempt to save Lord Sweetbriar from dangling on the gallows had the valet joined in this mad venture. "I am not certain, sir," he said aloud, "if peers *are* hanged."

"Hanged?" echoed Lord Sweetbriar, then glanced guiltily around him and lowered his voice. "Dashed if I know why you must be so Friday-faced. *You* was the one who wanted to come along."

It was not Mr. Brown's place, superior servant that he was, to point out that *some*one had to try and make his young master see sense. Since his attempts to do so had failed, the valet could only insure the family suffered the least possible ill consequence. Too, Mr. Brown thought that Lord Sweetbriar should marry Lady Regina, to whom keeping an amiable mooncalf in line would be child's play. Or so Mr. Brown had thought until recently. Now he had begun to wonder if Rolf's beloved was any less crackbrained than he. "I fancy, sir, that this is the entrance we seek."

"Aha!" Curious, Lord Sweetbriar gazed at that portal, which lay at basement level; then he tiptoed ponderously down the steps. Having waited hidden in the shadows while Nikki departed her little house en route to Covent Garden, the conspirators were now ready to housebreak. From his pockets, Rolf removed a center bit and pocketknife, borrowed from a footman with connections that weren't particularly nice. The footman had advised against a crowbar as too noisy, had explained how to use the center bit to drill holes along the edge of the doorstyle, close to the head of the panel, how to run the pocketknife from hole to hole until— *voilà!* The panel was removed. Enthusiastically, Lord Sweetbriar had practiced this new art until he was confident he had the hang of it, to the dismay of his servants, and the detriment of his house. That Lord Sweetbriar did not practice his art now was due entirely to his valet, who stepped forward with a long-suffering expression, and the house agent's key.

For any other servant, the penalty for such presumption would have been severe. Rolf stood in awe of Mr. Brown, whom he had inherited from his father, and who had an uncanny ability to make him feel as though he were still in leading strings. He stood aside and allowed the valet to precede him. Mr. Brown pushed the door open. They entered the nether regions of Lady Sweetbriar's hired house. A front and back
170

kitchen occupied the basement, with a hallway running beside. Voices came suddenly to the intruders. Recalling Mr. Brown's ghoulish comments regarding the gallows, Lord Sweetbriar clutched at his valet.

Calmly Mr. Brown disengaged himself, and with a trace of disdain; no valet of the previous Lord Sweetbriar would have long survived a faint heart. The previous Lord Sweetbriar had possessed no nerves whatsoever, and a subsequent contempt for anyone who did. In point of fact there had been precious little Master Reuben had *not* held in contempt, reflected Mr. Brown.

But this was no moment in which to ponder the deceased Reuben's character, or the lack thereof; the servants were mere yards away. The subject of their animated conversation seemed to be the additional tasks one was expected to perform in this small household, and the erratic fashion in which one was paid. So Lady Sweetbriar was in the suds again? Lord Sweetbriar seemed fascinated by the conversation. Mr. Brown hoped no lull would come therein, so that the speakers might hear Rolf's chattering teeth. They could not stand forever in the hallway, no matter how fascinating the complaints of Lady Sweetbriar's servants, nor how cold Lord Sweetbriar's feet. Rolf seemed as firmly rooted as a sapling. Though it offended his nice sense of what was proper, Mr. Brown grasped and tugged his master's sleeve.

"W—" gasped Rolf, and only in time broke the word off. As he realized how close he'd come to inviting discovery, he blanched. But no one appeared to apprehend them. Lord Sweetbriar's exclamation had gone unnoticed, so strident had been the cook's complaints. Again the valet tugged on his lordship's sleeve. The intruders crept down the hallway, the laments of the cook—who had come from a larger establishment where such onerous tasks as lighting fires and scrubbing kitchen tables, sweeping and dusting the dining room and front hall and doorstep, had been performed by house and scullery and kitchen maids—masking their cautious footsteps.

Past the kitchens tiptoed Lord Sweetbriar and Mr. Brown. Up the uncarpeted back stairs proceeded his lordship and the valet, until they reached the floor whereon Nikki's bedroom lay. His lordship's familiarity with the location of the chamber, Mr. Brown was too well trained to remark. For his part, Lord Sweetbriar was too *distrait* to notice that he had earned the disfavor of his valet. Rolf's earlier enthusiasm for this venture had fled. He was feeling as jumpy as a cat on hot coals. Only when they were safe in his stepmama's chamber, with the draperies drawn and a candle lighted, did he draw a relieved breath. Then, before his valet's astonished gaze, he leapt onto the gabled tent-bed. A wild thrashing ensued. At length, his lordship emerged from the draperies, looking red-faced.

"It don't *do* to take Nikki for granted." Lord Sweetbriar's explanation was prompted by the disapproving expression of his valet. "I *know* we saw her leave, but that ain't nothing to go by; Nikki will do almost anything to throw a rub in my way. Look at the clankers she told Lady Regina—or if she didn't *tell* them, she at least *implied!* I *don't* have a partiality for Clytie! I never did! And then Uncle Duke took up throwing the hatchet at Regina—all these people flirting when they don't *want* to, and it is all Nikki's fault!"

During this diatribe Mr. Brown had straightened the bedcovers and cast a knowledgeable glance around Lady Sweetbriar's bedchamber, which he summed up as neat but uninspired. Her ladyship had come down in the world, he thought, as he inspected the contents of the veneered wardrobe. There was not a gown therein that he didn't remember, despite her ladyship's efforts to disguise that sorry fact. Almost, Mr. Brown pitied Nikki, who he had always found as kind as she was disreputable. Sympathy did not blind him to his duty, nonetheless. The previous Lord Sweetbriar's will had stated that Rolf should have the family jewels, and so he must, no matter how many laws were broken in the process.

Thought of broken laws recalled to Mr. Brown the penalties for such undertakings as that on which they were currently embarked. Politely he suggested that Lord Sweetbriar might care to join in the search.

"I like that!" Indignantly Rolf divested himself of his
172

stifling many-caped greatcoat, revealing padded shoulders and calves and a valiant if misguided attempt at a wasp waist. "As if I wasn't doing just *that!* And so you would have known if you'd been with me the last time, because Nikki herself was hiding in that bed." He jabbed a tentative finger at the draperies. "Well, she wasn't *hiding* precisely; she was asleep! Yes, and when she woke up, damned if she didn't have a gun! It was enough to scare a man out of a year's growth!"

That his young master could well do without a year's growth, or several, Mr. Brown did not remark. "Do I understand you, sir?" he inquired, rather faintly, from the tallboy where he stood, searching swiftly through the narrow drawers. "You have been here before?"

The draperies having proven unrevealing, Lord Sweetbriar moved next to his stepmama's dressing stand. "Don't go jawing on about it," he said rudely, and poked at a painted festoon of flowers. "I know I made a rare mull of it, but I'll wager even *you* would bungle the thing no less completely was Nikki to pop up right now out of her bed. It's confounded disconcerting, I can tell you!" He smirked. "Nikki won't like having the tables turned on her, I'll wager—but there won't be a thing she can do."

It was Lord Sweetbriar who was currently inclined toward doing nothing, his valet thought; and also that little benefit would be derived from poking at the dressing table in that queer way. Mr. Brown watched his master grasp the table firmly and give it a shake. Little happened except to the items arranged thereupon, which danced about and fell over in wild disarray. Apparently dissatisfied with the results of his labors, Lord Sweetbriar gave the table another shake. Further chaos resulted. At this point Mr. Brown intervened, with a polite query as to what the devil his master was about.

"What am I *about?*" scornfully echoed Rolf. "What the deuce does it *look* like I'm about? I'm looking for Nikki's jewels, and so should you be! The *reason* I am looking for Nikki's jewels is that Regina will not have me without them—and there ain't no use in pointing out that she's a greedy chit! I know she is." He tried to brush rice powder off his sleeve. "They *both* are! Hang it, I don't even know *who* is dangling after my fortune at this point, but I don't mean anyone to have it but who *I* choose!" A sulky expression settled on his features. "And it *won't* be Uncle Duke."

Mr. Brown moved to tidy up the dressing table. "I doubt that Master Marmaduke harbors such unworthy ambitions, sir," he protested. "As a boy, he—"

"Hah!" interrupted Lord Sweetbriar, with irate tone and flashing eye. "I don't care what Uncle Duke was like as a boy, because he obviously ain't that way *now!* You needn't be tut-tutting at me, either. You'd feel differently if *your* uncle was a villain! Don't quibble! Uncle Duke told me he was one himself." Rolf frowned. "Or maybe that was *another* rapper. Never have I run into such a bunch of tarradiddlers! But I mean to marry Regina even if she *is* running mad for Uncle Duke, because *if* she is, it ain't *her* fault. Why are you fussing about with that dressing stand? I already discovered it don't have a secret drawer."

So that was why his master had so mistreated the table? Mr. Brown was glad to have one small mystery cleared up. He put forth an opinion that Lady Sweetbriar might have hidden her jewels elsewhere than her own room.

"No, no!" Lord Sweetbriar said irritably. "That horse won't trot! Nikki would want to keep the baubles as close as possible to her, since she knows I want them back. Or that Regina wants them, which is the same thing." He sighed. "Dashed if I don't wish she *didn't*, just like I wish Papa hadn't made that cursed will. I *like* Nikki, though I'm cross as cats with her. Maybe she truly thought I wanted Regina and Clytie both. That's what comes from rubbing shoulders with Uncle Duke!"

Did they not speed up the present proceeding, they would be rubbing shoulders with representatives of the law, as result of being caught whilst committing the highly illegal act of housebreaking. Due to the circumstances, and Lord Sweetbriar's exalted position, it was doubtful they would be taken for a criminal offense and lodged in Newgate prison; but the consequences were apt to be highly unpleasant just the same. These unpalatable facts, Mr. Brown diffidently pointed out. "The deuce!" muttered Lord Sweetbriar in response, and held his candle high, the better to see the far corners of the room. What he glimpsed in one of those corners caused him to utter a little shriek and clutch at his valet.

Mr. Brown performed the intricate mental exercise which enabled him to maintain his perfect record of having never once lost his temper during a lifetime of dealing with Sweetbriars. Then he freed himself from his master, who was shaking like a blancmange. "You can open your eyes, Master Rolf," the valet said gently. "It's only the likeness of Master Reuben which used to hang in the salon."

Likeness? Could it be that his papa had *not*, as Rolf had long anticipated, risen from the grave? Cautiously his lordship opened one eye. Then he opened the other, relieved to discover that the cause of his terror was indeed no more than the portrait which had once hung in Sweetbriar House, and which Nikki had taken when she left. Why his stepmama had wanted the dreadful thing, Rolf had never been able to discover, as he now could not imagine why she had hung it in her bedroom. The mere thought of his papa, let alone a painted likeness, was enough to inspire Rolf with nightmares.

No sooner was one fear put to rest than another took its place. The intruders heard movement in the hallway. Simultaneously they snuffed out their candles. Mr. Brown stepped behind the draperies as Lord Sweetbriar dived under the bed.

Not without difficulty did his lordship achieve his objective. Not only did he bang his head against the bedframe, he scorched himself with hot candle wax. These minor inconveniences signified naught to Rolf. His thoughts were wholly occupied with his dire fate, were Nikki to come unexpectedly home. *Would* she shoot him this time, once she discovered him cowering beneath her bed? Rolf was very much afraid she might.

He heard the door open, footsteps enter the room, a flint being struck. Faint fingers of candlelight crept close. Rolf remembered that he'd flung his greatcoat carelessly onto Nikki's bed. He closed his eyes and awaited the pistol that would dispatch him to eternity.

No such report was forthcoming. Instead the intruder hummed a snatch of song. That was not Nikki's voice, decided Rolf, opening his eyes. Nor would Nikki, despite her checkered history, have hummed that particular song. Lord Sweetbriar himself would not have known it, had he not numbered among his acquaintance some very ripe young bucks with a taste for establishments of low repute. It was a servant, then, who had interrupted them. Rolf was not half so fearful of servants as of his stepmama. In truth, judging from the conversation overheard earlier, Nikki herself should have been fearful, hirelings with wages in arrears being prone to raise the devil of a dust. His stepmama was grown very dilatory about meeting her obligations, it seemed. Rolf recalled the tiny legacy his papa had left her. A distinctly bilious feeling overcame Lord Sweetbriar as result of his sudden suspicion that his stepmama had contrived to land herself in the River Tick.

Perhaps it was the stifling atmosphere beneath the bed, and his dislike of dark enclosed spaces, that made Rolf feel as if he might at any moment cast up his accounts. What was the blasted serving wench doing, other than singing off-key? Gingerly Lord Sweetbriar inched forward and peered out from the concealing bed hangings. The girl—Nikki's abigail, she must be— stood before the dressing table, holding a gold openwork necklet against her throat. Then she lowered her hand, and turned away. Rolf cowered back among the hangings. No wonder the wench had failed to notice the smell of hot wax, he thought, inhaling a strong aroma of garlic as she passed. Poor Nikki, who had once been accustomed to the best. From these somber reflections, Lord Sweetbriar was roused by a violent twitching of the window hangings. Through them, a pale hand emerged to point.

Had Mr. Brown taken leave of his senses? wondered Rolf. As he thusly mused, the window hangings grew more agitated still. It occurred to Lord Sweetbriar that it might be interesting to discover what had inspired

176

his superbly self-possessed valet to such excitement. Cautiously Rolf emerged from beneath the far side of the bed, and peered around a curtain-draped post.

The sight that there awaited Rolf did indeed almost cause him to cast up his accounts, from an excess of joy. The abigail had swung back his papa's portrait from the wall. Behind it lay a cavity. In her hands she held a familiar jewel chest.

Chapter Twenty-one

It was no excess of joy that caused Miss Clough discomfort; she had little heart for the task which must be done. Yet if Marmaduke Thorne was a villain, then Lady Sweetbriar was a villainess, and at all events Sir Avery must be warned. Too, Clytie felt strongly in need of paternal guidance and advice. Her father having already departed the house when she arose heavy-eyed from her restless slumbers, Clytie set out also for the British Museum.

In the entrance hall, she paused distressed. *How* Miss Clough was to gently inform her papa that he was betrothed to a villainess, she did not know. Slowly Clytie mounted the stair. Sir Avery was in the new gallery, erected a few years earlier at the northwest corner of Montagu House and joined to it by a short corridor.

Down that corridor trudged Miss Clough, growing more morose with each step. The new gallery consisted of thirteen rooms, in which antiquities were displayed. In light of her recent luck, Miss Clough was not especially surprised to find her papa in the last. He appeared to be deep in contemplation of the fabled Portland vase, thought to date from about 25 A.D.

Clytie paused on the threshold, uncertain how best to proceed. Someone bumped into her from behind. With a murmured apology, Clytie stepped aside. "Can I help you, miss?" inquired the assistant whose way she had blocked.

Clytie shook her head. "I wish to speak to Sir Avery."

The assistant, being new, was more zealous than most; and furthermore possessed an appreciation for a pretty face. He crossed the room to stand at Sir Avery's elbow, and informed him that a lady was desirous of engaging him in speech. Immediately Sir Avery treated the assistant to a short lecture on the Portland vase, an excellent example of cameo glass, which depicted the marriage of Peleus and Thetis in white relief on a blue background.

Miss Clough walked toward her papa. Without turning, Sir Avery added: "Hullo, my dear! Have you come to talk to me again about the house? You need not have! You may purchase as many pictures as you please, so long as you don't hang hunting scenes in the dining room. I have never found my appetite improved by vistas strewn with dead hares. No, and I am not partial to Turkey sofas either. As for the bedchamber—" He swung around, Miss Clough having hastily cleared her throat. "You again, Clytie? I had thought you were Nikki. Have you come to ask me to wish you happy? Although I believe the fellow *should* have applied to me before making you a declaration—but I shan't make a fuss."

Miss Clough was visited by an uninvited vision of Marmaduke Thorne's swarthy face. Wish her happy? Precious little chance of that! With a cautious glance at the avidly listening assistant, Clytie moved closer to her father. "I wish very much to speak with you, sir. Privately."

"Ah." Sir Avery also looked at the assistant, in such a pointed manner that the zealous young man abruptly quit the room. Then the fond parent contemplated his daughter, so injudicious as to fall in love with a gentleman who went about kissing other ladies on the nose. Not that Sir Avery had anything against this habit. A fair-minded individual, Sir Avery could understand that another man might feel about noses as he himself felt about antiquities.

His daughter obviously did not share that tolerant outlook; Clytie was looking positively hipped. Sir Avery drew her hand through his arm and gave it a little pat.

She sighed. "Oh, Papa, everything is *such* a muddle! I can't think what to do next."

Wistfully Sir Avery glanced once more at the Etruscan vases displayed to such good advantage in the lofty, spacious room. Then he focused his keen intelligence upon his daughter. Even cloistered as he generally was within the timeless walls of the museum, Sir Avery had become aware that the large majority of his intimate acquaintances were going on in a very queer way. And even had he *not* noted it before, reflected Sir Avery, he could hardly fail to do so today. Clytie was positively blue-deviled. Gently, Sir Avery touched his daughter's cheek, and invited her to tell him what had chanced.

Clytie's expression was rueful. "I don't know where to begin! I tried to convince Nikki that she should stop trying to throw Rolf and I at one another, as result of which she decided Rolf should practice making his declaration to Regina—or so Nikki *said*." Clytie went on to describe the resultant kick-up, concluding: "I vow I am no longer certain how *any*one feels!" Then she glanced shyly at her father. "Papa, how *does* one go about getting up a flirtation? You must know, because of Nikki! I *thought* I knew all about it myself, but I must not have gone about the thing properly, else he would not have groaned!"

His usually clear-sighted daughter had not benefited from acquaintance with the jingle-brained Lord Sweetbriar, Sir Avery mused, as he led her out of the Etruscan vase room. "May I inquire with whom you sought to flirt?" he diplomatically inquired. *"Not*, one trusts, Sweetbriar?"

Miss Clough looked appalled. "Good gracious, no! If you must know, Papa, it was Mr. Thorne."

In response to this intimation that his daughter had sought to dally with a profligate, Sir Avery appeared not the least disturbed. In point of fact, he *appeared* a great deal more interested in the Crackerode collection of gems and coins and medals through which they currently passed. "You *did* persuade the fellow to kiss you, I presume?"

Anew, Miss Clough ruminated upon the eccentricity of her parent; most fathers would react far differently to the intelligence that their offspring had been embracing profligates. Clytie smiled weakly at the notion of her papa confining her to her bedchamber, there to exist upon a Spartan regime of bread and water, and inviting Mr. Thorne to engage with him in pistols at dawn. "Yes, Papa, he kissed me." She sniffled. "And I suspect he didn't like it one little bit, because he left without a word!"

This disclosure distracted Sir Avery from his contemplation of the Towneley marbles. "Capital!" said he.

"'Capital'?" Miss Clough stared at her eccentric parent. "'Capital'! You must not have heard me properly; I said he *groaned!* And then he left me without a by-your-leave!" She lowered her gaze to her gloves. "I think I must be very wicked, Papa, because I don't care a fig if Mr. Thorne is every bit as bad as Nikki says he is, even though Nikki should *know.* Except that she has been bamboozling everyone of late—oh, I do not know *what* to think! But this is not what I meant to talk to you about. I tried to warn you before, but you would not listen. I am afraid that Nikki—well, one has reason to have *doubts!*"

For his daughter's reasoning, Sir Avery exhibited scant enthusiasm. Nonetheless, he sought to allay her concern. "*You* may think you have reason to question Nikki's motives, but *I* am not such a clunch! Shortly after it became apparent that she had set her cap at me, I had investigations made."

"Investigations?" Her papa had known all along that he was betrothed to a villainess? Clytie's brown eyes opened wide. "One tends to forget that you are a *downy* one, sir! But don't you *mind?*"

"Mind *what*, my dear?" In truth, Sir Avery was most disturbed by the rapid deterioration of his daughter's usual good sense. "I wish I knew what has turned you into such a pea-goose! If it is Thorne who has you in such a taking, you are being tediously missish! Kisses are not so important. Did you *like* his kisses, you must invite him to do so again, when next you meet."

"Invite him—" Accustomed as she was to her papa's broadminded attitudes toward childrearing, this permissive attitude caused Miss Clough to gape. Then her

181

attention was caught by a figure in the doorway. It was Rolf, wearing a *distrait* expression, and clutching in his arms an ornate little chest.

"Ah!" said Sir Avery, whose attention had likewise been caught. "The jingle-brain."

Lord Sweetbriar pushed his way through the other visitors to the Towneley gallery—a number of such visitors were strolling through the rooms, this being an appropriate day and hour—to reach Sir Avery and Miss Clough. "I have come upon a very painful errand!" he gasped. "Hallo, Clytie! This must be your papa. We have never been formally introduced, but I feel as if I know you, sir. Yes, and I feel that I should warn you *not* to take up with the petticoats, because there ain't no telling which way they'll jump! But I'm forgetting you've already taken up with Nikki."

Sardonically, Sir Avery contemplated the flushed and breathless young man. Lord Sweetbriar had something of the aspect of a chubby puppy who'd run too far and too fast. "But I know which way Nikki will, er, jump," he gently replied.

Lord Sweetbriar's flushed features were skeptical. "That's more than the rest of us! When I think that—"

What Lord Sweetbriar thought was destined to remain undisclosed, alas; a commotion broke out at the doorway. Through the knot of people gathered there burst Lady Regina, looking very irate. "*Here* you are!" she cried, having espied Rolf. "I have been following you this age. Indeed, I even began to wonder if you were wishful of avoiding me!" Then she espied Clytie. "That creature again! You said she was nothing out of the ordinary way!"

Rolf, who keenly felt the perils of his position, rolled an anguished eye from his beloved to Miss Clough. Of all the predicaments in which he had lately found himself, this was perhaps the worst. "I didn't come here to see Clytie!" he protested. "I didn't even know she *was* here! I wished to speak to her papa."

"Wished to speak to—" Lady Regina could think of only one reason why a young man would wish to speak to a young lady's papa, which is an excellent demonstration of how overheated had grown her brain. "Wretch! Brute! You have trifled with my affections— oh! I cannot trust myself to speak."

For this blessing, Lord Sweetbriar was very grateful; the vigor with which Regina had denounced him had caused several curious heads to turn their way. "I ain't trifled with anything!" he protested, in his own defense. "I wish you wouldn't rip up at a fellow that way. Especially after he's gone to so much trouble to do what you wanted—yes, and even thought he'd seen a ghost." Just remembering that moment gave his lordship gooseflesh. "That was *worse* even than when Nikki caught me in her bedroom, because *had* it been Papa, he would have done a great more than sit upon my lap!"

Responses to this revelation were much as might be imagined: "I do not think I can permit you haunting Nikki's bedchamber," remarked Sir Avery, with a meaningful glance at the ornate chest; and "Upon your *lap?*" echoed Miss Clough. Lady Regina's reaction was the most severe. "Sat upon your—*oh!*" She stamped her foot. "My papa is right. You *are* a cabbagehead!"

This insult from the lady whom he had tried so hard to please was for Lord Sweetbriar the last straw. "*I* ain't the cabbagehead!" he therefore retorted. "*You* are! I don't think I *want* to be married to a cabbagehead, or a female who's forever railing at me and calling me names and looking like she wants to box my ears. I don't care either if it ain't gentlemanly to cry off!" He looked confused. "Or doesn't a fellow *have* to cry off if he ain't officially betrothed?"

Sir Avery roused from his absorption in the scene; it was to him that Rolf's question was addressed. "That is an interesting point," he allowed. "I haven't the slightest notion. But though you have broken off with this young woman, Sweetbriar—not that I blame you for it! To be leg-shackled to a female who is forever loading you with reproaches would be far too great a bore—you must not start dangling after Clytie. I will not forbid your friendship, but neither will I have you as a son-in-law. That I am going to marry your stepmama is bad enough! You have the oddest ability to set well-ordered minds at naught."

Lord Sweetbriar found in this evaluation nothing with which to quibble, perhaps because he didn't wholly understand the drift of it. Rolf did understand, however, that Sir Avery would not permit Clytie to marry him. "*That's* all right!" he responded; "I never wished to be leg-shackled to her. Not that Clytie ain't a good sort of girl."

Lady Regina, who had been rendered almost bereft of all her senses by the intelligence that Lord Sweetbriar meant to hedge off altogether, now trusted herself to give voice. "We must not be hasty!" she said. "Considering the difficulties under which we have had to labor, it is not wonderful if we are a little out of sorts! If I have been precipitate, I am sorry for it, Sweetbriar—but you must remember that your stepmama has tried very hard to make one think your preference lies elsewhere."

Frowning, Lord Sweetbriar studied Lady Regina, whose expression was contrite. Rolf liked that expression considerably more than the others he had glimpsed upon those incomparable features of late. Though his comprehension might be limited, Rolf realized that a ready acceptance of Regina's apology would be a dangerous precedent to set. Though Lord Sweetbriar still wished very much to marry his beloved, and did not enjoy having turn-ups with her, neither did he relish fretting his guts to fiddlestrings. "Hasty? Balderdash!" he said.

At this set-down, Lady Regina gasped. She had thought a simple apology would be sufficient to bring about a reconciliation. Since it had not been, she must try all the harder. If only she and Rolf were private, it would be a simple matter to twist him around her little finger—but they were not private. Regina cast a resentful glance at Miss Clough and Sir Avery and the various other individuals who displayed much more interest in the scene being so vigorously enacted than in Charles Towneley's collection of classical sculptures. Though she normally enjoyed being the focus of attention, Regina knew she did not currently show to good advantage. What her mama and her sisters would say when this tale reached them, she shuddered to think.

It was marriage to Sweetbriar now, or no one; and his lordship's sulky aspect strongly indicated the latter course. The incomparable Lady Regina Foliot was very likely to become an ape-leader. The prospect turned her perfectly ill.

The morbid tenor of her thoughts was reflected on Regina's face as she plucked at Lord Sweetbriar's sleeve. "I have been very foolish, I know, and I do not blame you for being very much disgusted with me, but I cannot bear that we should be on bad terms. Tell me what I must do to atone." When Rolf made no response, she leaned forward to peer up into his face, and consequently noticed what he clutched so tightly in his arms. It was a jewel chest. There was only one lady to whose jewel chest Lord Sweetbriar might lay claim.

All was not yet lost then, thought Regina, her green eyes alight. Why Lord Sweetbriar might be carrying his stepmama's jewel chest all about London, especially to the British Museum, it did not occur to Regina to ask. She snatched the case away from him and flung it open. Glittering up at her were Nikki's jewels. The diadem, necklace, and earrings of emeralds set in diamonds and hung with immense pear pearls; the set of Italian gold openwork; a silver necklace set with emeralds and rubies, foiled crystal, and topazes; the marquis diamond ring—

But something about the glitter of the lovely gems was not quite as it should be. Yes, and why was Rolf trying so hard to wrestle the jewel chest away? It was hardly a gentlemanly thing to do. Puzzled, Lady Regina took a closer look at the marquis ring. Within its facets lay revelation. "Paste!" she cried, and swooned.

Chapter Twenty-two

During those same moments when Lady Regina stalked Lord Sweetbriar through the streets of London, prior to the fit of vapours which overtook her in the British Museum, Mr. Thorne obeyed a summons to Fitzroy Square. Marmaduke had pondered long and hard upon his dilemma, or at least had tried to do so; he must not be judged too harshly if his thoughts invariably strayed to those ecstatic moments when he had clasped Clytie in his arms. Was Mr. Thorne granted his dearest wish, he would spend a large portion of his remaining lifetime in that activity. Unfortunately, Mr. Thorne's wish was not likely to be granted. Despite the various unflattering evaluations of his character currently existant, Marmaduke was a man of honor. In his past lay only one incident when he had not behaved as well as he might have done. As is the way with such incidents, it now rose to haunt him. Nikki was asserting her prior claim. Due to the drear nature of his reflections, Mr. Thorne's expression, as he applied himself to the door of Lady Sweetbriar's hired house, was grim.

Nikki herself flung open the door. "You came!" she cried. "I am very grateful to you for it, but we cannot stand here jawing on the doorstep." She took firm grasp of his sleeve and pulled. "Come in!" Having insured that her caller must do so, she then slammed and bolted the door.

Although Mr. Thorne no longer felt toward Lady

Sweetbriar as he had in years past, he still retained a fondness. She was on pins and needles, he thought, and wondered why. "Have your servants left you, Nikki? You should have let me know. I would have helped you contrive to be beforehand with the world."

Nikki's glance was tearful: "Dearest, *dearest* Duke! The best of *all* my flirts! It has gone beyond the point when *any*one can help me, I fear! There's no wrapping *this* in clean linen—and it is no more than I deserve. I *have* been enacting the slyboots! My conduct *has* been monstrous! And I do not wish to be the stumbling block in anybody's path, even Rolf's!"

Mr. Thorne struggled very hard to make sense of these disclosures, uttered in mournful tones as her ladyship preceded him up the stair. Not only in her stepson's pathway was Nikki a stumbling block, he reflected. Resolutely Duke prevented his thoughts straying to Miss Clough, a topic which inspired him to romantical excesses, but with little beneficial result. "If you won't let me haul you out from under the hatches, why did you not apply to Sir Avery?" he inquired.

Over her shoulder, Lady Sweetbriar showed him a woeful countenance. "As if I *could!* I may be on the dangle for a fortune, Duke, but that is your brother's fault. I am *not* an adventuress! Had I gone all to pieces *after* we were married, I would have applied to Avery for assistance, but I cannot in good conscience do so *before*. It would be to take shocking advantage of Avery's good nature."

"And a direct violation of your philosophy of value received." By the reminder of Nikki's betrothal to another man, Mr. Thorne's apprehensions were slightly eased. "But you have already given *me* good value, even if it was many years in the past! Therefore, in good conscience you may let me render your assistance."

"*Definitely* the best of all my flirts!" Sighing, looking rueful, Lady Sweetbriar continued up the stairs. "It's too late for that. I have been very foolish, and now I must abide the consequence."

Since it was very difficult to carry on a disagreement with a lady three paces ahead of him, Mr. Thorne temporarily refrained. Silently he trailed after her, marshaling his arguments. So preoccupied was he with those arguments that he paid scant heed to their progress up the broad stair with its massive balustrade in the old style, corniced and thick, and along the dark paneled hallway. Only when Lady Sweetbriar passed through a doorway did Mr. Thorne come to his senses, every one of which insisted that he refrain from entering her *boudoir*. This reluctance was a novel sensation for the dashing Mr. Thorne, whose acquaintance with feminine *boudoirs* was not slight. With the manner in which to casually enter such a chamber, without breaking the prevailing mood or causing last-minute doubts, Marmaduke was very familiar. About how to tactfully *refrain* from entering, however, he was much less certain. Attempting to look nonchalant, he lounged in the doorway.

The bedroom was in chaos, with articles of feminine apparel strewn everywhere—gloves and shawls and stockings, headgear, chemises and petticoats. The doors of the wardrobe gaped open; intimate articles of clothing spilled out of the narrow tallboy drawers. Mr. Thorne hastily averted his gaze from a pair of very daring opera drawers fashioned from elastic India cotton.

Gowns were flung carelessly upon the gabled tent bed. Bandboxes were piled haphazardly upon the dressing stand. In the midst of this confusion stood Nikki, gazing somberly upon an opened portmanteau.

That somber glance she transferred to Mr. Thorne, once she realized he had followed her no farther than the doorway. "What *are* you doing in the hallway, Duke?" she inquired, puzzled. "I wish very much to speak with you, and I am in a very great hurry, so I wish you would not dawdle there!"

"I am not dawdling but, ah, preserving your reputation, Nikki!" Mr. Thorne was very pleased to have thought of this excuse. "You will recall that you are betrothed."

That recollection did little to lighten Lady Sweetbriar's expression, the solemnity of which caused Mr. Thorne's premonitions to recur in full force. Nor did Lady Sweetbriar's next words ease his apprehensions.

"I *was* betrothed!" she sighed. "I doubt Avery will want to marry me once he discovers I have—And I had just settled on a claret-ground set of seven vases painted with mythological subjects in the manner of Hondecaeter—But there's no use crying over spilt milk! At least I furbished up Avery's house for him. He may thank me for that, if for nothing else. It was *so* exciting, Duke, the way we met."

"*What* was exciting?" inquired Mr. Thorne, from the doorway where he was still lodged. "The match between Cribb and Molyneaux?"

"No!" Lady Sweetbriar giggled. Then she recalled her woes. "Now it's bellows to mend with *me!* You are being tediously provoking! Do you mean to stay forever in my hallway, Duke? This concern for my reputation seems somewhat excessive. After all, we are alone in the house, and you have been in my bedchamber *before!* Even if it was a very long time ago!" She picked up and shook out a petticoat before cramming it absent-mindedly into her portmanteau. "I wish you would not be so stodgy! I have a great many things I wish to do in very little time, and it makes a person very cross to have to shout!"

It was the things Lady Sweetbriar wished to do that had caused Mr. Thorne's reluctance to cross her threshold, especially those things that concerned himself. But how could a gentleman inform a lady of whom he was fond that he wasn't so fond of her as all *that?* Duke hesitated. Nikki plucked out the petticoat which she had just packed into her portmanteau, and frowned. Perhaps actions might prove more eloquent than words, decided Marmaduke. He strode purposefully into the room, and swept Lady Sweetbriar up into his arms. With practiced skill, he kissed her. Then he briskly set her aside.

"Well?" inquired Marmaduke, his expression saturnine, his arms folded across his chest.

"*Well?*" echoed Lady Sweetbriar, looking astounded. "Egad! Have you taken leave of your senses, Duke? I tell you disaster has struck, and you take it as leave to kiss me? Or perhaps you thought you would cheer me up?"

If so, his efforts had not been successful, reflected Marmaduke as Lady Sweetbriar applied her petticoat to her damp eyes and reddened nose. "I begin to think I detect my nephew's hand in this," he murmured, ignobly cheered by his old friend's woe. Marmaduke did not enjoy seeing Nikki made unhappy, of course; but he rejoiced at her lukewarm response to his embrace.

Irritably, Lady Sweetbriar flung aside her petticoat; her patience was running thin. "What the devil has Rolf to do with you kissing me?" she snapped.

"Everything." Apace with her ladyship's ill-temper, Mr. Thorne's spirits rose. "He intimated that you had a *tendre*."

"A *tendre?*" Nikki emptied a drawer of a tallboy onto her bed. "Naturally I have a *tendre*. Rolf is a—"

"I know what Rolf is." Mr. Thorne watched Nikki rummage through the purses and reticules of straw and beads, steel and fabric, which she'd strewn across her bed. "He has stolen a leaf from your book, I think—because I do *not* think that you have a *tendre* for *me!*"

"For *you!*" Lady Sweetbriar's dark eyes opened wide in astonishment. "Poppycock! That is, I am very *fond* of you, Duke, and when you first came home I wondered—but I soon saw my mistake." She shook her head. "Rolf told you I still hankered after you? *Why*, I wonder? Either he is more of a gudgeon than I realized, or he is playing some deep game."

So very comfortable was Mr. Thorne rendered by these disclosures that he cleared a space for himself amid the various articles of feminine apparel tossed on Nikki's bed. "I suspect Rolf sought to divert me from Lady Regina," he said.

"And so he might!" Lady Sweetbriar paused in the act of folding a poppy-red scarf. "*You* have been behaving almost as badly as I. Throwing the hatchet at *both* Lady Regina and Clytie—why is it I never realized just *what* a rogue you are? Not that it will serve you, Duke! How very comfortable you look. Instead of taking your ease, you might make a push to help me pack." With a quizzical expression, Mr. Thorne picked up and folded her much-abused petticoat. "Zounds! This is almost like old times!" sighed Nikki.

For several reasons, Mr. Thorne did not especially care to enter upon a discussion of time past. "*Why* are you packing, Nikki?"

As diversion, this gambit was remarkably successful; Lady Sweetbriar flung out a dramatic arm. "The game," she cried, "is up!"

For an awful, appalled moment, Mr. Thorne thought he had been caught out lolling on Lady Sweetbriar's bed, clutching her petticoat, a situation far more compromising than that she had contrived for his nephew. Cautiously he poked his head out from among the bed hangings, glanced in the direction of her pointing finger—and swore.

Though Mr. Thorne was no happier to view his brother's likeness than had been his nephew, Marmaduke was quicker to realize that it was a portrait that he saw. Unappreciatively he gazed upon Lady Sweetbriar. "Confound it, Nikki! A sight like that could make a fellow cast up his accounts."

This viewpoint had not occurred to Lady Sweetbriar, long accustomed—both in the flesh and on canvas—to the unlovable aspect of her late spouse. "I hope it *did* get the wind up Rolf!" she muttered, as she crossed to the portrait and swung it to one side, revealing the cavity behind. "Because the wretch broke into my house *again*, and this time he *did* make off with my jewels. Now I am truly in the basket—which is why I wished to see you, Duke! Yes, and it was very good of you to come so quickly!"

As he extricated himself from the feminine fripperies strewn across Lady Sweetbriar's bed, Mr. Thorne mourned the sense of well-being which had been so short-lived. "I do not understand you, Nikki. Only moments past you said you would not let me help you, even though your pockets are to let. Now you hint that I might. I would be very glad to do so, if only you would make up your mind."

Whatever Lady Sweetbriar had expected from her old friend Marmaduke, it was not this selfish, bullying attitude. Had he changed so much during the years they had been separated—or had she? Anyone *must* change, after several years of marriage to a nipfarthing

191

cheese parer, she supposed. But Duke had not endured such a marriage, and he was no less altered than she.

"I hinted no such thing!" Nikki said crossly, as a glimpse in her dressing-stand mirror told her she looked as hagged as she felt. Would the poppy-red scarf which she still held cheer up her spirits as well as her white dress? It did not. "It was not to tell you that I haven't a feather to fly with that I summoned you, Duke, but to warn you that you must not let Regina beat you at the post. If she has not already done so! Yes, and to tell you also that you must content yourself with Rolf's money, can you but gain access to it, for which I do not hold you out a great deal of hope! Just days ago, I'd have laid a monkey that *I*'d never be outjockeyed by the chit."

So very much had Mr. Thorne altered, that the conversation of his onetime ladylove was in a fair way to giving him a headache. "But I don't *want* Rolf's money," he protested, plaintively. "I wish I knew what you are talking about!"

Lady Sweetbriar had gone back to packing, in her highly individualistic manner, which consisted of placing an item in the portmanteau only to remove it seconds later and toss it aside. "Do not try and bamboozle *me*, Duke!" she scolded. "*I* am the greatest bamboozler of all. I have known all along that there was something havey-cavey about your return to England. You didn't deceive *me* with those tarradiddles about Bonaparte invading Russia."

Wearing a very satiric expression, Marmaduke strolled across the bedchamber, halting before his brother's painted likeness. Unfondly, Duke gazed upon the portrait. Then he swung it aside. "You have not been paying attention to the newssheets, Nikki. Napoleon has departed St. Cloud for Moscow."

Lady Sweetbriar's delicate jaw dropped open. "Egad! You were telling the truth, after all." But the Corsican's designs on Russia held little interest for her at that point. "I am very sorry if I misjudged you, Duke, but what else was I to think? Your conduct *was* bizarre. Moreover, Rolf distinctly told me you were after Reuben's blunt. The young cawker! Lady Regina is welcome to him! Never did I think a stepson of mine could turn out to be so *low!*"

"Do not take on so, Nikki!" Mr. Thorne inspected the cavity which had until recently hidden the coveted Sweetbriar jewels. "So what if Rolf stole back the baubles? Clough will give you more."

To this optimistic declaration, Lady Sweetbriar responded with a renewed frenzy of packing, at the end of which plumes and ribbons and turbans were added to the existing chaos. "The deuce he will!" she wailed. "It makes me very sad to think Avery will not wish to marry me once he finds out what I have done, because I never wished to marry *any*one so much—no, not even *you!* But as is the way of things with me, I found it out too late! Confound it, Duke, don't just *stand* there! Come and help me pack."

Mr. Thorne allowed neckpieces and gloves and stockings to be piled into his arms. "Clough won't wish to marry you once he discovers Rolf has reclaimed the jewels? Nikki, that doesn't make sense. I can't imagine Reuben added extensively to the collection, and it was not worth all *that* much. Certainly it was not worth so much as must signify a button to Clough."

Upon this reminder of her *fiancé*'s enviable financial situation Lady Sweetbriar sighed and added a tippet of pale fur to the stack of her belongings which Mr. Thorne held. It slipped to the floor. She picked it up and draped it round his neck. "I know *exactly* what the things were worth!" she muttered, "and it is not that which will make Avery wish to wash his hands of me, but what they *aren't!* If only I could think what to take with me, but it is unlikely I will ever have anything so fine again, and I hate to leave anything behind."

"What they *aren't?*" Between his headache and his premonitions, Mr. Thorne was not at his best. "Nikki—"

"Don't *you* scold me, Duke! I do not think I can bear hearing another harsh word." Perhaps if she were to begin packing again, in a more orderly fashion, the business might more rapidly proceed. Lady Sweetbriar grasped the portmanteau and upended it on the bed. "Lady Regina has already said enough sharp words to last me for a *life*time, and it was very *hard* of her. Moreover, she was *right!* I have behaved abominably. Only the most *unconscionable* of females would stand in the way of Rolf's happiness, and bamboozle poor Avery as I have." She struck a selfless posture. "Although I do not mean to oblige that stiff-rumped female by turning up my toes, I quite see it will be best for everyone if I leave town."

"How do you propose to do that?" inquired Mr. Thorne, with distinct acidity. "You have just got through telling me, at some length, that your pockets are to let."

"I did not say that, precisely." Nikki scrabbled through the chaos on her bed, and at length triumphantly held up a heavy purse. "I have managed to set aside a little nest-egg. Do not tell me that in all conscience I should turn it over to Rolf; I know I should! But he doesn't *need* it, and I do. Beside," and she looked very sorrowful, "I have already done so many odious things that one more will scarce signify. My only hope is that *some*day everyone will grant me forgiveness."

Mr. Thorne had not been so long parted from her ladyship as to forget her talent for melodrama. "Cut line, Nikki!"

"Well, it *will* be best!" With a half-hearted smile, Lady Sweetbriar dropped the purse back onto the bed. "Especially for *me*. I don't want to be anywhere in the vicinity when Lady Regina discovers the jewels are paste. But that is not why I called you here, Duke, and I do not have time to stand here prosing on." She grimaced. "You will not like it, I think."

Mr. Thorne thought likewise. Additionally he thought that, were she allowed to go racketing about the countryside, Nikki would likely tumble into scrapes that were even worse. Casually, he glanced at her little purse. Could he possibly palm it without attracting her attention? Perhaps under the pretense of depositing upon the bed some of the diverse articles draped haphazardly about his person? "Do you want me to help you take French leave? I won't! The people you have been diddling deserve better from you than that, Nikki."

"So they may," agreed Lady Sweetbriar, whose attention was primarily on her packing, "but *I* deserve better than to end my days in Newgate, which is doubtless what Lady Regina will demand! Tell me truly, Duke; *do* you need a fortune? *Is* that why you threw the hatchet at Miss Clough?"

"No." It was the only word Mr. Thorne trusted himself to speak.

Lady Sweetbriar bit her lower lip. "I was afraid you would say that. You are not going to like this, but I persuaded Clytie you are a villain, Duke. I meant it for the best!" Before she could explain her reasoning, Mr. Thorne uttered a harsh oath, flung the remainder of his burden on the bed, and strode out of the room. The effect of his wrathful exit was in no way diminished by the fur tippet which he still wore around his neck.

Mournfully, Lady Sweetbriar gazed after Mr. Thorne, feeling as though she had been abandoned by her oldest friend. Then she recalled her predicament, and that Bow Street might come any moment calling, and scurried down the broad staircase, and bolted the front door.

Chapter Twenty-three

In the Towneley gallery of the British Museum, meantime, Lady Regina had been revived via the vinaigrette which Miss Clough had brought along in case her own spirits took an abrupt turn for the worse. Having been revived, Lady Regina was indulging in a tantrum. "How *could* you have been so negligent?" she inquired acerbically of Lord Sweetbriar. "How could you have let your stepmama *do* such a thing?"

"Dash it, I didn't *let* her!" As he tried to focus on the marquis ring which Lady Regina waved under his nose, Lord Sweetbriar's eyes slightly crossed. "Although I *might* have, had I known how things stood with her. A fellow don't relish his stepmama being dipped, no matter how much of a nuisance she's been." He darted a quick glance at Sir Avery who, having grown bored with the proceedings, had begun to compose a catalogue of the new gallery's contents. "No offense, sir!"

Sir Avery didn't look up from the Cottonian coins and medals. "Umm?" said he.

"Never mind, Papa," murmured Miss Clough. Denied a handy collection to catalogue, Miss Clough was occupying herself in wondering whether or not Marmaduke Thorne was a villain, and if she wanted to kiss him again in any event. "I do not think a response is required."

So it was not; the hostilities between Lord Sweetbriar and Lady Regina had not halted for comment. In point of fact, Lady Regina had during that brief interval once more made adverse comment regarding his lordship's mental abilities, as result of which his lordship was grown increasingly irate. "And you call yourself a pretty-behaved female!" scoffed Rolf, brandishing the jewel chest. "It would serve you right if I *did* leave you upon the shelf!"

It occurred to Lady Regina that a young woman did not enhance her standing with a gentleman by indulging in such audible fits of temper as were impossible to keep from reaching strange ears; and she clamped her teeth shut. Since her tongue was in an infelicitious position, she then winced. Realization that her bitter and ill-advised comments had been heard by other visitors to the Towneley gallery caused her further anguish. As ill luck would have it, there were an inordinate number of such visitors today. It took little imagination to realize the probable consequences of her injudicious temper tantrum. Did this story get around, she would be mortified. As result of these reflections, Lady Regina succumbed to chagrin.

"Rolf!" Lest he take it in his head to leave, she clutched his arm. "I have been a trifle too quick to speak. Try and enter into my feelings. You would not like it were the, er, object of your affections to seem to prefer another, I think!" Belatedly, she recalled that the object of Lord Sweetbriar's affections had seemed to do just that. "I mean—"

"Moonshine!" retorted his lordship, rudely. "I ain't so great a cabbagehead that I don't know what you mean, no matter what your father thinks—which ain't half as little as *I* think of him! You mean that it was all right for you to throw out lures to Uncle Duke, but it *ain't* all right for me to have a fondness for my own stepmama." He looked indignant. "And you called *me* a jingle-brain!"

Lady Regina closed her eyes and counted slowly to a thousand. "*I* did not call you a jingle-brain," she said, at length. "I never even *thought* such a thing. Oh, this is all your stepmama's doing! If only she had not—"

"Twaddle!" interjected Lord Sweetbriar, more rudely still. "It ain't Nikki's fault you was so determined to have her accursed baubles. Well, you wanted them;

now you may have them! Much good they will do you."
He thrust the chest at Regina, so roughly that she
gasped. Then he turned on his heel.

That his lordship did not make a precipitate departure, so wroth was he with his beloved, was due to some
excessively quick thinking on that young lady's part.
Inspired to fast action by the realization of impending
spinsterhood, Lady Regina tucked the jewel chest under
one arm, took firm grasp of Lord Sweetbriar, and dug
in her feet. Lest Rolf drag the lady whom he had wished
to marry across the floor, he was forced to halt. "What
is it you want *now?*" he inquired irritably. "Ain't
Nikki's jewels enough?"

Lady Regina's own temper was not unfrayed, despite
her attempts to be contrite. "But I do not *have* Nikki's
jewels," she pointed out. "I have paste *imitations* of
Nikki's jewels, which is not at all the same thing. You
are wonderfully calm about this business, Sweetbriar!
Your stepmama sold jewels that were not hers *to* sell.
That is a criminal offense, surely." Regina's tone was
wistful. "One for which a person could be confined to
a prison such as Newgate!"

This callous arrangement of his *fiancée's* future
roused Sir Avery from his absorption in the Cottonian
coins. "I do not think Nikki would care for Newgate,"
he remarked judiciously. "And I also do not think I can
allow any of you to do something for which Nikki would
not care."

Lady Regina stared at Sir Avery. Perhaps *here* was
someone who was not immune to reason, she thought.
"Consider, sir!" she pleaded. "Lady Sweetbriar has sold
jewels that were not hers *to* sell, and has substituted
copies made of paste. No one with a proper way of thinking can approve such grave misconduct!"

Sir Avery's expression made it very clear that the
current subject of his disapproval was Lady Regina
herself. "Pea-goose!" he remarked, and returned to his
work.

Pea-goose? Lady Regina felt this rudeness so very
keenly that she did not trust herself immediately to
speak. As she sought to regain her self-control, Lord
Sweetbriar twitched himself out of her grasp. "I don't

think there's anything left to say!" he said. "You have what you wanted. I will bid you good day."

"No!" Regina placed herself smack in his pathway. "I don't! That is, what I wanted was for you to show me that you favored *me*."

"And so I did! I gave you Nikki's baubles! Dashed if I know what else it is you want." Lord Sweetbriar stuck out his lower lip. "Now I think on it, dashed if I know why you made such a kick-up in the first place! Anybody could have seen all along that I favored you. Hang it, I wasn't trying to marry Nikki!"

"I never said you were!" Regina tittered. *How*, she wondered, had things gotten so out of hand? Sweetbriar had been dangling at her slipper strings for months, yet now he showed every indication of *not* coming up to snuff. There was a valuable lesson to be learned from all this, supposed Regina. She had sought to revenge herself upon both Mr. Thorne and Lady Sweetbriar— and had wound up in the suds herself instead. It was enough to make a damsel consider changing her ways. "All I ever wanted," Regina said sadly, "was a mama-in-law who wouldn't put me to the blush."

"Devil take it!" Having at last gained the upper hand, Lord Sweetbriar was not about to give it up. It was long past time that his beloved was delivered up a few home truths. "It ain't Nikki who's put anyone to the blush, it's *you*. I'll wager that in all her life Nikki never made a public rowdy-do. People will be talking about your family soon enough, but not because of Nikki. All *she* did was kiss a couple fellows, neither of which counted, because she is betrothed to Sir Avery, and as for Uncle Duke—" Guiltily Rolf glanced at Sir Avery, who in response quirked an ironic brow. "Well! And since I am her stepson, it don't signify if she *did* sit on my lap."

Lady Regina's horror at being thus addressed was not abated by her suspicion that his lordship's complaints were not without basis in truth. "It may not signify for *you!*" she said bitterly. "You may not expect so blasé an attitude from your wife."

"Wife?" Lord Sweetbriar looked confused. "I don't *have* a wife! Oh, you mean when I *do!* When I have a wife, Nikki won't need to sit upon my lap, because someone else will be!"

After due reflection, Lady Regina decided that Lord Sweetbriar's somewhat incoherent speech had indicated a strong desire to cuddle his own wife. So overset were Lady Regina's spirits that she herself would have greatly benefited from some cuddling at that point. However, Lord Sweetbriar had given no indication of wishing to cuddle *her*. To make matters even worse—which hardly seemed possible—his comments about laps and wives had attracted notice. "Pray moderate your manner!" Regina murmured, eyes modestly downcast.

"Why should I?" Lord Sweetbriar was feeling pugnacious. "You didn't moderate *yours*. Scolding me for dangling after Clytie, when all the time you was dangling after Uncle Duke. I don't blame you for it! Uncle Duke's a nonpareil." He frowned. "Now I remember! It was *you* who said he coveted my papa's fortune, and I don't know why you should've, because he *don't!*"

This comment penetrated Miss Clough's self-absorption. "He don't—doesn't, that is? Are you certain, Rolf? Nikki distinctly told me Mr. Thorne is a villain."

"Did she?" Lord Sweetbriar's stern brow lightened when he looked at Miss Clough, Lady Regina was not pleased to note. "Nikki has been telling a prodigious lot of rappers lately." He glanced back at Regina, his expression again severe—remarkably so for a young gentleman who'd been telling a fair number of rappers of his own. "Eyes like stars, just fancy! Face beyond compare! Moonshine!"

"But, Rolf!" Surely was she patient, Sweetbriar would come around. "Your stepmama tried to throw a rub in our way."

"Can you blame her for it? You was determined to have her baubles, and she wasn't wishful that you should discover they was only paste. Hang it, I'd have done the same thing in her place." Rolf eyed his beloved. "And so, I'll warrant, would you!"

Lady Regina did not care to discuss the point, on which she suspected they would reach no agreement. Regina could not imagine herself ever engaged in so underhanded an enterprise. Marrying a gentleman for his fortune was a straightforward business, not at all like replacing family heirlooms with paste imitations, as must be obvious to anyone who had a sense of what was nice. But if she was going to marry any gentleman at all, Regina would have to make a push. And push is precisely what she did, if in a ladylike manner, as result of which Lord Sweetbriar found himself rubbing shoulders with various Egyptian antiquities. Hastily he stepped away from an especially repulsive mummy. "Your stepmama," persevered Lady Regina, "tried to trap you into a compromising situation with Miss Clough."

So she had. In retrospect, Nikki's cunning amused as it appalled. What was that drivel she had had him spouting? "I am mad for you! Absolutely enraptured!" he recalled. "I have an income of—Dashed if I can remember the rest of it! Clytie would know."

"I daresay you can remember." A diabolical plan had presented itself to Lady Regina, one in which there was no place for Miss Clough. "Do you but *try*."

Rolf was not reluctant; he screwed up his brow. "I have a great regard for you. There is no other woman with whom I could ever think of settling in matrimony." He paused. "Sounds dashed silly, don't it? It ain't quite so bad when a fellow's down on his knee."

Egyptian antiquities not being of consuming interest to the individuals who this day visited the Towneley gallery, Lady Regina and Lord Sweetbriar were temporarily without an audience. Lady Regina therefore grew so bold—and desperate—as to give his lordship another shove. "Show me!" she said.

"Show?" Lord Sweetbriar also ascertained that they were alone. Then he awkwardly dropped down onto one knee. "What came next? I have it! Darling Clytie—er, Regina! Say that you will be my bride."

Lady Regina pursed her lips. Was this any moment to quibble over a proposal addressed to Miss Clough? She looked down into Lord Sweetbriar's face. Something in his expression told her it was not. "Yes!" she said.

"Yes?" Stiffly, Lord Sweetbriar clambered erect. "Yes, *what?*"

"Yes, I will become your bride." Oddly, Regina felt no triumph at the success of her sly scheme. "I want to marry you. That is—if you still want to marry *me.*"

Though Lord Sweetbriar's mental facilities may have been focus of various unkind comments, he was wise enough to refrain from explaining to Lady Regina that he had never ceased to wish to marry her, even during the worst of her kick-ups. "There are conditions," he said firmly. "I don't wish to be badgered about Nikki. If she is to be your stepmama-in-law, you must be civil to her."

Be civil to the lady who had employed sleight-of-hand in regard to the jewels Regina had long thought of as her own? She wondered if she could. Consideration of her prospects, were Rolf to hedge off, prompted Regina to hastily respond: "I will try."

"Nor do I wish to be badgered about my friend Clytie," continued Rolf, who was deriving definite pleasure from his beloved's submissive attitude. "And there'll be no more flirtations with Uncle Duke, or anyone else, mind!"

Lady Regina's experience with flirtations was not such as enticed her to further such endeavors. "As you wish it, Sweetbriar," she replied.

As he wished it? Rolf thought he must discover the extent of this newfound docility. "And you will also sit on my lap when the occasion warrants!" he decreed. Regina bowed her head. He stared. "Dash it! You *will?*"

"Naturally I will, if that is what you require. Say what you may about my papa, he *did* tell us girls how we must go on. There are so many of us, you see, and so little money—frankly, we must be more amiable than most." Regina thought her words had had effect. "I know I have been very silly. My sisters were not wrong to claim I grew puffed up with conceit. I can only hope you will not hold my foolishness against me, Rolf."

Lord Sweetbriar shifted his weight from one foot to the other. "Not a bit!" he responded, made uncomfortable by Lady Regina's humble speech. "I was a teeny bit foolish myself. Thought you wanted Uncle Duke.

Thought I didn't want to be married for my money, too. I mean, look at m'father and Nikki! It don't work."

Though this comparison to Lady Sweetbriar could hardly please Regina, she merely flinched. Regina had come too close to losing her wealthiest suitor altogether to quickly take insult. "Nikki wasn't fond of your father!" she pointed out. "I *am* fond of you."

Lord Sweetbriar looked astounded. "You *are?* I don't know why!"

Lady Regina was little less surprised. "Nor do I, but there it *is!* Can you forgive me, Sweetbriar?"

Certainly his lordship could. After a further exchange of compliments, the effect of which was to put them both in great good humor, Lord Sweetbriar exited the Egyptian antiquity chamber. Beside him, still clutching Lady Sweetbriar's jewel chest, was his newly acquired *fiancée*. Back through the various rooms of the Towneley gallery they slowly walked. Sir Avery and Miss Clough were as last glimpsed, one contemplating the Cottonian coins, the other deep in thought.

"I *like* Nikki!" explained Lord Sweetbriar to his beloved, as they entered the room. "Even if she *did* threaten to blow my brains out—*not* that you must take her seriously, you know. Dash it, I always *did* like Nikki! It was Papa who always complained about her tumbling into scrapes—and why I should agree with my papa on that head, when I never did on any other, I'm sure I don't know!" Lady Regina did not look as if she especially cared for the topic of conversation, he thought. Generously, Rolf changed it. "You must not mind too much about Nikki's baubles; I will buy you more! Dash it, if I'd known—I *did* know Papa had treated her shabbily, but I never thought she'd have to pop her—my!—jewels." Lord Sweetbriar's genial gaze alit upon his stepmama's husband-to-be. What would Nikki's husband be to him? Rolf mused. Steppapa? Steppapa-in-law? "We may trust Sir Avery to look after her better in the future! Not that I mean to imply that Nikki is marrying you for your money, sir!"

"I know precisely why Nikki is marrying me." Sir Avery set aside the catalogue he had been compiling, it clearly being useless to attempt further work. As he did so, he caught Lady Regina's guilty expression. During his acquaintance with Nikki, Sir Avery had learned to recognize the look of a lady who had meddled where she should not. Of where Regina had meddled, he had little doubt. With an impatient exclamation, Sir Avery strode toward the door.

"Papa!" By her parent's odd behavior, Miss Clough was roused from trance. "Where are you going? Surely you aren't angry at what Rolf said!"

"That Nikki is marrying me for my money? But she's not." Sir Avery paused on the threshold, at his most formidable. "And I am going to tell her so."

Chapter Twenty-four

Sir Avery having departed to inform his *fiancée* of the true state of her feelings, and Lord Sweetbriar having departed with his *fiancée* in search of more secluded quarters in which to explore their newfound mutual inclination to cuddle, Miss Clough withdrew into the museum's garden, where she strolled aimlessly along graveled paths which wound through a shady grove of trees and amid pretty flower beds. Thus far her peaceful surroundings had had as little effect on her spirits as the vinaigrette which she occasionally inhaled. Not that Clytie's spirits were deflated. She had a curious sensation of awaiting some portentous event.

Miss Clough did not wait long. Toward her, down one of the graveled paths, strode Mr. Thorne. She paused, watched him approach. Was that a *fur tippet* that he trailed after him? Villain or no, adorned or not by a highly inappropriate fur piece, Marmaduke was a damnably handsome man. "Why are you in the dismals, my darling?" he inquired, as he flung the tippet over his shoulder, and boldly grasped Clytie's hands.

Apparently he had *not* taken her in disgust, decided Clytie. A gentleman with a disgust of a lady would not gaze down upon her so warmly, she thought. "Alas!" she sighed. "I fear I have fallen in love with a rogue. I am in a very bad way, sir—as Rolf would have it, *quite* midsummer moon!"

"Rolf?" Thus reminded of the considerable time passed by Miss Clough in his nephew's company, Mr.

Thorne might have released her, had not she held him fast. "I wish you would make up your mind! Do you want my nephew or no?"

"You wish I would make up *my* mind?" Miss Clough arched her brows. "*I* am not the one who has been making sheep's eyes at Lady Regina."

Mr. Thorne grimaced: "Sheep's eyes! That will put me in my place. Shame on you, my darling! You know that I only danced attendance on Lady Regina to persuade her to look more kindly upon Rolf's suit. And had I anticipated how *tedious* it would be, I would not have!"

With that answer, Miss Clough was satisfied. "I do not think that is why you have been kissing Nikki," she remarked.

Was this young lady who grasped his hands so firmly not only adorable but prescient to boot? It would be an uncomfortable talent to live with—not that Duke intended to allow any potential discomfort to sway him from his chosen course. "Kissing Nikki—how did you *know?*" And then he realized that Clytie must refer not to the salute which he had just bestowed upon Lady Sweetbriar, but the previous incident when he had kissed her nose. The ironic expression on Clytie's face warned him that it would do no good to try and equivocate. At least she had not flung away from him in a temper. "It's nothing but a habit!" he explained. "Do you but let me kiss *you* at whim and I'll break it easily enough."

Apparently he had not disliked kissing her all *that* much or he would not contemplate kissing her again. Clytie wished that Mr. Thorne would do more than just think about it. "If Papa doesn't mind your habit of kissing Nikki," she allowed, "I suppose I must not. You should have been here earlier; you missed the *most* diverting scene! Lady Regina discovered that Nikki had sold off the Sweetbriar jewels and substituted paste— and *what* a taking she was in! She thought it would be an excellent notion if Nikki was clapped in Newgate. Then Rolf took her to task for *her* behavior, and the upshot is that your nephew and Lady Regina *are* to tie the knot." She smiled at Marmaduke's disinterested expression. "I will spare you further details."

"Thank you!" Belatedly aware that to stand so long clasping Miss Clough must rouse comment from the next visitor to venture down the graveled path, Mr. Thorne released one of her hands, and drew the other through his arm. In so doing he brushed his nose against the fur tippet, which remained draped across his shoulder, and consequently sneezed. What the deuce was he to do with the thing? Duke did not like to casually dispose of Nikki's belongings, else he would have tossed the tippet aside. And what the deuce must Clytie think of him, thusly adorned?

Perhaps if he just ignored the accursed fur she would respond likewise. "Rolf and Lady Regina are a tedious pair. I'm sure I wish them joy of one another! Perhaps now that they are out of the way, we may concentrate on more personal matters."

Although Miss Clough would have liked nothing better than to have all of Mr. Thorne's concentration focused on herself, she had not forgotten her reservations concerning his character. Those reservations were not set at rest by the casual manner in which he wore a lady's fur piece. Clytie stopped, making it necessary that her companion did also, and stared up into his swarthy face. Marmaduke's blue eyes moved over her own features, almost hungrily.

Clytie felt faint. "Gracious!" she breathed. "Papa said if I *liked* kissing you, I must invite you to kiss me *again,* sir—and I wish you would!" But he was already doing so. Clytie surrendered herself up to bliss.

Some moments later she was set back down on her feet, with her pulses deliciously racing and her bonnet askew. The latter abuse, Mr. Thorne remedied. About the former he could do little, his own pulses being in little better case. "Goodness!" sighed Clytie. "I thought I had done something *wrong* the last time, so quickly did you leave me; I thought you had taken me in disgust."

"Disgust? My foolish darling! You did everything *right.*" Lest he impulsively take her into his arms for further demonstrations, Mr. Thorne retreated a pace. In so doing, he came perilously close to tripping on the trailing end of the fur piece. Irritably he snatched it off his shoulder. Further demonstrations of his approval of Miss Clough's conduct were definitely in order, but not in the gardens of the British Museum. "Rolf had told me Nikki still had a *tendre,* and I felt responsible. Until I knew that she did *not,* I could not declare myself." He frowned. "But have I mistaken you? Did you not tell me some moments past that you are in love with a *rogue?*"

If she was, she could not regret it. "Oh, yes!" Clytie satirically contemplated the fur piece. "A rogue, a scoundrel, a profligate—a veritable villain! I have Nikki's word on it. I could not decide if she wanted you herself, or if she simply hoped to spare me a hopeless passion, but she was quite adamant on the point."

"Spare you—" Mr. Thorne abandoned his intention to carve out the rogue's heart. "Clytie, you *minx!*"

"I have not been able to make up my mind whether or not you are a villain," Miss Clough generously allowed. "Sometimes I think you must be, so many ladies have you made the object of your gallantries—and other times I wonder if association with Nikki and Rolf has merely turned my brain. Not *everyone* is on the dangle for a fortune, surely? Oh, yes, you were also accused of being a gazetted fortune hunter. Between you and Nikki, at least half of London was in peril! I *think* it was Rolf who hinted at that."

Mr. Thorne drew Clytie into the shadows of the garden shed. "But I do not need a fortune!" he protested, as he settled her comfortably within the shelter of his arms. "We may not be quite so plump in the pocket as my nephew or your father, but we will command life's elegancies. Set your fears at rest, my darling; I am *not* a villain. This is more of Nikki's doing. I think I may wring her neck."

Miss Clough was not especially concerned for Lady Sweetbriar's safety; Marmaduke's threat had been delivered in a very bemused tone. As result of Mr. Thorne's boldness, Clytie was feeling somewhat bemused herself. The shed, and the shrubbery which pressed in all around them, rendered them virtually invisible to all but the most prying eyes. *"Not* a villain?" she echoed, with a disappointed expression. "I had just gotten used to the notion that you *were!* And I had just decided that I must be every bit as wicked as you are, because I didn't *care!*"

Not surprisingly, as result of this pretty confusion, Mr. Thorne was inspired to enfold Miss Clough in another embrace. Several moments were passed in this delightful manner, moments during which Mr. Thorne kissed every one of Miss Clough's freckles, and Miss Clough felt abandoned indeed. At length, and reluctantly, he disentangled the three of them—himself, the fur piece, and Miss Clough. "I think that I had better speak with your papa straightaway," he said ruefully. "Else Sir Avery will be threatening to carve *my* heart out! Clytie, you *will* marry me?"

"Is *that* what you consider an adequate proposal?" Miss Clough was feeling thoroughly giddy, Marmaduke's intoxicating kisses having gone straight to her head. "From you, I would not have expected such paltry stuff! *You* have lived among the Russians, remember? *Rolf* compared my eyes to stars, and vowed he could not live without me, which was very entertaining, even if he *was* pretending I was Regina. Instead of kissing Nikki, you should have told her you wished to make a lady your declaration, and asked for her help!"

"But your eyes *aren't* like stars!" protested Marmaduke, as with a tender finger he traced the outlines of Clytie's face. "Stars aren't brown. And I *can* live without you; I just don't *want* to. However, if you wish to hear romantical high-flights—"

"I don't, especially." Clytie caught Marmaduke's hand and stared very seriously up into his dark face. "I am not the least bit *missish*, I fear. I do not have an especially high sense of decorum, like Lady Regina— although you would not believe it of her had you been here earlier."

Mr. Thorne was very grateful that he had not been. "The devil with Lady Regina!" he remarked.

"Nor are my habits especially elegant," continued Miss Clough, determined to catalogue her failings lest Mr. Thorne discover that he had purchased a pig in a poke. "Or my principles upright! In truth, I am a very ordinary person, and I do not understand why you should want to—but you obviously *do* want to, so that's all right!"

"Definitely I want to." By the tacit compliment just paid him, Mr. Thorne was very moved. "I have wanted to ever since I first laid eyes on you. The only difference is that now I know I want to do so for the remainder of my lifetime. And if you keep looking at me in that manner, my darling, I will forget my good intentions to speak with your papa." Suddenly he looked appalled. "Good God!"

Had Marmaduke come abruptly to his senses, realized he didn't want to marry her after all? Warily, Clytie watched his swarthy face. Had he suffered last-minute doubts? If so, Duke was indeed a villain. No gentleman who was uncertain of his feelings for a lady should subject her to so very passionate an embrace. "I beg your pardon?" Miss Clough delicately inquired.

"My darling, you must not look *so!*" In the most reassuring of manners, Duke kissed the tip of Clytie's nose. "You are utterly adorable, and I mean to devote a great deal of my life altering your undeservedly low opinion of yourself. We shall have a townhouse built, don't you think—as well as Thornewood, which is in Surrey—but I digress. The reason that I swore, *galoubchik,* was Nikki. Which reminds me that she charged to bring you this tippet, in case you grew cold!" Relieved to find an explanation for his encumbrance, he carefully draped it around Clytie's shoulders.

That explanation, Clytie found highly suspect. How had Lady Sweetbriar known Mr. Thorne would find her in the museum garden? No matter; Clytie would learn the true story of the fur tippet someday. So Nikki had driven Duke to curses? Miss Clough suspected that a great many people had been similarly inspired of late. Another subject was of far more immediate importance to Miss Clough than either of the preceding. *"Galoubchik?"* she inquired.

"My little pigeon." Marmaduke's smile, as once more he adjusted Clytie's bonnet, was wry. *"What* a distraction you are! Would you like to travel, my darling? Perhaps, when Bonaparte is done terrorizing Russia—or vice versa!—we may even return there. You would

210

like to visit Moscow and St. Petersburgh—the sledges decorated in bright colors with strange carved work and iron whirlgigs; the Convent of the Virgins, which contains the tombs of the Russian dead; the trade fair where gather merchants from all over the world." He smiled. "Then there is the hunting. The Russians are great hunters of the wolf as well as the bear. I have told you the legend of the fortieth bear."

Much of Miss Clough would have liked to pursue this topic, a lifetime of association with her aloof father had taught her to be practical. "What *about* Nikki?" she gently inquired.

"Um?" Mr. Thorne was engaged in counting Clytie's faint freckles. "Ah! The reason that I came here was to seek out your papa. I have just come from Nikki, who was in a dreadful taking because Rolf had filched back her jewels." Marmaduke looked reluctantly admiring. "I didn't think my nephew had it in him! Anyway, Nikki has taken it into her head that she's a thorn in everyone's side and has decided to leave town."

"Leave town! Duke, we cannot let her!" Clytie was appalled. "We must *do* something! How can you be so calm?"

Mr. Thorne did not consider that he *was* calm, a state of nerves which had nothing to do with Lady Sweetbriar. "Do not take on so!" he soothed, catching and holding the hands which Clytie was absentmindedly pounding against his chest. "I *have* done something, as I will explain, do you but cease to abuse me."

"Abuse—oh!" Made aware that she was pummeling the gentleman whom she revered above all others, Miss Clough blushed. "I am so sorry! But I have grown very fond of Nikki, and there is no one whom I would rather have as a stepmama—yes, and I felt no differently even when I thought she was a villainess!"

"Nikki a villainess?" Mr. Thorne looked amused. "Absurd child! Now you know otherwise, I think."

Miss Clough grinned. "I think I do. And I know also that Nikki will suit my papa perfectly—do we but prevent her running away from him! He has gone to tell her that she is *not* marrying him for his fortune, have I said?"

"You have not."

Miss Clough having exhibited no desire to wreak further physical violence upon his person, Mr. Thorne felt safe in releasing her hands. One of his own hands he placed into his pocket, and withdrew a lady's purse. "Nikki will not go far without funds!" he said.

Miss Clough clapped her hands together. "You *are* a scoundrel, Duke!"

"And you," said Mr. Thorne, succumbing to temptation, "are a *darling!*" Miss Clough offered him no resistance, went eagerly into his arms. No little time was passed by them in very personal pursuits into which it would be highly improper to pry. The shadows grew longer and the garden cooler until it would have been a hardy visitor indeed who chose to wander along the gravel paths. Had such a visitor existed, had he passed near the garden shed, the whoops that suddenly issued from behind it might have given him pause. Certainly they affected Mr. Thorne in that manner. "What the devil?" he inquired of Miss Clough, who—minus bonnet and trippet—was dissolved in giggles on his chest. "My darling, this is *not* the way to encourage a gentleman!"

"Gracious!" gasped Clytie, and availed herself of Duke's handkerchief. "Of course I wish to encourage you, Duke! That was not what made me laugh! I had just thought—" She struggled heroically to restrain her mirth. "You have not realized that Nikki is going to be your mama-in-law!"

Chapter Twenty-five

The prospects for Lady Sweetbriar becoming Mr. Thorne's mama-in-law were not especially encouraging at this moment, however; it looked very much as if Sir Avery Clough would be denied admission to her little house. Certainly he had stood for several moments rapping on the front door without raising a response. But Sir Avery was a man of considerable patience and resource. When his knuckles began to ache, he raised his voice instead. "Nikki, if you do not open this door, I will break it down!" The door did swing inward in response, at least sufficiently for a suspicious dark eye to be applied to the resultant crack. Sadly, the eye blinked. Then the door opened wide, and Lady Sweetbriar darted forward, clutched Sir Avery's arm, and tugged him inside.

"Egad!" Having slammed and bolted the door, Nikki leaned back against it, and sought to catch her breath. "Calamity after calamity! Never did I think I would be brought to so much of a standstill—and by the best of all my flirts. That *abominable* man! Every time I think of it I vow I could spit nails!"

Sir Avery gazed thoughtfully upon his *fiancée,* whose posture still suggested that she sought to forcibly bar the door. Nikki wore an ankle-length carriage dress of a textile he recognized as anglo-merino, nearly as fine as muslin, manufactured at Norfolk from the king's merino flock. Sir Avery remembered the gown, its pretty bodice with the antique frill. He did not think that Nikki was used to wearing it with a poppy-red scarf wound around the neck, which in combination with her melancholy expression gave the unsettling effect of a lady whose throat had been cut. "Cheer up, my dear!" Sir Avery said bracingly. "I assure you things are not in so worse a case."

"I wish I could believe that." Sighing, Lady Sweetbriar stepped away from the door. "Not that I mean to accuse you of telling rappers, Avery—though if you have not been, you are the only one! Rolf and Clytie have both been telling whiskers, and as for Duke—the wretch!" In a very suggestive manner, she yanked the scarf from her neck and tightened it in her hands.

The sight of his *fiancée* looking very much as though she was prepared to strangle Mr. Thorne brought an ironic expression to Sir Avery's aristocratic face. "You have been telling a few rappers of your own, I think, Nikki."

"So I have." Trailing her scarf on the floor behind her, Lady Sweetbriar approached the staircase. "I *told* you I was a designing female! Not that telling you so excuses me for behaving scaly. Avery, there is something I must confess."

Careful not to tread on the scarf, Sir Avery likewise mounted the stair. "I wish you would not," he said. "All has worked out for the best. Sweetbriar is to marry his starched-up chit, and he has decreed that she must be civil." He looked saturnine. "The jingle-brain *likes* you, my dear, even if you *do* wish to blow his brains out."

"Blow out—" Casting her eyes heavenward, Nikki very nearly missed her step. Sir Avery caught her arm. Mournfully she looked at him. "You are prodigious *good*, Avery! If only—but I understand perfectly why you would rather *not!*"

"Who says I would rather not?" Sir Avery escorted Lady Sweetbriar into the drawing room, and solicitously settled her in an overstuffed chair. "You are being foolish beyond permission, my dear."

Undeniably Nikki had been foolish; no one knew it better than she. Sadly she studied her *fiancé,* who had dropped onto a nearby chair. Sir Avery's muscular legs were stretched out before him, his arms folded across

214

his chest. "You don't know the half of it! I have been more foolish than you realize. If only there were some way in which I might atone—but there is not!" Sadly Nikki contemplated the fine, lean lines of Sir Avery's calf and thigh. "I have made my bed and now I must sleep in it, and just to think of such a thing makes me very dismal, because I shan't like it above half."

"My dear." Sir Avery watched Lady Sweetbriar gaze somberly upon his pale yellow pantaloons, his own expression wry. "This is unnecessary."

"You would not say so, if you had on your conscience what I have on *mine!*" With effort, Lady Sweetbriar elevated her gaze. "I have been a—a *block*head, Avery! But I did not wish to apply to you for assistance, and there was no other way! Yes, and I would probably do the same thing all over again, did the situation arise. Except that I would never turn my back on Duke! It makes me very cross to think that the oldest of my friends filched the last little bit of money I had in the world. I suppose he will not even visit me in jail, the wretch! Oh, Avery, I am so sorry about this—but I know Lady Regina will persuade Rolf to bring charges against me. I *had* meant to go away and spare you all the fuss, until Duke made off with my purse." She sniffled into the red scarf. "That *Duke* should be the one to bring me to *point nonplus* makes it all the worse. He *knew* how important that purse was, because I told him so. And he is the oldest of all my, er, friends!"

"Don't put yourself in a pucker, Nikki." Sir Avery crossed his handsome legs at the knee. "I'm not one to kick up a dust over trifles. Oh, yes, this business *is* a trifle. You had better tell me exactly what that stiff-rumped female said to you, I think, or we will never see an end to this business."

"She *is* stiff-rumped, isn't she? I have always said so!" For emphasis, Lady Sweetbriar waved the scarf. "Nonetheless, she has a point. There *has* been a sad want of openness about my behavior. I *have* exhibited a shocking unsteadiness of character. You *can't* wish to marry such a conniving and unscrupulous female."

Because Lady Sweetbriar had fixed him with a distinctly hopeful dark eye, Sir Avery smiled. "Can't I just!" he said.

"*Can* you?" breathed Nikki, and then her expectant expression faded. "But I am forgetting that you don't know what I've done! Avery, I popped the Sweetbriar jewels! Those I have been wearing are only paste, and now Rolf has filched them, and when Lady Regina finds out—" She shuddered. "I don't *want* to go to Newgate!"

Despite these dire disclosures, Sir Avery's voice was calm. "My dear, I promise you will not. Why did you not tell me you were so badly dipped, Nikki? Could you not bring yourself to trust me?"

"Oh, no!" Lady Sweetbriar's expression was horrified. "You must not think that! I trust you more than anyone, Avery. Nor must you think I set out to diddle you, because I did not. There has been plain dealing between us; everything has been quite aboveboard." She recalled the manner in which she had contrived to meet him. "Or *almost!* But it was bad enough of me to marry you for your money. The least I could do was wait until the knot was tied!"

Sir Avery looked very sardonic. "But you are *not* marrying me for my money!" he said.

Nikki's glance was reproachful: "I know that! But I *didn't* know it when I popped the gems. You are not a very *ardent* fellow, Avery—at least you have not been since the occasion of our first meeting, though you were all a lady could wish *then!* When you made no effort after that to, ah, sweep me off my feet, I thought it must have been a fluke! And so I thought I didn't love you, which is entirely your own fault, because you gave me so little opportunity to discover otherwise!" She clenched her fists. "Do you know, I am not convinced Reuben has not had some part in this? It is *just* the sort of thing he would like best, because he always wanted me to be miserable, and I have never been more miserable than this! I would not put it past him to try and make me come a cropper even from beyond the grave."

Sir Avery unclasped his knee. "You need not be made miserable, Nikki."

"No?" Lady Sweetbriar's glance was arch. "You are not properly conversant with the penalties for selling

216

what isn't yours, I think. Neither do I know exactly what the penalties are, but I am sure they are very bad! Lady Regina will do her worst for me, you may be sure."

"I think not. Any scandal that involves you must reflect upon her, as your stepson's wife." Sir Avery gazed with keen appreciation upon his *fiancée*, whose posture was suggestive of a wilting flower. "All this fuss over some jewels! A shabby lot, I always thought. It is your decision, but I would advise letting the jingle-brain and his starched-up chit have the wretched things. I will buy you others that are much more fine."

No wonder Sir Avery had seemed so tolerant, Lady Sweetbriar sadly thought; he had somehow failed to comprehend the enormity of her sin. "You do not understand; I cannot give them back—though could I, I would, because I never want to set eyes on them again! Were you paying attention, Avery, you would have heard me say I *popped* the accursed things."

"It is you who do not understand." Sir Avery was amused by the fierce concentration with which Nikki frowned at him. "The jewels Sweetbriar filched from you are paste; the ones *I* have in safekeeping are not. You must do with them as you wish, but I would suggest giving the things back. They have already been much more trouble than they're worth."

"You have—" Lady Sweetbriar wrinkled her nose. "I'll be hanged if I know what you're talking about, Avery!"

"No, my dear, you will *not* be hanged, or go to prison either, so you may relieve your mind on that score." Sir Avery sounded faintly apologetic. "I had an agent buy them up, once I realized you were run aground. Several times I almost told you I had done so, but the occasion never seemed quite right. Then I decided to give them back to you as a bride gift."

"What a *good* man you are!" Looking very melancholy, Lady Sweetbriar sniffled into her scarf. "I know I do not deserve it—or you! Do not fear, I will not hold you to our betrothal. You will not wish to throw the handkerchief in my direction *now*. Not that you probably ever did, but you could not help yourself, so thoroughly had I bamboozled you!" In a very dejected manner, she blew her nose. "Now you want nothing more to do with me. I cannot like such a thing, because I would like to have a great deal more to do with you, but I fully enter into your feelings! Lady Regina was right! I *am* a dreadfully designing slyboots, and no gentleman who had *not* been bamboozled could ever wish to marry me!"

To this very moving speech—which had been accompanied by a full battery of sideways glances and wistful sighs—Sir Avery responded promptly: "Come here," he said. Looking curious, Lady Sweetbriar rose and approached the chair. Sir Avery grasped her wrist and pulled her down onto his lap. "I am quite satisfied with you just the way you are, Nikki. You must not feel guilty about bamboozling me, because I have never been more pleased with anything in my life."

"Pleased that I *bamboozled* you?" Lady Sweetbriar was briefly diverted from snuggling very comfortably against his chest. "I think you must be trying to flummery me. Not that I am complaining, mind! As long as you realize you do not *have* to do the civil! But if you truly *want* to, that is quite another thing." She paused to ascertain if Sir Avery did in fact appear to be doing other than following his inclinations. He did not. Due to the nature of those inclinations, Nikki dimpled and giggled and fluttered her eyelashes. "Deuced if you don't have a *dandy* lap!"

"Thank you!" responded Sir Avery, much moved. "I do not mean to restrict your movements, Nikki, but I think I must ask you to eschew other laps once we are wed. As for the gentlemen who have taken to haunting your bedchamber—*not* that I think there is anything in it, of course—"

"I should hope you don't!" With a futile and altogether enchanting attempt at severity, Lady Sweetbriar sat up. "You must not be jealous of Duke; *that* was done with a very long time ago. Not that I blame you for wondering if I still hankered after him; I did myself. But I knew when he kissed me—er." She looked adorably guilty. "And so did he!"

218

"I am glad to hear it." Sir Avery was wry. "Because I expect he is going to marry Clytie."

Lady Sweetbriar's dark eyes opened wide. "Marry— egad! Then it is *not* a hopeless passion. I am so glad! Or perhaps I'm not. Have you thought that Duke may be on the dangle for a fortune? It is difficult to believe it of him, but the wretch *did* steal my purse right off my bed!" She realized the implications of that last remark. "You will be wondering what Duke was doing in my bedchamber, I daresay. You must not blame Duke; I invited him there!" That explanation was no better, she decided. "Oh, *rats!* I do not suppose you will believe that I was *not*—"

"I know you were not," interrupted Sir Avery, taking a firmer grip on Lady Sweetbriar, who in her agitation was bouncing about. "It is you who are the harsh judge, Nikki. I suspect Mr. Thorne relieved you of your purse only to prevent you taking French leave."

"Twaddle!" Lady Sweetbriar snuggled very close to her *fiancé,* her arms around his neck, her breath warm on his cheek. "Why should Duke care if I left or not? He has no partiality for me. Moreover, that doesn't explain why he took away my fur tippet, too! But if you say he is not on the dangle for a fortune—"

"He is not." So unadverse was Sir Avery to Lady Sweetbriar's snuggling that he held her closer yet, and turned his head so that their lips brushed. "I know it for a fact. I had investigations made. I suppose I had better confess, Nikki, that I also had investigations made when I met *you.*"

"Hmm?" How could she have been so shortsighted as to think Avery was not ardent? mused Nikki. If his current activities were any indication, he was wonderfully so. "Investigations?"

"Um." Sir Avery's mind was not on the conversation either. "So you see you did *not* bamboozle me." And then he abandoned all further attempt at rational discourse and kissed Nikki's pretty lips, and chin, and throat.

"Avery," she murmured, some time later. "I do not deserve you, and I know it, but I am determined to *try!* I shall not flirt with anyone but you ever again, and

I am resolved to never fall into another scrape." She nuzzled his neck. "I am grown *prodigious* fond of you! But that reminds me that you have never said *why* you wish to marry me."

Sir Avery saluted her delicate earlobe. "Because I love you," he said simply, before embracing her again.

"Avery," whispered Lady Sweetbriar, later still, when his kisses had reached a point best left undisclosed. "Why the devil have you waited so long to do this?"

Sir Avery raised his head, his expression so extremely ardent that Nikki's breath caught. "Because I knew that once I started, I wouldn't wish to *stop!*"

Dimpling, Lady Sweetbriar tangled her fingers in her *fiancé's* sandy hair, drew his head back down against her breast. "Then don't stop! *Ever!*" she replied huskily.

In this highly satisfying manner, the dilemma of Lady Sweetbriar was at last resolved; and in years to come Nikki and Sir Avery did in fact devote a large proportion of their time to snuggling and related activities. Sir Avery did not give up all interest in other pursuits, and wisely diverted his wife's excess energies—or what little excess energy was left after all their cuddling—to the British Museum. Nikki became a figure as familiar within those hallowed halls as Sir Avery himself, and only the most small-minded of the staff complained about their affectionate manner, which on one never-forgotten occasion inspired Sir Avery to kiss the tip of her nose in the presence of royalty.

A similar felicity was granted to the others involved in the last of her ladyship's scrapes. No less affectionate toward one another were Sir Avery's daughter and son-in-law, though less prone to public display. In years to come, Mr. and Mrs. Thorne traveled extensively, first of all to Russia, where they passed a winter enjoying the theater in St. Petersburg, the Convent of the Virgins, and the Polrovsky Cathedral and the Kremlin in Moscow, and somewhere between the two gave birth to their first son in a sledge. So little overset were Mr. and Mrs. Thorne by this bizarre occurrence that scant days later they were engaged in a bear hunt, which both immensely enjoyed.

Lord Sweetbriar and his lady also snuggled frequently, which his lordship secretly suspected was why Regina turned into a remarkably biddable wife, even managing to be civil to Nikki, which was the one stipulation made by Sir Avery when he restored the Sweetbriar jewels. But even though she at last had possession of the gems she had so long coveted, Regina was the only participant in Nikki's final scrape who was left less than content. Perhaps it was in her nature to be a teeny bit dissatisfied. Or perhaps Regina's lingering chagrin was the fault of Sir Avery, who had a secret resolution that Regina's jewels would never be so fine as those of her stepmama-in-law.

GREAT ADVENTURES IN READING

□ **FREE FALL IN CRIMSON**   14441 $2.95
by John D. MacDonald
Travis McGee comes close to losing his status as a living legend when he agrees to track down the killers who brutally murdered an ailing millionaire.

□ **THE PAGAN LAND**   14446 $2.95
by Thomas Marriott
The story of a bold journey through the wilderness of nineteenth century South Africa in search of a homeland and of love.

□ **CAPTIVE OF DESIRE**   14448 $2.75
by Becky Lee Weyrich
Even in the arms of the king, young Zephromae's cries are for her childhood sweetheart, Alexander. But Alexander can no longer protect her from the sly priest, the lust-mad prince, or the bitter queen.

□ **MARRAKESH**   14443 $2.50
by Graham Diamond
Magic and miracles, satanic evil and everlasting love. This is an exotic adventure even more enchanting than the Arabian Nights.

□ **BRAGG #1: BRAGG'S HUNCH**   14449 $2.25
by Jack Lynch
The first book in a new action series. Bragg finds himself in the middle of a deadly crossfire when he is hired to investigate who's been threatening the life of an ex-hood.

Buy them at your local bookstore or use this handy coupon for ordering.

COLUMBIA BOOK SERVICE, CBS Inc.
32275 Mally Road, P.O. Box FB, Madison Heights, MI 48071

Please send me the books I have checked above. Orders for less than 5 books must include 75¢ for the first book and 25¢ for each additional book to cover postage and handling. Orders for 5 books or more postage is FREE. Send check or money order only. Allow 3-4 weeks for delivery.

Cost $_____	Name_____
Sales tax*_____	Address_____
Postage _____	City_____
Total $_____	State_____ Zip_____

The government requires us to collect sales tax in all states except AK, DE, MT, NH and OR.

Prices and availability subject to change without notice.   **8239**

CLASSIC BESTSELLERS
from FAWCETT BOOKS

] THE LIVELY LADY by Kenneth Roberts	24482	$2.95
] THE LAST ENCHANTMENT by Mary Stewart	24207	$2.95
] SELECTED SHORT STORIES OF NATHANIEL HAWTHORNE Edited by Alfred Kazin	30846	$2.25
] MAGGIE: A GIRL OF THE STREETS by Stephen Crane	30854	$2.25
] SATAN IN GORAY by Isaac Bashevis Singer	24326	$2.50
] THE RISE AND FALL OF THE THIRD REICH by William Shirer	23442	$3.95
] ALL QUIET ON THE WESTERN FRONT by Erich Maria Remarque	23808	$2.95
] TO KILL A MOCKINGBIRD by Harper Lee	08376	$2.75
▌ THE FLOUNDER by Gunter Grass	24180	$2.95
▌ THE CHOSEN by Chaim Potok	24200	$2.95
] THE SOURCE by James A. Michener	23859	$3.95

CURRENT CREST BESTSELLERS

☐ **THE MASK OF THE ENCHANTRESS**   24418 $3.25
  by Victoria Holt
  Suewellyn knew she wanted to possess the Mateland family castle,
  but having been illegitimate and cloistered as a young woman, only
  a perilous deception could possibly make her dream come true.

☐ **THE HIDDEN TARGET**   24443 $3.50
  by Helen MacInnes
  A beautiful young woman on a European tour meets a handsome
  American army major. All is not simple romance however when she
  finds that her tour leaders are active terrorists and her young army
  major is the chief of NATO's antiterrorist section.

☐ **BORN WITH THE CENTURY**   24295 $3.50
  by William Kinsolving
  A gripping chronicle of a man who creates an empire for his family
  and how they engineer its destruction.

☐ **SINS OF THE FATHERS**   24417 $3.95
  by Susan Howatch
  The tale of a family divided from generation to generation by great
  wealth and the consequences of a terrible secret.

☐ **THE NINJA**   24367 $3.50
  by Eric Van Lustbader
  They were merciless assassins, skilled in the ways of love and the
  deadliest of martial arts. An exotic thriller spanning postwar Japan
  and present-day New York.

Buy them at your local bookstore or use this handy coupon for ordering.

COLUMBIA BOOK SERVICE, CBS Inc.
32275 Mally Road, P.O. Box FB, Madison Heights, MI 48071

Please send me the books I have checked above. Orders for less than 5 books
must include 75¢ for the first book and 25¢ for each additional book to cover
postage and handling. Orders for 5 books or more postage is FREE. Send check
or money order only. Allow 3-4 weeks for delivery.

Cost $_____	Name_____
Sales tax*_____	Address_____
Postage _____	City_____
Total $_____	State_____ Zip_____

*The government requires us to collect sales tax in all states except AK, DE,
MT, NH and OR.

Prices and availability subject to change without notice.   **822**